DARK PRINCE'S ENIGMA

THE CHILDREN OF THE GODS BOOK 29

I. T. LUCAS

DARK PRINCES'S ENIGMA

Copyright © 2019 by I. T. Lucas

NOTE FROM THE AUTHOR:
Dark Prince's Enigma is a work of fiction!
Names, characters, places and incidents are products of the author's
imagination or are used fictitiously and are not to be construed as real. Any
similarity to actual persons, organizations and/or events is purely coincidental.

LOKAN

*A*s Lokan's awareness returned, it was accompanied by a throbbing headache, nausea, and disorientation.

Drugs.

He must've been pumped with shitloads of them. Other than a severe injury, drugs were the only thing he could think of that could cause an immortal to experience such symptoms.

And if that wasn't bad enough, Lokan couldn't open his eyes more than a crack without it feeling as if someone was sticking needles in them.

With a groan, he let his lids drop. The room was steeped in such complete darkness that there was no point in forcing it. He couldn't see anything anyway.

If Lokan had ever wondered what being drunk and drugged felt like, he knew now and was doubly glad for never allowing himself to drink excessively or touch drugs.

Why people would want to deliberately impair their faculties baffled him. Getting shit-faced was the prerogative of plebs, not leaders. Lokan couldn't allow himself to partake in excess even if he was ever tempted to. His very survival depended on him always being sharp and alert.

The ever-present competition for positions of power and influence in the Brotherhood was demanding and subject to the whims of a despot. The fact that his competitors were his half-brothers and the despot was his father only raised the stakes and made the game more dangerous.

Was one of his brothers responsible for this?

And what exactly was 'this'?

The bed he was lying on was superbly comfortable, like what he would expect to find in a luxury hotel, and the sheets smelled freshly laundered.

Was he in a hotel room?

Why couldn't he remember what had happened to him, or how he'd gotten there?

Was he suffering from drug-induced amnesia?

Fighting the mental fog, Lokan went back to the last thing he remembered, which had been calling his pilot and telling him to have the jet ready for takeoff.

Why had he done that, though?

He had just returned to Washington from his mandatory visit to the island, and his next scheduled report wasn't until next month. He had work to do, meetings with politicians and lobbyists to attend, and a couple of powerful telepaths to snatch from their government's clutches...

Fuck! Suddenly it all came rushing back.

He'd failed.

The mighty son of Navuh had been outmaneuvered by fucking humans. For that failure alone, his father was likely to execute him. And if Navuh was merciful enough to spare his life, he would definitely demote him like he'd demoted Losham.

Except, whatever his brother had done to prompt his fall from grace couldn't have been nearly as bad as what Lokan had gotten himself into.

Which meant that Navuh could never find out about this fiasco.

And that wasn't even the main reason why his father could never know about this. It would be difficult to explain why Lokan had invested so much effort and had taken such unreasonable risks to capture two telepaths who could only communicate with each other.

No one was supposed to find out about this personal acquisition of his.

First of all, because the mission he needed them for was top secret, and if discovered would cost him his head for sure. And secondly, because the dream-sharing ability that had allowed him to set the trap for the telepaths needed to stay forever hidden from the Brotherhood and especially from his father.

Navuh wouldn't tolerate anyone in his organization having an advantage over him, not even his own son, and not even if the talent was pretty useless.

Until meeting Ella, Lokan hadn't found any practical purpose for the dream-sharing. Provided that it was used wisely, however, it was an asset nonetheless, and as far as Lokan knew, he was the only one on the entire planet who possessed it.

Much good it had done him, though.

Where had he gone wrong?

After weeks of dream-sharing with Ella and charming her into trusting him, he had realized that she'd been attempting to use her meager feminine wiles to lure him into a trap of her own. But since the girl was too young and inexperienced to devise a plan like this, and he didn't think she had any real motive for trying to entrap him, he had concluded that she'd been doing it on behalf of the agency holding her and her mother captive.

Most likely under duress.

Lokan still believed that his plan to snatch both telepaths from under their handlers' noses had been ingenious. He was sure that it had failed not because of any mistake on his part, but because of the unprecedented level of military support the agency responsible for collecting paranormal talents evidently had access to.

He hadn't expected such an obscure and highly classified department to get Special Forces backup.

It had been clear to him that Ella's rescue from the Russian mafioso and the faking of her death had been orchestrated and executed by highly trained professionals, but what he knew about government agencies and how they operated had led him to believe that it had been a one-time collaboration.

Lokan thought it probable that Vivian had revealed the truth about her and Ella's telepathic connection in a desperate attempt to get the government to rescue her daughter.

It seemed that she had succeeded in that, but the price was her and Ella's freedom, as well as that of Ella's younger brother. As far as Lokan was concerned, Vivian might have saved her daughter from sexual slavery, but to do so, she'd sold her soul and the souls of her children to the devil.

Evidently, the agency had been willing to put just as much effort into getting their hands on a dream walker as they had into securing the telepaths. After all, his talent was just as rare as the mother and daughter's ability to talk to each other in their heads.

That agency must have other exceptional talents as well.

As more and more details of what had happened were coming back to him, Lokan remembered that the guy who'd shot him knew his real name.

"Game over, Lokan," he'd said.

Since Ella had only known him as Logan, and so had all of his Washington contacts, Lokan figured that the only way the guy could've known his real name was by entering his mind, and that was the most alarming development of all.

Because he could've learned much more than Lokan's name.

Humans were not supposed to know about the existence of immortals or the secret island that served as their base. But that was only the tip of the iceberg. It was basic information that could've been obtained from any captured member of the Brotherhood.

What they could learn from Navuh's son, however, was much more damming than that.

Humans possessing such strong paranormal abilities was something neither Lokan nor his father had anticipated.

Nor had he expected to ever get caught by them.

The plan he'd constructed had seemed foolproof. No one born in this century knew about the secret tunnels running under the university and, given the wild goose chase he'd sent Ella and Vivian's handlers on, there should have been no way for them to stop him.

They had outmaneuvered him with the airport shutdown, something only a powerful government agency could have pulled off.

There was no point in dwelling on his failure, though. What he needed to focus on was devising a new plan of action before they came in to question him, especially if they brought the mind reader along.

He decided he would have to kill that human first and then deal with the others.

The problem was that they seemed to be aware of his ability to compel and would no doubt bring in immunes to deal with him, which meant that thralling was out as well.

Those who couldn't be compelled couldn't be thralled.

Lokan would have to rely on his basic immortal super traits

of strength and speed, which the humans wouldn't be expecting.

First, though, he should try to dream-share with Ella and find out as much as he could from her. After more than a month in the place, she should be familiar with its personnel and safety procedures.

Ella might be still angry at him, but there was no reason for her to hide what was going on and what he was up against, and perhaps she would even use the opportunity to gloat.

It was most likely that she was somewhere nearby, perhaps even in the same facility. Not that distance played a factor in his ability to dream-share with her.

He had done it from the other side of the world.

It had been early afternoon when he'd been captured, and unless the room was devoid of light because the shutters were closed, Lokan assumed it was night, so she should be sleeping.

Drifting into dreamland while his head was throbbing was a challenge, but he'd practiced doing so at will. Taking a deep breath, he imagined what he wanted to dream about and then counted back from ten.

CAROL

"*Y*ou're bouncier than usual." Wonder handed Carol a plate of sandwiches. "These are for table six. What's going on?"

"I'm excited."

"About what?"

"Let me finish with that order first."

Lifting the tray with the cappuccinos and sandwiches Wonder had made, Carol headed toward her waiting customers with a spring in her step and a big smile on her face.

Navuh's son had been captured, and she couldn't wait to talk about it with someone. Was she allowed, though? Or was it a secret?

Wonder probably knew because Anandur had told her, and the same was true for the other Guardians' mates.

Thank the merciful Fates for the earpiece Brundar had given her and had never asked her to return. That little device was keeping her in the loop. Listening to the communications between the Guardians, Carol was getting the latest news before everyone else.

She wasn't supposed to share what she'd learned, but this was big news, and Carol was sure it was going to spread throughout the village like wildfire. After all, there was no point in keeping it a secret. It wasn't as if the information could be shared with outsiders.

Humans didn't know immortals existed, and keeping it that way meant that none could be told about the capture of one of the most prominent figures of the Devout Order of Mortdh Brotherhood, the son of their evil leader no less, or how incredible it was for the clan.

Bottom line, even if everyone in the village knew about Lokan's capture, there was no way the news could get back to his father.

From what she'd heard over the earpiece, the idea was to make it look as if Lokan had deserted. If Navuh discovered that the clan had his son, the consequences would be disastrous.

Unable to retaliate against them directly, he would strike at humans, knowing how much it would hurt the clan.

It would be a matter of ego for the despot.

She wouldn't be surprised if Navuh tried to blackmail the clan into releasing his son by threatening to nuke a large city. Not because he loved Lokan, but because his son probably knew things about the Brotherhood that Navuh couldn't afford his enemy to discover.

It was better to let him think that Lokan had deserted, or even gotten killed by having his private jet explode in the middle of the ocean.

In her opinion, the second option was better. With no one searching for Lokan, they would have all the time they needed to milk him for information. Finally, they were going to learn the location of that freaking island the Doomers called home, which meant that Kian could finally approve her mission.

Well, there was one small detail that might still prevent it, but she planned on taking care of it as soon as possible.

Returning with the empty tray, Carol put it on the counter and wiped it with a rag. "Is Anandur going to stop by this morning?"

From her spot next to the cappuccino machine, Wonder glanced at Carol over her shoulder. "Maybe in the afternoon. Kian is on his way to pay a visit to you-know-who, and he took Anandur and Brundar with him."

Carol leaned closer and whispered, "Is the one you're referring to supposed to stay a secret?"

"I'm not sure. Until I'm told it's okay to talk about it in public, I'm going to assume that it should."

Tucking a curl behind her ear, Carol leaned against the counter and crossed her arms over her chest. "A spy in our midst would be the only reason to keep it a secret. But if there was one, discussing you-know-who would be the least of our worries. Our location would've been compromised, and we would have been attacked by Doomers a long time ago."

"Not necessarily." Wonder turned to stand next to Carol and glanced around, making sure no one was close enough to eavesdrop. "With the self-driving cars and the hidden tunnels, the village's residents don't know where it is. So even if there is a spy amongst us, he or she can't disclose our location."

"That's true. But what are the chances of a clan member spying for the Brotherhood? Unless you suspect the ex-Doomers." Carol huffed. "I can assure you that Robert is not a spy, and neither is Dalhu. Both are happily mated and would never betray their mates."

"I don't suspect them or anyone else. I'm just saying that it's possible."

"Perhaps, but it's highly unlikely." Carol pushed away from

the counter. "I'm going to call Anandur about the hunting lesson he's supposed to give me."

"Didn't you say that you were not going to do it?"

"I changed my mind. No guts, no glory, eh?"

"I guess." Wonder grimaced. "But it's gross."

"Can't argue with that. It's just that I've realized that eating meat but not being willing to hunt for it is hypocritical. It's time for me to woman up." She could have lived with the hypocrisy, but she had to do it if she wanted Anandur to approve her for the mission.

"Good luck."

"I'll call Anandur from the playground so I can have some privacy while I grovel. Are you going to be okay here by yourself for a little bit?"

Wonder waved a hand at the tables. "All the customers have been served, and there are no new ones in line."

"It won't take long."

The playground was about a minute's walk from the café, and as usual, there was no one there. Kian had built the place with hope for the future, but in the meantime, there were only two kids in the entire village. Phoenix was a toddler and Nathalie brought her to the playground from time to time, but Ethan was still too small to play.

Hopefully, Merlin's fertility treatments were going to work, and the clan would be blessed with many more babies.

Not that Carol was interested in having kids herself, but there was nothing like the happy squeals of playing children to boost morale and hope for the future.

Sitting on one of the swings, she placed the call.

"What's up?" Anandur answered on the second ring.

"Are you stopping by the café anytime today?"

"Maybe later. Why?"

"I want you to take me hunting. I'm ready."

"Oh, really. What made you change your mind?"

"I decided that I have no problem killing freaking coyotes. When I hear their howling at night, I'm ready to get my shotgun."

Anandur laughed. "They howl to mark their territory and to court mates. They are not as bad as people think they are."

"Oof. Don't tell me that. You wanted me to hunt to prove that I'm capable of killing. And now that I'm finally ready, you make even coyotes sound innocent?"

"Of course, they are innocent. They are animals fighting for survival. They don't harbor sinister plans to conquer the world or kill for the fun of it."

"Like the Doomers."

"Precisely."

"Can I practice on them?" She waved a hand even though he couldn't see her. "I'm just joking. Can we skip the hunting thing, though? I'm sure that I can kill in self-defense or to protect others."

A long moment passed before he answered. "What prompted your reawakened interest? Does it have anything to do with Lokan's capture?"

She rolled her eyes. "Of course, it does. When we extract the island's location from Lokan, Kian might finally approve my mission. I'm ready to go and start planting the seeds of revolt in the hearts of Doomers."

"I bet you are. But we don't have the location yet, and it might be a while until we get it out of him. Then we need to figure out how to get you there, how to communicate with you, and how to extract you if needed."

"You are not telling me anything new. Knowing where the freaking island is will make all of this doable, while before it wasn't. So, I figured that the only thing still preventing me from going is your stupid condition that I kill an animal and take out its heart."

"How about we cross that bridge when we get to it?"

"We are practically there, Anandur."

KIAN

"You ou shouldn't hold the phone while driving," Kian said as Anandur ended the call with Carol. "Why didn't you link it with the car's system?"

"Carol called me. Not you, Andrew, or Brundar."

In the back seat, Andrew chuckled. "We all heard her anyway."

Anandur shrugged. "I know, but it's a matter of decorum."

Kian cast him a sidelong glance. "If you were concerned with propriety, you should've told her that you were in the car with us before letting her talk."

"Maybe, but then all of you would've thought that Carol and I were keeping secrets. Besides, it saves me the trouble of repeating what she said." He glanced at Kian. "Are we still considering that crazy plan?"

"That depends on what we learn from Lokan."

"Is he even awake yet?" Andrew asked.

"Arwel said that he woke up and then dozed off again." Kian removed his sunglasses and put them in his pocket. "Probably because of all the sedatives we've pumped into him."

"I'm surprised you didn't demand that Lokan be awakened last night when they brought him."

"I wasn't ready to talk to him yet. I wanted to talk with Turner first and get his opinion. I also wanted to hear Ella and Vivian's versions about what went on while Lokan had them. Their insight into his personality was very helpful. According to them, he seems smart, educated, well-mannered, and full of himself."

"Wasn't pumping him with shitloads of sedatives dangerous to his brain?" Anandur asked.

"It's not. Bridget approved it. She said that keeping him asleep will allow his body to repair the damage he sustained."

"I thought that Turner shot him in the legs." Anandur frowned. "Did he shatter his kneecaps?"

"No, but after getting shot, Lokan fell back down the jet's stairs and hit his head on the last rung."

"That's not a big deal either."

"We needed to keep him sedated until he was locked down in the keep's dungeon. A few more shots to keep him asleep throughout the night weren't going to make a difference."

"Do you think he realizes who has him?" Andrew asked.

"Unless he figured it out when Turner shot him, I don't see how he could. It was lights out for him seconds later."

Andrew chuckled. "I wish I could peek into his head and see what he imagines happened to him. That should be interesting."

"He's a Doomer," Brundar said. "He probably thinks one of his brothers set him up. Dalhu says they are constantly competing for positions and for their father's approval."

Kian didn't want to speculate. What he'd been itching to do since Lokan's capture was to start the interrogation.

Last night, it had been too late to question Ella and Vivian about their interactions with Lokan and what they had learned from him. Ella had gone home with Julian straight from the plane, and Kian had no doubt the two had been busy celebrating her safe return.

The same was true of Vivian and Magnus.

This morning, Kian had waited for as long as he possibly could before calling them up to ask a few questions. The rest would have to wait for Monday after all the celebrating was done.

The main thing Ella had warned him against was how good of a liar Lokan was. That was why Kian had called Andrew and asked him to come along. His brother-in-law's lie-detecting services were needed.

The second thing Ella had warned him about was Lokan's chameleonic adaptive ability. Apparently, the guy knew how to make himself likable when he wanted.

Not that it was going to work on Kian.

As someone who'd witnessed the atrocities committed by Doomers, Kian's hatred for them ran deep. The only reason he'd accepted Dalhu and Robert into the clan was the sacrifice each of them had made to prove themselves worthy.

But it hadn't been easy to do. It had taken him a long time to accept that not all Doomers were evil, and that some managed to escape their leader's relentless brainwashing and maintain some basic decency.

That, however, could not be true of Navuh's sons. They were privy to the backstage of their father's propaganda, and they were the ones in charge of executing his evil plans.

No one would ever convince him that they had any decency left in them at all. Except perhaps for the one who had gotten away.

Kalugal.

What Kian had managed to piece together was that Kalugal had faked his own death during the Second World War and escaped to the States. Sometime later, he'd had a chance encounter with Eva, activating her dormant genes and turning her immortal without either of them realizing it.

Even a skeptic like Kian had to concede that the Fates had something to do with that. The chain of events was just too fantastic for it all to have happened by chance.

As Kian's phone rang, he accepted the call, and Arwel's voice came through the car's speakers. "He is getting out of bed. Any instructions?"

"Get him breakfast," Anandur said.

"I'm not his servant."

"The dude needs to eat."

"So, you get it," Arwel said.

Anandur huffed. "Fine, I will. I'll get him stuff from the vending machines."

"Bring some for me too."

"I'm not your servant, buddy."

As humorous as the exchange was, the truth was that Kian would have to make arrangements for the Doomer and his keepers to have their meals delivered.

Last night, Arwel had volunteered to stay down in the dungeon in the cell adjacent to Lokan's and head the team of Guardians assigned to him. Evidently, deep underground or high in the sky were the only places Arwel could escape the bombardment of emotions normally assailing him. This assignment was perfect for him, and he'd jumped at the opportunity.

The problem was that they hadn't figured out the logistics yet. Until they did, the Guardians on rotation in the keep would have to take turns bringing in meals for Lokan and those in charge of keeping an eye on him

Kian's other option was to bring Okidu to prepare meals

for them, but then he would be giving up his butler for the fucking Doomer.

Wasn't going to happen.

Whatever the solution, he was going to address it later when he got back to the office. Right now, he was too jazzed up about interrogating his prisoner and getting game-changing intel out of him.

Was Lokan going to be a hard nut to crack?

The Doomer was old and experienced, a seasoned soldier, but the question was how loyal was he to his father? If they were lucky, Lokan hated Navuh and would cooperate freely, but Kian didn't like to indulge in wishful thinking.

"I'm curious to see how different Lokan is from the other Doomers," Andrew said. "Even Dalhu, who was a unit commander, and Robert, who was Sharim's right-hand man, knew very little of use to us. I think Navuh keeps information highly compartmentalized. Lokan might know more than Dalhu and Robert, but not much."

Anandur shrugged. "We will soon find out. I bet it's going to be interesting, though. From what Ella and Vivian said about him, Lokan is charming and smart. His plan to kidnap them was brilliant. If not for Turner's connections and quick think-ing, the Doomer would have succeeded in snatching them from under our noses despite all the men we had in place. Not only that, he would have done it with significantly fewer resources at his disposal. I can despise what he attempted to do, but I have to respect his smarts."

LOKAN

*L*okan opened his eyes and groaned. He hadn't found Ella in dream world, and his head was still throbbing.

She was either awake, or he was somehow being blocked from entering her dream.

How long had he been asleep?

As before, the room was still completely dark, and he had no sense of time or space for that matter. To familiarize himself with his surroundings, he had to get out of bed and search for the light switch.

No pain in his legs meant that his wounds were all healed by now. Which implied that the human hadn't hit any bones and had caused only flesh wounds.

Still, the guy had caused him injury, so summoning aggression and imagining sinking his fangs into that human's throat was easy.

As Lokan had expected, his eyes started emitting a subtle glow by which he could see enough to orient himself. He made sure it was dim, nothing that would show up on the surveillance cameras that he was sure were there, but for an immortal it sufficed.

He was in what looked like a nicely appointed hotel room, and a glance at the ceiling confirmed the camera he'd expected.

Peeling the duvet off, Lokan swung his legs over the side of the bed. His pants were in tatters, but that had been done to treat his wounds. His thighs were bandaged, which was good because he needed to hide the fact that they were already healed.

But that wasn't the only thing he noticed. He had cuffs on both his wrists and ankles. Whatever purpose they served, he could probably break out of them, but that would give away his immortal strength, which at the moment was the only advantage he could surprise his jailers with.

Shuffling as if he were in pain, he pretended to pat the walls until he found the switch and turned the lights on.

The first door he opened led to a small walk-in closet where he found his two suitcases lying on the floor. They were both closed, but he had no doubt they had been searched. The second door led to a small living room and the third to a very nice, spacious bathroom.

Not bad. It seemed that the American government wasn't stingy when it came to hosting its paranormal talents.

After using the facilities, he went back to the closet and opened one of his suitcases. Whoever had gone through the contents had folded everything nicely but without bothering to put things back in the same order.

The message was clear. They wanted him to know that his stuff had been searched, but also that it had been treated with respect.

This indicated that they wanted his cooperation, which was a good sign.

Lokan was a master manipulator. If given half a chance, he would find a way out of this mess.

A change of clothes and his toiletries in hand, he headed back to the bathroom and turned the water on in the shower.

Those watching him on the surveillance cameras would tell whoever was coming to talk to him to wait until he was done showering and got dressed, which meant that as long as he was standing under the spray, no one was going to come in, and he would have time to think.

Thankfully, there was no camera in the bathroom. Not because he minded his jailers seeing him nude, but because he wanted to take the bandages off and examine his wounds.

As he had suspected, no trace remained, and his thighs looked perfectly healed. Lokan left the bandages on the vanity's counter and stepped into the shower. Normally, he would have burned them so no trace of his blood remained for anyone to examine, but he was sure that his jailers had taken blood samples from him when he'd been out.

Besides, unless there was a fireplace in the living room, which he didn't remember seeing, he didn't have the means to do that.

It was a minor concern, though. His biggest one was his father, but Lokan had almost an entire month until his presence was required at the island. He worked independently and reported only to Navuh, so no one was going to look for him until he failed to show up for their next meeting.

That was good. A month was plenty of time to get himself out of this situation. A powerful immortal with nearly a thousand years of experience in manipulating humans should have no problem outsmarting a bunch of bureaucrats.

This wasn't the movies, and this place wasn't run by X-Men mutants possessing extraordinary abilities.

In fact, this could be an opportunity to find more humans with paranormal talents. He could walk out of here with a bunch of them in tow.

Perhaps the best strategy was to at first play along and learn as much as he could about where he was and who he was up against. If he could stall until nightfall, he could attempt to dream-share with Ella again and find out more.

When he was done with his shower, Lokan got dressed, sprayed some cologne on, and walked into the living room area of his apartment. There were no windows, so he assumed it was underground, and when he checked the front door, it didn't even have a handle.

A quick search of the walls revealed no buttons to press and no intercom. Unless someone opened the door from the outside, there was no way out, and judging by the sound it made when he knocked on it, the thing was at least a foot thick.

Maybe it was a mutant base after all, and this was a holding cell for intelligent gorillas. Humans used doors like that for their bank safes, not inside their jails.

Despite how desperate his situation seemed, Lokan chuckled. They either thought of him as a priceless jewel or a dangerous gorilla.

Glancing up, he checked the air-conditioning vents, but they were the new kind, which was a long slit instead of the square grate of years past. Knocking on the walls, he wasn't surprised to find them made from concrete.

As he headed to the bar area, the phone rang. He picked up the receiver. "Yes?"

"Please take a seat on the couch and don't move. You are about to receive visitors."

"Thank you for the heads up, but I can see that there is a refrigerator in the bar, and I was wondering if I could get something to drink."

The guy on the other side of the line chuckled. "Sure, there are bottles of water and beer in there. Get yourself a drink and then sit on the couch. Don't make any sudden moves if you don't want to get shot again."

"I would very much like to avoid that."

"I thought so."

These people weren't playing games, and they were very cautious. Until he had a better grasp on the situation, Lokan was going to act as the perfect guest.

5

MAGNUS

"$\mathcal{M}$agnus, sweetheart, as much as I would like to spend all day hugging and kissing, I can't make lunch while you are holding me." Vivian smiled as she pushed on his chest.

"So, don't."

Since waking up this morning, Magnus hadn't been able to wipe the grin off his face or keep his hands off Vivian. They'd made love all night without any barriers between them, and if not for his worry over her transition, all would have been well in his world.

"I already invited Ella and Julian to lunch, and you know that I promised Parker to make his favorites today."

"His favorite is a juicy steak accompanied by another juicy steak."

"Yeah, but we are out. I'm making his other favorite dish. He asked for the salmon that I made while you were away. And anyway, you need to take Scarlet out for a walk." She waved at the dog who was sitting by the front door and wagging her tail expectantly. "Just look at her. She missed her daddy."

That reminded him that he still needed to talk to Edna

about the adoption papers. With everything that had been going on, he hadn't given it much thought, but now that Vivian could enter transition at any moment, it became urgent to take care of the adoption.

"Fine. It seems that you want to be rid of me."

Vivian slapped his chest playfully. "Don't be silly. Take her for a walk and then come back and help me set up the table. Parker is still sleeping, and I don't have Ella here to make the salads."

He pulled her into his arms again. "Are you sad that she is moving out?"

"Well, a little. My baby is leaving the nest. But mostly I'm overjoyed for her. I know she's going to have a wonderful life with Julian."

"I'm happy for them, too." He glanced at Scarlet, who started whining softly. "I'd better take her out before she has an accident."

Since it was daytime and Scarlet had learned to come when he called for her, Magnus decided to forgo the leash. "Let's go, girl." He opened the door.

She bounded out but kept close, running in circles around him.

"Good girl, Scarlet. Stay close." He was tempted to add, stay close to Daddy, but that was silly.

Pulling out his phone, he searched the clan's directory for Edna's office number.

"Edna Brook's office, how may I help you?" the judge's human assistant answered.

"Can I talk to Edna? This is Magnus MacBain, her cousin."

The woman chuckled. "Edna sure has a lot of cousins."

"We are a big family. An entire clan." He made his accent come out thicker than usual.

"Lucky you. I'll check if she can take the call."

Several seconds later, Edna came on the line. "Congratulations on a successful mission, Magnus. I heard everything worked out well."

"It did. But we had a few scary moments."

"I heard that too. I'm glad everyone is safely back home. I guess that you are calling about adopting Vivian's children?"

"Vivian is ready to attempt transition, and I thought it would be best to make everything legal before that. Just in case."

"Are you talking in future tense, or has the attempting already started?"

"We started."

"Then it is indeed urgent. You should have called me weeks ago."

"You're absolutely right, I should have. But Vivian wanted us to get married first, so in my mind we had time. Then this morning I realized that she would be less stressed about the transition knowing that this was taken care of, and that if, Fates forbid, something happened to her, her children would have a father."

"Then get married, or rather mated. It's as simple as pledging yourself to each other in front of two witnesses. You can have the big ceremony later if you wish."

"In my mind, I'm already mated, but Vivian comes from the human world. For her it's not going to be official until after the ceremony."

"Hmm. I think I can help you out with this as well. Humans can get married by a judge. What if I draw up some official documents and marry you?"

"That would be terrific."

Or not. Vivian would agree and go through the motions, but he was afraid she would be disappointed.

"You don't sound as if you mean it."

"I want to make Vivian happy."

"This is the best I can offer you. But you can give Amanda a call. If anyone can pull off a wedding party on short notice, it's her."

"That's a great idea. Thank you."

"You're welcome. I'll have those adoption papers ready for you by tomorrow. I need to do some research before drafting the first adoption document in the clan's history."

After ending the call with Edna, Magnus tried to think of the best way to present it to Amanda. He couldn't just call and ask her to arrange his wedding. Perhaps he could pretend to ask her advice and wait for her to offer her help?

Yeah, that was good. Even if she saw right through him, this was a more polite way to ask for her help. If Amanda didn't want to be bothered, she wouldn't have to say no, just play along and offer her advice.

Since only those who'd gone to Washington had taken the day off, Amanda should still be at the university, and it was better to text her first to make sure she wasn't in the middle of a lecture.

I'm sorry to bother you at work, but I have some questions regarding organizing a wedding that I thought you could help me with. Call me when you can.

His phone rang five seconds later. "Congratulations, darling. When is the happy day?"

"As soon as I can arrange it. Vivian and I started working on her transition, and I want to adopt Ella and Parker before she enters it. But Vivian wants us to be married first. So, I'm in a bit of a rush."

"You don't say. I'm a pro at this, but even I can't organize a same-day wedding. I might have been able to do it on Saturday, but Callie and Wonder are having a village square barbecue to celebrate your safe return. The best I can do is Sunday."

He'd expected her to say a week from now at best. But Sunday?

"Are you sure?"

"Well, I can't promise anything lavish, but I can probably make it as festive as Parker's transition party."

"That's more than I hoped for. Tell me what I need to do."

"Pfft. Leave it all to me, darling. You just worry about getting a tuxedo for you and Parker. Vivian needs a wedding dress, and Ella needs something nice to wear too. Oh, boy. We need bridesmaids' dresses as well, but I can take care of that. We had a bunch made for Eva's wedding and ended up using the saris instead, so the ladies are covered. You should go shopping today, though, and tell your groomsmen to get tuxes too."

"Right. I didn't even tell Vivian about it yet."

"Then hurry up and talk to her. A wedding is not something a woman wants to be surprised with. If there is any change in plans, call me right away. Call me either way, so I know whether to go into turbo mode or not."

"I will. And thank you so much. I owe you big time for this."

"Yeah, yeah. It's my pleasure. I love organizing parties. Maybe I should quit the university and open a shotgun wedding service."

6

KIAN

*A*rwel's door was open when Kian and his entourage got to the dungeon.

"Come in." He waved them inside.

"How is Lokan doing?" Kian asked.

Arwel motioned to his open laptop, which was running a live feed from the neighboring cell. "He's acting so nonchalant that I'm positive he doesn't know who's got him. He must think he is dealing with humans."

Kian wasn't sure at all that Lokan didn't know he'd been captured by the clan. The arrogant son of a despot wasn't going to show fear.

"How is the feed working? Did you experience any glitches?"

Arwel shook his head. "Works as perfectly as ever."

Now that the keep's security department was made up entirely of humans, the feed from areas the clan still used was redirected to the village's security office, and the monitoring was done from there. Arwel was getting his live transmissions from them.

Freshly showered and looking like he'd stepped out of a

fashion magazine, Lokan was sitting on the couch with an arm stretched over its back, one leg crossed over the other, and sipping on a bottle of Snake's Venom.

"Who gave him that?"

Turner had advised treating Lokan well, but that didn't include pampering him with imported beer.

"It was probably left over by Magnus and Vivian," Anandur said. "When Okidu cleaned the place, he left it in the fridge."

Yeah, that made sense. Okidu knew to check labels for expiration dates, and he wouldn't throw away anything unless it was time to do so.

"Okay." Kian turned to Brundar. "If he makes a wrong move, show him the error of his ways but don't maim him."

Brundar nodded, but the Guardian's hand was hovering over the pommel of his sword, and his lips were curled in a hint of an evil smirk.

"Whatever you do, don't chop his head off. We need him."

"Don't worry, boss. I got it."

As Anandur entered the code into the keypad, Kian put a hand on his shoulder. "I know that you and Brundar want to get in first and secure the scene, but I just have to see the look on his face when he realizes who's got him. He's unarmed."

"He's not planning anything," Arwel said. "He is in watch and learn mode."

A grimace twisting Anandur's face, he nodded. "You are the boss, Kian."

Damn right he was. But when it came to his safety and his disregard for it, his bodyguards rarely obeyed his wishes without argument.

As the heavy door finished moving on its track, Kian strode into the room, his eyes trained on the Doomer.

A barely audible intake of breath was the only indication that Lokan was taken by surprise. His eyes were so dark that it was difficult to distinguish the irises from the pupils, and Kian couldn't tell whether they had dilated or not.

And as far as scents went, whatever Lokan emitted was masked by the cologne he'd doused himself with. Turner shouldn't have left it in the suitcase when he'd checked Lokan's belongings and removed everything that could be used as a weapon or a communication device.

"Good morning, Lokan." Kian walked over to the armchair and took a seat.

As the brothers and Andrew pulled out chairs from the dinette, Arwel put down a paper cup and a wrapped sandwich on the coffee table. "Your breakfast."

"Thank you," Lokan said. "You seem to know who I am, which puts me at a disadvantage." He smiled. "An additional one." He lifted his cuffed wrist and saluted Kian with the beer bottle. "May I have your names, gentlemen?"

For a brief moment, Kian debated how to introduce himself. Annoyed by Lokan's ability to keep a calm façade, he decided to go for his full title. "I'm Kian, Annani's son and her American regent."

Surprising him, Lokan put his beer down and leaned forward, offering him his hand. "A pleasure to meet you, cousin. I am Lokan, Navuh's son, and his liaison to Washington, but then you seem to know that. May I inquire how?"

Not one to refuse a challenge, Kian shook the hand he was offered. "Do you really think you're in a position to ask questions?"

Lokan dipped his head in mock respect. "Only if you don't mind answering them, of course."

Well, that was reasonable.

Fuck. The Doomer was acting all rational, calm and collected, making Kian feel like he was the bully in this situation.

Leaning back, he crossed his legs and put his arms on the armrests, affecting the same nonchalant attitude the Doomer was fronting.

"I'll make you a deal, Lokan. For every question you answer truthfully, I'll answer one of yours."

A big grin spread over the Doomer's handsome face. "Deal accepted. I assume you want to go first?"

"Naturally. Why did you want Ella and Vivian?"

"I had a special mission in mind for which I required their unique talent. Undetectable communication."

"Truth," Andrew said from behind him.

"What kind of a mission?"

Lokan shook his head. "I believe it is my turn."

"Go ahead."

"What have you done with my men and with my jet?"

Out of everything he could have inquired about, Kian hadn't expected Lokan to show concern for his men. It was uncharacteristic for a Doomer leader.

"That's two questions, but I'm feeling generous. Your men were put in stasis, and your jet was hidden in a hangar in Mexico. Why is it important to you? I wasn't aware Doomers cared for their underlings."

"My men and the abandoned jet could have alerted my father to the fact that I was kidnapped."

"Truth," Andrew said.

"Would he have come after you?"

"Obviously."

Andrew chuckled. "Lie."

Lokan lifted the beer bottle and saluted Andrew. "I was testing him. He's good."

"Yes, he is. We call him the lie detector." Kian crossed his arms over his chest. "So, tell me, Lokan. What will your father do when he discovers you are gone?"

"It depends on how well you covered your tracks. If you did a good job, he will assume I defected. If you didn't, he will come after you with a vengeance."

"Truth."

Kian lifted a brow. "He doesn't know where to find us. Otherwise, he would have done it a long time ago."

"He knows where to find your allies."

"Truth."

"My turn. What do Ella and her mother have to do with the clan? What's the connection? And why did you rescue her from Gorchenco? Do you need their talent as well?"

"That's four questions. Ella and Vivian are Dormants. Not for long, though. They will transition soon."

For the first time since their conversation had started, Lokan looked stunned. "I had no idea. If I'd known..."

Kian uncrossed his arms and leaned forward. "You would've done what?"

Casting a quick glance at Andrew, Lokan shook his head. "Because of him, I can't lie even to be polite. Dormants are precious. No wonder you went to such lengths to rescue them. Both Ella and Vivian are beautiful women, each in her own way, but I wasn't overly interested in either, as humans, that is. The possibility of having immortal offspring though, that would have made a big difference in the level of their desirability to me."

"Truth."

7

LOKAN

*L*okan never thought he would be thankful for the years of practice he'd had hiding his thoughts from his father. He was an expert on guarding his expressions and keeping his emotions running on neutral, which was crucial to throttle the potency of any emotional scents he emitted.

Not many immortals could pull that off as well as he did.

The trick was disassociation. Since a young age, Lokan learned to take himself out of the scene and pretend that whatever was happening wasn't happening to him, and that he was just an uninvolved observer.

Except, it was difficult to do when facing imminent execution.

Unless he could prove exceptionally valuable to the clan, he was going to be dead soon, same as his men. What had made Kian come up with the ridiculous story about putting them in stasis?

Why would anyone do that?

Stasis was a temporary state, a result of a grave injury. Immortals didn't stay in stasis indefinitely. Their bodies repaired themselves, and they were back up to fight another day.

But Kian's reasons for lying were not important right now. What Lokan needed to figure out was how to convince his cousin to spare his life.

If he told Kian everything he wanted to know, he would have no further need for him. Perhaps he could convince Kian that his father would trade for him?

It could've worked if not for the lie detector guy. But perhaps he could fool him by saying things that were mostly true and only slightly exaggerated or twisted a bit to serve his purpose.

First, though, he needed more information. "My turn. Back to my original question. How did you know who I was? And did you put Ella in my path on purpose?"

Kian chuckled. "You are doing it again. Asking several questions as if they are one. We didn't put Ella in your path. Fate did. Your meeting with her happened purely by chance. Later on, she recognized you from your picture. And that was how we found out about you."

"How did you come by my picture?"

Kian shook his head. "It's my turn to ask. What did you need Ella and Vivian for?"

"I told you already. I needed them for a mission to get information that couldn't be transmitted by ordinary means."

"I need more than that."

This was Lokan's most guarded secret, but that was because it could have meant his death if his father found out. Except, Navuh wasn't going to hear it from Kian, his arch-nemesis's son.

"My father's harem is inaccessible to immortals. The way it works, the only ones who can get in are the humans who serve there. If they are ever allowed to leave, it's without their

34

memories. I wanted to find out what he was hiding in there because it must be pretty damn important for him to go to such lengths to seclude his ladies."

"Truth," the lie detector announced.

So, it worked. Lokan could get away with telling partial truths and choosing his words carefully.

Kian nodded. "If you could get one telepath inside, she could communicate what was going on to the other."

"Precisely. And since Ella and Vivian can only communicate with each other, there was no fear of their mental conversations getting picked up by someone who wasn't supposed to hear them. I would've coached them on how to keep their shields up, so it wouldn't be as easy to peek into their heads as it was for me when I first met Ella."

He chuckled. "When I couldn't do that the second time around with her, it should've clued me in. But I assumed that she was doing it on her own."

"Who did you think was aiding her? You obviously knew that we were setting a trap for you. You just didn't know who we were. Am I right?"

"I believe it's your turn to answer my question first. How did you obtain a picture of me?"

"One of your men crossed over to our side. He's a talented artist, and he drew portraits of the Brotherhood's leadership for us."

That was another shocker Lokan had not been ready for. He could understand a Doomer seeking asylum with the clan, but he couldn't conceive of the clan granting it. He would have asked about it, but it wasn't worth wasting his questions on.

"You look surprised," Kian said.

"I am. Why would you grant asylum to one of us?" He waved a dismissive hand. "Forget I asked. I don't want to waste my question on that."

"As you wish. Now answer mine. Who did you assume was helping Ella and Vivian?"

"The government. I knew that they'd been collecting people with special abilities for decades. I thought that Vivian had revealed her and Ella's telepathy in exchange for their help rescuing Ella from the Russian. After that, I assumed that the entire family had been taken into the program, and that Ella had told them about my dream-sharing ability, which they wanted to get their hands on as well."

"Are you sure about the collecting of paranormal talents? I've never heard about a program like that."

From everything that Lokan had told Kian so far, this seemed to pique his interest the most. And not only his. He could smell the other immortals in the room emitting scents of excitement.

Why were they so interested in the government's paranormal warfare division?

Could this be his ticket to longevity?

Lokan lifted a finger. "I'll answer that, but then you'll owe me a question. Yes, I'm sure. I was trying to find out where they were hiding the talents, and with my ability to compel it shouldn't have been a problem, but I've never gotten close to anyone who had inside information that could lead me to them. Still, the sources I learned this from were very reliable. Given more time, I would have found out where the talents were being held."

"Fascinating," Kian murmured. "How come we've never heard about this?"

It was a rhetorical question, but if he answered it, Kian would owe him one more.

"It's highly classified. And the only reason I found out was that I had a meeting with a congressman who knew about it, and I peeked into his head. After that, I started looking for

36

more information. Mainly because I wanted to find out if there were more dream-walkers out there, but also because I could use talents like that for a variety of projects. Why is it so interesting to you, though?"

Kian regarded him with a peculiar expression on his face, condescending but also pitying, as if Lokan was stupid for not figuring out the answer to that himself.

"What do you know about Dormants, Lokan?"

"You didn't answer my question."

"Humor me. This is part of the answer."

"Dormants can be turned immortal by getting bitten by an immortal male. The propaganda my father spreads is that females are not worthy of being turned, and that is why we don't allow them to become immortal. But I know the truth. Female Dormants have the same fertility rates as other human females, and they can produce many Dormant children. Once they are turned, however, the fertility rate drops significantly. In order to keep growing our army of immortal soldiers, we need the female Dormants to remain as fertile as possible."

8

KIAN

*K*ian found it astonishing that even someone as highly positioned as Lokan didn't know about paranormal abilities being a possible indicator of Dormants.

To be fair, the clan had discovered this only recently, but that was because they hadn't had any Dormants to observe until Amanda had come up with her hypothesis. Just as some immortals exhibited special abilities, traits that they had inherited from the gods, so should Dormants. She'd then proven it by testing students at her university and finding Syssi and Michael.

The Brotherhood, on the other hand, had bred plenty over the millennia. Someone should have noticed that Dormants were much more likely to exhibit paranormal abilities than the general human population.

Except the male Dormants were induced at a young age, before those abilities manifested, and the female Dormants were regarded as inferior, suitable only for breeding and otherwise ignored. Furthermore, the attitude toward them affected the females' self-esteem, which probably made them doubt and stifle any extraordinary talents they might possess.

Could it be that even Navuh wasn't aware of the treasure trove he possessed?

After all, the Doomers kept their female Dormants secluded, and the males were separated from their mothers upon reaching puberty, and activated. After that, they had no more contact whatsoever with the female Dormants, ensuring that the immortal males didn't induce the female Dormants' transition.

Still, over the thousands of years that Navuh had the breeding program going, someone must have noticed something and connected the dots.

"Well?" Lokan prompted.

Kian pinned him with a hard stare. "You had a treasure trove of paranormal talent under your nose and didn't even know about it."

"What are you talking about?"

"Dormants exhibit special abilities in a much higher percentage than ordinary humans. I'm sure your abhorrent breeding program is full of them. But you wouldn't know that because you were probably not allowed in there the same way you were not allowed into your father's harem."

Lokan's reaction wasn't as satisfying as Kian had hoped it would be. If anything, he looked skeptical. "I spent my childhood inside the Dormant enclosure. I would have noticed if anyone exhibited anything out of the ordinary."

"How old were you when you were extracted from there, thirteen? Until then, you were probably busy playing with the other boys and didn't pay attention to the women."

"I was twelve when I went through my transition, and before that, I spent most of my time with my tutors. I'm not stupid, and I wasn't as a boy. I would've noticed if any of the females had extrasensory perception."

Twelve was a little young for inducing transition, but

maybe Lokan had hit puberty earlier. After all, Parker had done it at twelve and a half.

"They might have been afraid to show their abilities."

Lokan nodded. "That's possible. I didn't tell anyone about my dream-sharing ability. I would have kept the compulsion to myself as well, but I didn't know I had it until I told my tutor to kiss my ass and he did."

Behind him, Kian heard the men snicker.

"Your tutor was human?"

"Naturally. Back then, only priests and monks were literate." Lokan chuckled. "The guy ran to complain to the headmistress, who informed my older brother, who told my father. Imagine my surprise when, instead of a punishment, I received praise. But that was also the end of my childhood. My father ordered my induction, and I was put to work."

Grudgingly, and against his better judgment, Kian was starting to sympathize with the guy. Ella had warned him that Lokan could be charming when he wanted to be, and that he was cunning and manipulative. But even though he'd been prepared for it, Kian couldn't help the affinity, for lack of a better term, that he felt for the son of his arch enemy.

Was it because they were related?

Nah, there wasn't enough shared blood to justify that. The explanation was much simpler than that. Just like Lokan, Kian hadn't had much of a childhood.

Both of them were the sons of leaders, both had to assume the mantle of responsibility at a young age, and both had spent their long immortal lives in the service of their people.

The difference was that Kian had been busy doing good, while Lokan had been busy doing the opposite and undoing as much of Kian's work as possible.

"Your coffee is getting cold." He pointed to the cup and the wrapped sandwich that Lokan hadn't touched yet. "I promise you that nothing has been poisoned."

Lokan glanced at the sandwich and then at Kian. "It's rude to be the only one eating. I'll save it for later. Back to the issue of paranormal abilities and Dormants. Am I to understand that you wish to find where the government is hiding its paranormal talents because you believe that you'll find Dormants among them?"

The guy was sharp, which was another trait Kian appreciated.

"Correct."

"Perhaps I can help you with that."

"And you'll do it because?"

"In exchange for my life, naturally."

Kian leaned forward. "We are not going to kill you. But if you want to keep getting the royal treatment and save yourself a lot of pain, helping us find Dormants isn't going to cut it. I want the location of your fucking island."

Lokan's good mood seemed to vanish in an instant. "I can't tell you where it is."

"Can't or won't?"

"Both."

Kian hadn't expected it to be easy, and he'd already shown Lokan the stick as well as dangled the carrot. Perhaps a demonstration was needed?

Except, he had a feeling that torture wasn't going to work on Navuh's son. And in any case, it was prudent to start with persuasion and up the ante as needed.

"In here, you shouldn't fear your father's wrath, only mine."

"I'm well aware of that. But I can't allow you to annihilate my people. I might not agree with my father's policies, and there are many individuals whose demise I won't mourn, but there are tens of thousands of people living on that island who don't deserve to die."

"Truth," Andrew said.

"Unlike your father, I'm not a monster, Lokan. I would never kill indiscriminately."

Leaning back, Lokan crossed his arms over his chest. "I've been a military commander long enough to know that you don't have any other options available to you. You don't have enough men to storm the island. You can bomb it, but that will only kill the humans, or you can nuke it and kill everyone."

Sadly, it was a logical conclusion for someone like Lokan, who grew up in the Brotherhood and absorbed its disregard for life, human and immortal alike.

"I'm not going to nuke the place. For better or worse, we are all that is left from our people, and by *we,* I mean your people and mine. As much as I despise everything you stand for and everything you've done, I can't annihilate your people even if I could target just the soldiers and spare the civilians. I need the location to launch spying missions."

Lokan shook his head. "I don't buy it. What is it that you hope to learn by sending spies to the island? I can probably give you all the information you want, except for the location, that is."

Reaching into his suit pocket, Kian pulled out a box of cigarillos and a lighter. "Do you smoke?"

Eyeing the box, Lokan nodded. "It's an indulgence reserved for special occasions. But then, I never expected to meet you, cousin." He smirked. "I guess that's special enough to celebrate." He reached for the box and pulled one cigarillo out.

9

LOKAN

*W*as the cigarillo a condemned man's last perk?

As he leaned toward Kian's lighter and lit up, Lokan cast a sidelong glance at the other immortals in the room. They didn't look like they had murder on their minds. Even the blond, who Lokan had sensed was the most dangerous of the three, seemed disinterested.

Did he believe Kian, though?

Not even for a moment. The guy sounded so sincere while delivering his little speech, but Lokan could sense the smoldering hatred under Kian's calm and collected façade.

He took a puff. "It's really good. Where do you get them?"

"My wife commissioned them for me."

Lokan nearly choked on the smoke he inhaled with the intake of breath, releasing it through his nose and doing his damnedest not to cough. "You have a wife? I thought clan members were all the descendants of one goddess and that you have a strong taboo against intermingling, so to speak."

Kian smirked. "My wife, the love of my life, was a human and a Dormant. Now she is an immortal and a clan member."

Although Lokan had never wished for a mate of his own,

the adoration in Kian's eyes and the pride in his voice sparked a strange yearning in his gut.

If he'd only known that Ella and Vivian were Dormants.

Ella was still a kid, but Vivian was suitable mate material. Except, he hadn't been attracted to either for some reason. Not in real life, anyway. While dream-sharing with Ella, he'd gotten aroused when they kissed, but she hadn't evoked that response in him when they met in person.

He wondered why. Usually, the chase made him lustful, but not this time. Could it be that he had a premonition that it wasn't going to end well?

Or maybe it was something else.

"Are Ella and Vivian mated as well?"

"They are."

Perhaps it was a built-in mechanism that was particular to immortals, warning them to stay away from other males' mates. Something about Ella and Vivian's scents must have been different, and even though he hadn't discerned it consciously, his subconscious had recognized it and had adjusted his libido accordingly.

Lokan had so much to learn about his own physiology and that of dormant and immortal females. If he ever got out of this predicament, and if by some miracle he managed to persuade his father to allow the activation of female Dormants, this information would be invaluable.

"Are they about to transition?"

Kian nodded. "The Fates smiled upon us, gifting us with an entire family of Dormants. Ella's younger brother has already transitioned."

One thing was obvious. Dormants, whether male or female, were even more precious to the clan than to the Brotherhood, and Kian would be willing to pay any price to find out where the government had a whole bunch of them stashed.

If he were in Kian's position, Lokan would have preferred to get that information over the location of his enemy base. Especially since knowing where to find the island wasn't going to benefit Kian half as much as growing his puny clan in one fell swoop by getting his hands on a large bunch of Dormants.

"Congratulations. It seems like those Fates of yours have sent me to you because I can find many more Dormants for you."

Kian blew out smoke, then leveled his intense eyes on Lokan. "I need the island's location. Everything else is secondary to that."

Damn.

There was one more potential ace Lokan had up his sleeve. "What if I can get Gorchenco off Ella's back?"

Kian waved a dismissive hand. "He's no longer looking for her."

Lokan smirked. "That's where you are wrong. It was a bad idea to sell her engagement ring. He bought it back and is now convinced that she's alive and hiding from him."

"Truth," the lie detector said.

"Fuck! I knew we should have killed the son of a bitch."

Lokan smiled. "As I said, I can have him off her back."

"How?"

"I have dirt on him. But I'll disclose it in exchange for your vow not to kill me or torture me."

"I can vow not to kill you, but unless you tell me the island's location, I can't promise to spare you the other."

"I can't give you that."

"What if I vow not to nuke the island, which I really have no intention of doing?"

"I can't risk it."

"And yet you are willing to trust my word to spare you."

"That's different. I can gamble with my life. I can't gamble with the lives of thousands."

"He means it," said the guy with the haunted eyes.

Did they have two lie detectors? Or was the other one an empath?

Thankfully, his father didn't have anyone like that. They had spread rumors that Hazok could detect lies, but that wasn't true. His half-brother was an excellent sniffer and could differentiate subtle nuances, which was useful for lie detecting, but his ability didn't come anywhere close to Kian's guy.

Shaking his head, Kian tapped his cigarillo, dropping the ash into the cardboard tray that had come with the coffee. "I can't believe I'm saying this to a Doomer, but I respect and admire your dedication to your people. What if I can prove to you that we are not seeking the annihilation of all Doomers?"

"How do you propose to do that?"

"I can prove to you that we don't kill your people unless it's in the heat of battle and unavoidable. Most of the Doomers we've captured over the years are not dead. They are in stasis."

Again with the stasis.

This was such a ridiculous notion that Lokan felt insulted. Did Kian think he was an idiot?

"Do you want to tell me that you have them locked up in a dungeon and someone is knocking them over the head every time they regenerate? Because we both know that no one stays in stasis indefinitely."

The snickers from the men in the back confirmed his suspicion. But Lokan was surprised they allowed themselves to behave so disrespectfully toward their leader. Apparently, the clansmen lacked discipline and respect for the proper chain of command.

Shaking his head, Kian stubbed out his cigarillo and pulled a new one from the box. "No offense, Lokan, but I can't believe how ignorant you are. Not your fault, though. You guys are kept in the dark about the most basic things. A deep state of stasis can be achieved by injecting venom to the brink. The body doesn't regenerate spontaneously in that state. It has to be revived."

"What does it mean to inject to the brink?"

"Stopping just before the heartbeat winks out. It requires precision, but my men are all trained to do that."

"How is the reviving done?"

Kian smiled. "I'm not going to tell you that. But if you want, I can take you on a tour of our catacombs and show you that many of your missing men are not dead."

"That I would like to see. But first, if you don't mind telling me this, why do you bother? We are your enemies, and those men would not have hesitated to kill you."

A grimace twisted Kian's handsome face. "If it were up to me, none of them would have been spared. But my mother doesn't allow it. To her, every immortal is precious. She hopes that one day your father will be overthrown and that a new era of peace and cooperation will begin. She also believes that in the absence of his relentless brainwashing, these men can be revived and then reconditioned."

Lokan found this as hard to accept as Kian's other incredible claims.

"Your mother is a romantic."

"That she is. So, do we have a deal? If you see proof that your men are alive and in stasis, are you going to tell me the island's location?"

Kian was probably planning a trick. He was going to show him one or two men in stasis, who for all Lokan knew could be clan members who had transgressed and had been punished.

"How many men are we talking about?"

"Let's put it this way. We will soon need to expand the cata-combs because we are running out of space."

"How would I know they are mine? What if they are clan members who got punished?"

"We have only one of ours in that state, and he's in a different section. The rest are dead, killed by your people. It's not difficult to differentiate between them. Our dead are in closed sarcophaguses, yours are in more modest caskets. The live ones are laid in open niches. They are not pretty to look at, but if you listen carefully, you'll hear a very faint and slow heartbeat."

"I need to think about it."

"I understand." Kian pushed to his feet. "When you are ready, pick up the phone and dial zero. My guy will let me know."

At the door, he stopped and turned back. "Before I forget. Don't think about visiting Ella at night. If I hear that you've bothered her, I will be much less friendly the next time we meet. Am I clear?"

Lokan gave him a two-finger salute. "I'm not going to bother her. But I would appreciate it if she came to visit me. With her mate, of course. I'm curious to see the male she chose over me."

VIVIAN

"*I*t smells so good." Parker walked into the kitchen in his pajamas. "What're you making other than the salmon?"

Vivian pulled him in for a hug and squeezed hard. He was an immortal now, and her human strength was nothing to him. "Fettuccine Alfredo with mushrooms. I made two kinds of salmon, and I'm curious about which one you are going to like more."

He wiggled out of her arms. "What, no salad?"

"Ella is not here to make it. I didn't think you'd miss it."

"I don't. Is Ella coming back at all? Her stuff is still here."

It was sweet. Parker didn't like it when they told him that his sister was moving in with Julian. He'd even suggested that instead of Ella going to live with her boyfriend, he should come live with them.

Vivian would have loved nothing more, but a young couple needed their privacy. With the cost of housing not a consideration, it was a no brainer for Ella and Julian to live on their own.

Hopefully, they would come to visit often, and perhaps Ella would invite her family over to her new house as well.

"Ella and Julian are coming for lunch, and I invited Bridget and Turner as well. You should get dressed."

Parker narrowed his eyes at her. "Is this like an official engagement lunch or something?"

"Or something. Go already. They should be here in half an hour."

He waved a dismissive hand. "That's plenty of time. I can get dressed in five minutes. I want to eat."

"Take a small snack. I don't want you filling up before lunch."

"I'll get cereal. May I eat it in my room?"

Usually, she didn't allow it, but this weekend Parker was going to get a pass on a lot of things.

He'd earned it.

"Yes, you may. But don't get used to it. After the weekend, it's back to normal."

"Yes, ma'am." He saluted and then scurried away with his bowl before she could change her mind.

When a few minutes later the front door opened and Scarlet trotted in with Magnus in tow, Vivian waved him over to the kitchen.

"Just in time. Can you cut up some veggies for a salad?"

"Sure thing."

Magnus opened the sliding doors to the backyard, let the dog out, and then came over and washed his hands in the kitchen sink.

"I made a couple of phone calls while walking Scarlet," he said.

"I hope you didn't invite more people. I already called Bridget and Turner, and with Ella and Julian that makes seven. I don't think what I made can feed more."

Leaning against the counter, he reached for her hand and pulled her against him. "I called Edna about the adoption papers, and I called Amanda about organizing a wedding for us."

Vivian swallowed. "Not that I'm against either, but don't you think you should have talked with me first?'

"I should have, but it kind of snowballed while I was talking with Edna. It all started with your daddy comment. I thought about what we did last night and that you might enter transition any day now. I figured that knowing your children would have a father to take care of them if anything went wrong would ease your mind."

Lifting on her toes, she kissed his cheek. "I know that you will do that with or without official papers."

"I will. But I thought that you would like something more official, so I called Edna about drafting the paperwork. Then I mentioned that you wanted us to be married before the adoption, and Edna offered to marry us in a civil ceremony, but I said that you might be disappointed with that, so she suggested that I call Amanda about arranging a party."

Vivian shook her head. "So, you just called her and asked her to drop everything and start working on our wedding?"

"No, I asked for her advice."

Sweet Magnus. He was an awesome guy, but that was as subtle as a sledgehammer. "I see. And what advice did she give you?"

"That we should go shopping for a wedding dress and a tux because the party is this Sunday."

"That's crazy, and not only because there is no way she can pull it off, especially with the barbecue tomorrow, but because it just is." Vivian put a hand over her heart. "I need time to mentally prepare."

Leaning, he whispered in her ear. "Do you want to go back to condoms? Because if we keep going without, you'll enter transition. It's your choice, of course. We can also get married after you are an immortal. Edna can take care of the adoption regardless of our marital status. And besides, according to our law, a mating is official when we pledge ourselves to each other in front of two adult witnesses. We don't need a ceremony to make it official."

Having options was good.

Vivian relaxed. She didn't have to rush. She could wait with the wedding until after her transition. Or she could wait with the transition for after the wedding.

"What do you think we should do?"

Magnus smiled. "I say we go for it, but then I'm a guy, and I never had wedding dreams. It's up to you, love, and what will make you happy. That's all I want."

She glanced at the microwave display to check the time. "Can I decide after lunch? We have guests arriving in ten minutes, and the table is not set yet. And we don't have a salad."

"Amanda needs an answer as soon as possible, but it can wait for after lunch."

11

CAROL

*A*s Carol crossed her living room for the fiftieth time, Ben waved a hand. "Stop that annoying pacing. If you have to do it, please don't do it in front of the screen."

As if his yelling and jumping up and down when his team scored wasn't annoying as hell.

Her roommate was an easygoing guy, and most of the time she liked having him around, just not when he was watching sports games and cheering his teams from the couch.

Weren't guys supposed to do it together? Meet up in someone's house, drink shitloads of beer, and eat nachos?

"Don't you have friends that you want to share this joyous activity with?"

He cast her a sidelong glance. "Do you want me to watch the game in my room?"

"No. That's fine. I'll go out for a walk."

It was Ben's home too, and if he wanted to watch TV in the living room while munching on pizza, it was his right. Usually, the yelling and jumping wouldn't have bothered Carol, but she was humming with nervous excitement, impatient to hear all about Ella's adventures in Washington and get all the juicy details about what had happened with Lokan.

Except, the girl was celebrating with her guy, and it would have been rude to call her up and interrupt all that loving.

It was about time those two moved in together, but Carol hadn't expected it to happen so soon. It had been quite a surprise to hear it from Ray when he stopped at the café yesterday, complaining about Julian kicking him out because Ella was moving in with him. Julian had called him from the plane, giving him only a few hours' notice, and the guy had been looking for a place to crash for the night.

Carol could only imagine the steam coming out of that bedroom. It seemed that whatever had been blocking Ella's attraction to Julian had been taken care of. Those two were probably not going to leave their bed for days.

Damn, she really wanted all that juicy gossip.

During the day, she had been busy in the café, so it had been easier to keep herself from picking up the phone, but now she had nothing to do except think about it.

Not in the mood for a walk, she decided to sit on the rocking chair on her front porch and watch the sunset.

How lame.

It was pitiful to live vicariously through an eighteen-year-old's adventures, but that was what Carol, at one time Paris's most coveted courtesan, had been reduced to.

Between running the café and teaching the beginners' self-defense class, she had little time or energy for anything else. And if she cared to be honest with herself, after having been with Robert, human males didn't excite her nearly as much as they used to. Never mind that Robert had been far from her ideal lover. Even a mediocre immortal lover was better than the best of humans.

Besides, the type of men she liked didn't hang out in clubs

and bars. Successful, powerful men didn't waste their time in places like that.

With a sigh, she pulled out her phone and glanced at the time. It was after seven in the evening, and probably safe to call Ella. After all, the girl was still human, and her stamina should have run out a long time ago.

Just to be safe, though, she decided to text instead of calling.

Are you still celebrating? Or do you have time for your friend who is dying to hear all the juicy details you can't tell anyone else?

She watched the little icon as Ella typed her answer.

I'm taking a short break from celebrating. Come over.

Right. She could imagine the stink eye Julian would give her if she showed up in his house the day after his girl had moved in.

I don't want to intrude.

Julian went grocery shopping because we have nothing in the house. I'm all alone. Come.

That gave her an idea. Perhaps if she showed up with dinner, Julian wouldn't mind the intrusion.

I'll cook you something yummy to replenish your energy stores.

We had lunch at my parents, and I'm stuffed. Don't bring anything. On second thought, bring cream. I'm making coffee and we are out.

On my way.

Carol wasn't going to show up with just the cream no matter how stuffed Ella claimed to be.

It was a good thing that she always cooked too much, and her freezer was full with the extra portions she'd saved for later.

"What are you doing?" Ben asked as she started taking out containers from the freezer.

"Don't worry. I'll make more. I'm bringing Ella and Julian a frozen house warming gift." She chuckled.

"Good idea." He went back to watching his game.

A large insulated bag slung over her shoulder, Carol headed toward Julian's house, but found herself taking a detour.

The office building wasn't on the way, but it would add no more than five minutes to her walk. She just had an urge to take one more peek at the infamous Doomer's picture.

She'd seen all the portraits Dalhu had drawn of the Brotherhood's elite, but she hadn't paid that much attention. Now that Lokan had been captured, though, she wanted to have a face to go with the stories Ella was going to tell her.

Last time she'd collected packages from the building's lobby, the portraits had been hanging on the wall of the first floor corridor. Hopefully, Dalhu hadn't removed them yet.

Good thing that no one had wanted to buy those. Dalhu's landscapes had all been snapped up, even though the artist himself claimed that they weren't good enough yet.

Carol wasn't an art expert, but she thought they were all beautiful, and even bought one to hang in her living room where she could see it from the kitchen when she cooked. There was something soothing and relaxing about that landscape, and gazing at it while cooking made the activity even more pleasurable than it already was.

Some people knitted, others colored, Carol cooked.

When she got to the office building, though, none of the portraits were there.

Damn, that was a shame.

She was about to head out when she saw Bridget coming down the stairs.

"Working late?"

"Yeah. I took a long lunch break and had to come back to finish up. What are you doing here so late?"

"I was looking for Lokan's portrait, but I see that Dalhu took all of them down."

Bridget snorted. "I asked him to. They were getting on Kian's nerves. He didn't say anything, but I could see his reaction every time he glanced at one of them. Fates know that Kian doesn't need additional reasons to get angry. But if you want to see Lokan's picture, I have it on my phone. I snapped photos of all the portraits."

Bridget took her phone out of her purse and scrolled until she found it. "It's not the best. But it will give you an idea."

"Can you share it with me? I have a bunch of frozen meals I need to put in Ella and Julian's freezer."

"That's so thoughtful of you. I should have done it. Ella said that they have nothing in the house." She chuckled. "I would have ordered it from a restaurant, though. I don't have time to cook."

"I'm sure it would have been just as appreciated. Thanks for the photo."

"No problem."

Carol waited until she was alone on the trail to take a look. Lokan was handsome, but that wasn't his most striking feature. She could see so much in those dark eyes of his. Intelligence, mischief, secrets.

He should be fascinating to talk to.

The question was whether Kian would allow her to see him.

Perhaps she could help with the interrogation?

Men usually underestimated her, letting their mouths flap secrets they were sure she was too dumb to do anything with—a misconception Carol encouraged enthusiastically.

12

SYSSI

*I*n her bathroom, Syssi stood in front of the mirror and rubbed her tummy, wondering how immortal females knew when they had conceived.

With no periods, there was nothing to miss. She could be pregnant already and not know it. In fact, she had a feeling that she was.

Or maybe it was just wishful thinking. A placebo effect of drinking Merlin's potion twice a day and praying that it would work.

Kian was doing his best to calm down, and since everyone in the office building knew about Merlin's theory, they were trying to minimize Kian's annoyances.

Was it helping?

Not really. Even when he was happy, Kian was stressed. Capturing Lokan was a cause for clan-wide celebration, but there had been some scary moments on the way. Lokan had almost succeeded in kidnapping Ella and Vivian despite the army of Guardians Turner had with him.

The guy must be really smart, which wasn't surprising. His

father might be insane, and his grandfather had certainly been unstable, but no one doubted their superior intelligence.

She wondered about his mother. Navuh wasn't a god, so the only way for him to produce his many sons was if he had Dormants or immortals in his harem. Probably immortals because the Dormants would have turned after several biting sessions.

Poor women. They didn't even get to raise their children, which could have been the only solace for being kept secluded in a closed-off harem no one was allowed into. Not even their children.

Rubbing her tummy again, Syssi smiled as she imagined it swelling with her and Kian's child.

Assuming the win, so to speak.

Perhaps she should ask Bridget for a pregnancy test?

Except, Syssi was too scared to do it. If the result was negative, she would be disappointed, and a bad mood was not conducive to conception.

She could wait a little longer. Maybe ask Eva if there was a way to know before the pregnancy progressed enough for her scent to change and for other immortals to sniff it.

But what if Merlin's potion was not good for the baby, and she should stop taking it?

Suddenly panicked, she rushed into the bedroom and snatched her phone off the charger.

"Syssi, what a pleasant surprise," Merlin answered as soon as she dialed his number. "What can I help you with?"

"I have a question. Is the potion dangerous to a developing fetus?"

"Why? Do you have good news for me?"

"I'm not sure. Immortal females don't menstruate, so how would I know when to stop drinking it?"

"First of all, you can relax. It's not dangerous to the baby.

And you'll know when you hear the heartbeat at about forty days after conception, or if you get a pregnancy test."

She waved a hand even though he couldn't see her. "Why would I get a test? It's not like I'm going to be late and have a reason to do it."

"True. But if you are impatient and don't want to wait for the heartbeat, you can just pee on a stick every other day or once a week. It's not difficult, and the tests are not costly."

"I'll think about it. Thanks, Merlin."

"My pleasure."

After disconnecting, Syssi took a deep breath and grabbed her tablet. While Kian worked from home, she liked to sit on the couch in his office and read. They both enjoyed the closeness.

The problem with being married to an immortal, though, was that he could sense her emotions with ease.

Lifting his head from the report spread out on his desk, Kian smiled at her. "You seem excited. Any good news?"

Had he heard her talking with Merlin?

The bedroom door had been closed, and the soundproofing in the house was excellent. Kian couldn't have heard her.

Perhaps he was just as anxious and impatient as she was. In any case, Syssi wasn't about to share her suspicions with him. If it was nothing, at least he wouldn't be disappointed.

Luckily, she had some other good news to impart. "Magnus called Amanda at the lab today. He and Vivian are working on her transition, and since she's worried about what will happen to her kids if anything goes wrong, he wants to officially adopt them right away."

"Good for him. But that's Edna's department, not Amanda's."

"Right. So, he called Edna first and mentioned that Vivian wanted them to be married first, and Edna told him to go for it.

So, he called Amanda with the lame excuse that he needed her advice. Long story short, there is going to be a wedding on Sunday, and Amanda is making it happen."

Kian shook his head. "And I thought that our wedding was rushed."

"By now, Amanda has so much experience in organizing parties that she can pull it off."

"Do we need to do anything?"

Tucking her legs under her, Syssi leaned against the sofa's armrest. "I'm in charge of the decorations. Amanda is already assigning everyone tasks. I'm telling you, that woman could have been an army general."

He chuckled. "No doubt."

For some reason, thinking about an army and generals reminded her that Annani should be informed about Lokan's capture, and not through the grapevine. Or maybe it was the talk about the wedding that had prompted it. Annani loved presiding over weddings.

"By the way. Did you call your mother with the good news?"

He arched a brow. "You just told me about it. When was I supposed to do that?"

"Not the wedding. I meant about catching Lokan."

"Not yet. I want to get the island's location out of him first. Then I will really have good news for her. Lokan himself is not important. It's the information we can get out of him."

"She's going to hear about it from someone else and get mad at you for not calling her with the news as soon as we got him."

Waving a dismissive hand, Kian snorted. "It won't be the first or last time. I'm used to my mother being peeved at me."

"Don't be an ass. Call her. She'll appreciate it."

"Fine, but speaking of asses, there is a board meeting at

Perfect Match next week, and as the majority stockholder, you need to attend."

"Only if you come with me. But what does it have to do with asses?"

He smirked. "Just one ass. Yours. Have you given a thought to the fantasy you'd like to experience? All the testing is done, and the service works without a glitch. It's safe."

Butterflies taking flight in her tummy, Syssi put the tablet down. "We can try it out?"

"That's what I said."

"When?'

"Whenever you want. Just give me a couple of days' heads up, so I can get William to supervise."

No way. She was not living out her fantasies with William watching. It was a deal breaker.

Syssi waved a hand. "Then forget about it. I don't want anyone to be privy to our adventure."

"Neither do I. William will just make sure that after we are done, the records of our playtime are erased, and that no one made copies."

That was acceptable. "Are you sure he's not going to see anything?"

"William is not going to defy me in this or anything else. I trust him."

Did she?

Yeah, William was okay. He wouldn't betray their trust.

"Give me a few days to come up with a cool adventure that won't be too girly for you."

Kian got up, walked over to the couch, sat down, and lifted her onto his lap. "I will gladly participate in whatever you can dream up. Don't modify a single thing on my account. I love your imagination."

13

CAROL

*C*arol put the last container into the freezer and waved Ella over. "The main dishes are on the right, and the side dishes are on the left. Each container has enough for two."

"Thank you, but you really shouldn't have. I can cook, you know. And I'm eager to start playing house."

Carol shrugged. "Think of it as emergency rations for when you are not in the mood or your fridge is empty. I always cook large quantities and freeze portions for later. That way I always have something, and I don't need to cook every day."

"Smart."

"How come you didn't go grocery shopping with Julian?"

Ella's lips curled in a smug smile. "I'm exhausted. After lunch, we came home and decided to take a nap before going out, but naturally we didn't, so Julian suggested I rest while he did the shopping. I made him a list, though. Otherwise, he would have come back with frozen pizzas and cereal."

Carol rolled her eyes. "Men. But then there are exceptions, like Gerard. He's a master chef."

"Who's Gerard?"

"A clan member with a fancy restaurant named By Invitation Only. I interned with him for a little while, but I realized that cooking in a restaurant is not the same as cooking at home. I do it to relax, and a restaurant kitchen is one of the most stressful places there is. I don't think there is as much tension in firehouses and emergency rooms."

Ella leaned against the counter and crossed her arms over her chest. "I hope that doesn't happen to me with running the fundraiser."

"How is it going?" That wasn't what Carol wanted to talk about, but this was important to Ella.

"So far, great. Not huge amounts, but more than I expected."

"I'm glad. Now come sit with me and tell me all about Lokan and what happened. I know that you're probably tired of telling the story, but I only want the juicy tidbits that you didn't tell anyone else."

Giggling, Ella let Carol pull her to the couch. "So, I was right about Lokan compelling my attraction to him. He was very clever about it. The way he phrased it, he made me feel guilty anytime I got intimate with Julian. I interpreted that guilt as being unworthy and soiled and other nonsense like that. Once he removed the compulsion, it was like a suffocating blanket was lifted off me, and my desire for Julian flared like oxygen-infused fire."

"How did you get Lokan to remove the compulsion?"

"He thought that he had gotten us and felt cocky enough to be magnanimous. Apparently, Turner was right about him. Lokan was playing me the same way I was playing him, and he wasn't interested in me romantically at all. He wanted to lure my mother and me into a trap because he needed two strong telepaths for some secret mission."

That sounded interesting. "Did he tell you what it was?"

"No. But I'm sure Kian is going to get it out of him one way or another."

Carol grimaced. "I hope they are not thinking of torturing him."

"Yeah, I hope not. Even after all he did to me, I can't help but like him a little. Which is weird because he used to scare me so much. I often thought of him as Lucifer." She chuckled. "He certainly is a handsome devil."

With a sigh, Carol grabbed a throw pillow and hugged it to herself. "As one who's been through torture, I don't wish it even on my enemies. Besides, I'm proof that it's not effective. If I could keep my mouth shut and not betray my people, I'm sure that an experienced soldier won't do it either. The only way to get the information out of him is to prove that we are the good guys, and that we mean his people no harm."

Ella frowned. "Is it true, though?"

"Of course, it is. Our goal is not Doomer annihilation. We are defending ourselves because they want to annihilate us and rule over humanity. All we want to do is start a revolution, so their leader gets overthrown and someone more reasonable takes his place."

"Yeah, but that leader happens to be Lokan's father."

Carol waved a dismissive hand. "Navuh is not the kind of father who inspires loyalty. More like burning hatred. Did Lokan talk about his family with you? I know he wouldn't mention Navuh by name, but, in general, like whether he gets along with his brothers sort of thing."

"He mentioned having many brothers, but he didn't elaborate. The one thing I took notice of, though, was his resentment over not knowing who his mother was and if she was still alive."

"Hmm. I can use that."

"For what?"

"To manipulate Lokan into revealing things, of course. I'm

going to talk to Kian and ask his permission to play with Lokan." She waggled her brows.

Ella cast her a curious glance. "Play as in softening him up so he will talk, or the other kind of play?"

"Both. How do you think I'm going to soften him up? I'm a courtesan. I have my ways."

"Is it that easy for you?"

Carol pulled out her phone and scrolled for the picture Bridget had shared with her. "Just look at him. I would do him for fun any day and twice on Sunday. He's gorgeous."

"I can't argue with that. But he is also the enemy."

"That's why I need a good excuse to play with him." Carol winked. "I'm training to be a spy, an instigator of a revolution. What better way to practice my rusty feminine wiles than to do so on someone as close to the throne as Lokan?"

14

ANNANI

*A*nnani returned her cell phone to her gown's pocket and pushed to her feet. "I cannot believe Kian. Navuh's son was captured on Wednesday, and I only hear about it now, and not from him, but from Sari." She started pacing. "Sari did not hear it from Kian either. Her assistant heard it from one of the Guardians and told her."

Alena, in her usual stoic manner, waited for the temper tantrum to be over before responding. "Which of the sons?"

"It does not matter." Annani waved a dismissive hand. "Any of the sons would know more than the simple soldiers. I need to talk to him. And this is precisely why Kian did not tell me about it." She huffed. "He should have called me right away, but he doesn't want me anywhere near Lokan. What is he afraid of? That Lokan is going to attack me? I can take hold of his mind in an instant and freeze him in place. Kian keeps forgetting how powerful I am. He wants to keep me wrapped in goose feathers."

"It's bubble wrap, Mother. Not goose feathers."

Alena was a wonderful daughter, but sometimes she had the sensitivity of an ice cube.

Annani was in no mood for a language lesson. "It is of no importance what metaphor I choose, and if I want to make one up, it is my prerogative." Annani pulled out her phone. "I am going to call Kian."

Tapping her foot, she waited for him to answer.

"Mother, I was just about to call you."

"To tell me about Lokan's capture? You are a little too late. Sari already told me."

He sighed. "I should have known news like that would travel fast."

"I should have been the first one you called. Why do I have to wait two days to hear about an important development like this? Am I not the head of this clan?"

He sighed. "I apologize. Syssi told me to call you right away, but I hoped to get the island location out of Lokan first so I could surprise you with the good news. His capture in itself is not important."

That mollified her, but only a little bit. "Do you have the location now?"

"Not yet. Lokan is a hard nut to crack. Not surprisingly, he doesn't believe that I have no intention of nuking his island. He's trying to play the hero and protect his people. Or maybe he's just buying time. He is hard to read."

"I want to see him. I can probably get him to tell me whatever I want."

"He is immune to compulsion."

Annani huffed. "I was not going to use it on him. Besides, my compulsion ability is mediocre at best. For a goddess, that is. But Navuh was rumored to have almost god-like powers. His sons might be very powerful too."

"Lokan certainly is. And his dream-walking is a unique talent. Do you think Navuh could have it as well?"

"I do not know. We did not see each other often, and we

never talked." She sighed. "But I remember thinking that he was not as bad as his father, and that he had some compassion in him. He certainly seemed infatuated with Areana. I wonder what happened to him."

"Insanity is hereditary. Navuh got it from Mortdh."

"Perhaps. Mortdh was smart too, and very powerful, but he was a lunatic who murdered his own people and more than half of the human civilization that had been flourishing in our area."

"Navuh kept up the good work. How many wars did the Doomers instigate? And how much more progress could humanity have achieved if they didn't keep undermining it time and again? By now, Navuh has much more blood on his hands than Mortdh ever had."

"That is unfortunately true. And that is why I want to talk to Lokan. I want to ask him about his father. Also, he might know whether Navuh is holding Areana prisoner."

Annani sat down in her favorite armchair and sighed. "I do not know which fate is worse, being Navuh's captive for thousands of years or perishing with the rest of our people."

"If Navuh has Areana, he keeps her hidden in his harem, which is inaccessible and guarded as if it is his greatest treasure. The sons don't even get to grow up with their mothers. That was what Lokan needed Vivian and Ella for. He wanted to find out what, or rather who, his father was hiding in the harem. Only compelled humans are allowed in the enclosure. No one knows what goes on in there."

Annani's eyes widened. "Oh, that was so clever of Lokan. He could smuggle one of them inside, and she would report to the other what she found out."

"That was his plan. But we spoiled it for him."

"He must know more than he is admitting. I am going to fly over. Unfortunately, I cannot leave tonight or tomorrow, but I can leave early on Sunday morning and arrive late morning at our airstrip."

"That's wonderful. Perfect timing."

Wonderful? Kian had never sounded so enthusiastic about her visits.

Annani's heart skipped a beat. Could it be that Syssi was pregnant? That would be the best news Kian could give her. "Is there a cause for celebration that I am not aware of?"

"If you could have made it by tomorrow, you could have celebrated with us Vivian and Ella's safe return. We are having a barbecue in the village square. But that's the small celebration. Sunday, Vivian and Magnus are getting married. I know how much you like presiding over weddings, and they will be overjoyed to have you bless their union."

Fabulous news, just not what she had been hoping for. "It is indeed wonderful. But why the rush? Is there more good news?"

Perhaps Vivian was pregnant?

It was not as exciting as Syssi and Kian having a child, but every new baby was a great blessing.

Kian chuckled. "As far as I know, the answer is no. But they've started working on Vivian's transition, and Magnus wants them to be married before she enters it. He's officially adopting her children too. Vivian is in her mid-thirties, so the transition might not go as smoothly for her."

"It is good that I am coming, then. I can give Vivian my blessing."

The codename 'blessing' had been coined when Annani had secretly helped Syssi transition with a small injection of her godly blood, and it had stuck. Sharing the secret of her blood's miraculous healing properties with Alena and Kian had been necessary, but Amanda and Sari remained blissfully ignorant in that regard.

"My thoughts exactly. You might want to plan a longer visit, though. I don't know how soon her transition is going to start."

"Very well. I am bringing Alena with me and my Odus, of course. You might want to give me one of those new houses you built. Just make sure to stock the kitchen."

It would be easier for everyone if she did not stay in Kian's or Amanda's house. Especially if she was going to be there for a week or longer. That way, she could invite people over without burdening her children with a stream of guests.

"Are you sure that you don't mind?"

"I love spending time with you and Syssi and with Amanda and Dalhu, but this time, I would like to hold audiences with as many clan members as I can. I have been remiss lately, and I feel like I am losing touch with my people, especially since hardly anyone comes to the sanctuary anymore. You need your peace of mind at home, and so does Dalhu. A stream of guests would be very disrupting."

"None of the homes are fancy."

She laughed. "I do not need anything special to meet my family. A living room with a couch and a couple of armchairs will do."

15

LOKAN

*T*he phone ringing next to his ear jolted Lokan from a deep, dreamless sleep. Patting the nightstand for the receiver, he grabbed it and brought it to his ear. "Yes?"

"Heads up, Lokan. I'm bringing in your breakfast in about ten minutes."

"What time is it?"

"Time to get up, buddy."

"I'm up."

Lokan had spent most of the night searching his brain for an angle that would get him out of the cell. This wasn't how he wanted to spend the rest of his immortal life, and since no one was coming to rescue him, he had to come up with the solution himself.

His best option was to appear cooperative and get Kian and his men comfortable around him. They might let something slip that would give him an idea.

The cell's walls were built from solid concrete, and so were the floor and the ceiling. No breaking through those. The door was reinforced steel and about a foot thick, so that wasn't an option either.

On top of that, he had the four strange cuffs attached to his limbs that were made from some super strong alloy that was impossible to break apart. He'd tried last night. Why four though? And what were they for?

Trackers?

He had a feeling that their purpose was more nefarious than that. Did they contain a poison? A tranquilizer calibrated for immortals?

Perhaps he could coax the empath who was in charge of guarding him to talk. The guy seemed more easygoing than Kian and his bodyguards. Besides, other than them, Arwel had been the only one to enter Lokan's cell, so he was the only option.

Realizing that he'd already wasted two of the ten allotted minutes, Lokan rushed to finish up his morning routine. When the door to his cell started moving, he was already seated on the couch, legs crossed at the knee, and affecting the same nonchalant attitude he'd had the day before.

"Good morning, Arwel," he greeted the Guardian. "Thank you so much for breakfast."

"You're welcome." The empath put a cardboard tray with two paper cups on the coffee table, and then fished out two wrapped sandwiches from a paper bag.

It seemed that Arwel didn't get fed any better than Lokan, and the Guardian was subsisting on the same vending-machine fare.

The meager servings didn't fit what he knew about the clan's riches or the luxury of his cell, which led him to believe that he was the only prisoner in the clan's dungeon, and that they didn't have a system in place to feed their captives or the Guardians in charge of them.

This was good. It meant that Arwel was not a trained jailer.

As the Guardian lifted one of the cups and was about to

turn, Lokan asked, "Would you care to join me? We are both stuck here with no one to talk to."

Arwel chuckled. "For me, it's an advantage. The only emotions I'm exposed to are yours, and I have to admit that they are surprisingly mild. You are either not very emotional, or you have superb self-control."

"A little bit of both."

Taking his cup with him, Arwel sat in one of the armchairs. "I actually volunteered for the babysitting job. The many layers of earth between us and the surface muffle the human emotions that usually float through me, leaving their slimy residue on my soul."

That was a lot more information than Lokan had expected, and certainly not in the first ten seconds of their conversation.

First of all, Arwel had just confirmed his suspicion that they were underground, and then he'd continued revealing personal information like they were the best of friends and not sworn enemies.

He was either a very trusting soul, or he believed that Lokan was never leaving this cell, and therefore it didn't matter what he knew.

"What about immortal emotions? If you feel mine, then you must feel other immortals' as well."

"I do, but not as strongly as those of humans. It's like comparing a whisper to a shout."

"Can you feel me through the walls? They seem quite thick."

Arwel smiled. "They are. But I'm right next door to you in the adjacent cell, so yeah. I get your emotions."

"I'm sorry about that. I hope that at least you were given a cell as nice as this one."

Shaking his head, Arwel pulled a sandwich out of the paper bag. "My cell is smaller. I have a studio, not an apartment." He unwrapped the sandwich and bit into it.

Following the Guardian's example, Lokan lifted the cup of coffee, took a few sips, and then went for the sandwich. With what they were feeding him, he was constantly hungry, but since Arwel was eating the same crap, he could not even voice a complaint.

"If being underground is easier for you, why aren't you stationed here permanently?"

"Nothing to do here. We normally don't get prisoners."

Lokan chuckled. "That explains it." He lifted his sandwich. "Is this Kian's idea of torture? Because it might just work. I'm so hungry that I keep fantasizing about potatoes, and I hate the suckers."

Arwel laughed. "A Doomer with a sense of humor. That's refreshing."

Good, his tactic was working. Lokan hated the derogatory nickname Kian and his men had invented for the Brotherhood, but this wasn't the time or place to mention it.

Lokan took another sip of coffee. "What about the other Brother? The one who drew my portrait? Does he have a sense of humor?"

Arwel waved a dismissive hand. "Dalhu doesn't talk much. So, I don't even know if he has one or not. He's not stupid, though, and he really is a gifted artist. In fact, he drew that picture hanging behind you."

Lokan turned to look at the portrait of a dark-haired beauty with a mischievous smile. "Very well done. Who is she?"

Dalhu. The name sounded vaguely familiar, and Lokan tried to link a face to it, but failed. The guy must have been a simple soldier or a low-level commander.

"His mate."

"Oh." That was a good enough reason to take another look. "Now I understand why he defected. She is a stunning female."

"Yeah. She is." Arwel seemed like he wanted to say more.

"Is she anyone important?"

"You could say so." The Guardian put his cup down and reached into the bag for his second sandwich. "Did you think about Kian's proposition?"

So Arwel wasn't as free with information as Lokan had hoped. Some things he'd remained tightlipped about.

"I'm curious to see the catacombs, and I want to see with my own eyes the warriors Kian claims are in stasis."

"He's telling you the truth. Don't judge him by your standards, Lokan. Kian is a fair and honest male."

There was some truth to that insulting statement. Lokan was a liar and a manipulator, so naturally he assumed everyone else was as well.

Most of the time that assumption was correct, though, and he had no reason to believe Kian was any different.

Leaders didn't have the luxury of taking the moral high ground, and Lokan didn't believe the clan would be as rich if Kian were an honest businessman.

16

CAROL

*T*alking to Kian always made Carol nervous. Especially when showing up at his office uninvited and making a request that he was most likely going to shoot down. She imagined that it was what a human woman felt when asking her stern father for permission to do something dangerous.

Kian was an authority figure, which in itself wasn't a big problem even though she didn't deal well with authority. Carol was too independent and too stubborn. The problem was that he was immune to her charms, and she couldn't manipulate him by batting her eyelashes and smiling innocently like she did with most other males.

Even her cousins bought her act and made concessions for her that they would not have made for anyone else. Then again, they might have been indulging her because of the hero status she'd gained after withstanding torture and not revealing the keep's location.

With Kian, however, she wouldn't get far by using charm or relying on his compassion. Logic and clever arguments were the only things that would help her persuade him to let her take on Lokan. Regrettably, as one who hadn't had much use for such intellectual methods, she wasn't good at them.

"Are you going to just stand there?" Kian called from the other side of the door. "Come in. It's open."

She wasn't a coward, and Kian's bark was much worse than his bite.

"Well, here goes nothing," Carol murmured under her breath as she pushed the door open. "Do you have a few moments?"

"No, but I'll make time for you. How can I help you?"

Given the slight smirk lifting one corner of his mouth, Kian suspected the reason for her coming to see him.

Pulling out a chair, she thought about the way to start, but nothing clever came to mind, so she just went for it.

"I want to talk to Lokan and get more information about the island from him."

Kian put his pen down and leaned back in his chair. "He didn't divulge its location yet, but once I prove to him that I'm not a murderous sociopath like his father, I believe he will."

Excitement bubbling up in her stomach, Carol rubbed her hands. "All the more reason to let me see Lokan so I can get all the info out of him. Knowledge is power."

"About that. Turner suspects that Navuh has the entire island's population under his compulsion, which means that they will stay loyal to him no matter what. This blows our initial plan out of the water, because you won't be able to incite anyone into revolting against him."

"You said that Turner suspects it, which implies he's not sure."

"He is not, but after talking with Dalhu, I'm of the same opinion. It explains so much. Think about it." He waved a hand. "Why are the Doomers loyal to a cause that doesn't make sense, and they do so with the intensity of religious fervor? Why are they willing to be treated with such disregard and still follow their leader?"

Carol arched a brow. "Charisma? Brainwashing? Navuh is not the first evil leader to inspire an obsessed following. I'm sure you don't need me to recite names of humans who incited their followers to commit unthinkable atrocities."

Kian waved a hand. "But that's the thing. What if a cult-like following is the result of compulsion? What if some rare humans possess the ability? Perhaps those humans are possessors of our godly genes?"

Carol put a hand over her heart. "Fates forbid they were related to us. I don't need the guilt by association."

"What about the Brotherhood? We are related to them."

"Yeah, but I would like to think that it's not genetic and that they could be good if not for the brainwashing by their insane and incredibly powerful leader. But back to what I came here for. Verifying Turner's suspicion is even more of a reason to let me coax Lokan into talking." She smirked. "I might be able to get more with honey than you do with a stick."

Amusement dancing in his eyes, Kian crossed his arms over his chest. "And how do you propose to do that? What excuse are we going to give him for letting you into his prison cell?"

The obvious explanation would have been providing Lokan with a professional as an incentive, but Kian would balk at that and rightfully so. The clan held itself to much higher moral standards.

"I can come as the maid. The Doomers expect females to be doing traditional jobs, so it won't seem suspicious to him that a woman brings in his meals and tidies his place. Who is serving his meals now?"

"Arwel."

She rolled her eyes. "And where does he get the food? I'm sure he doesn't cook for the Doomer."

"Of course not. So far, I believe he has gotten everything from the vending machines. But that's not a solution. He needs to order meals to be delivered to the guard station in the lobby."

"I can take over that part of Arwel's job and do a much better one. You know what they say about the best way to a man's heart, right? It's through his stomach." Carol fluffed up her hair. "In addition to my more obvious talents, I'm also a very good cook. I can move into the keep and prepare meals for Lokan and for Arwel. That would give me the perfect excuse to visit him three to four times a day." She smirked. "I'll have him eating out of the palm of my hand in no time, so to speak."

"Perhaps. But Lokan is a manipulative bastard, and he might get you talking instead."

"Don't worry about it. I can talk circles around him. I'm not going to give him anything he can use against us, even if he somehow manages to escape, which he will not."

He arched a brow. "I still remember putting you in jail because you blabbered in bars about your infamous past in revolutionary Paris."

"Pfft." She waved a dismissive hand. "That was different. No one believed me. They thought I was either drunk or loony. You overreacted."

"You were drunk."

"I was just having fun. I wasn't so wasted that I didn't know what I was doing."

Tapping his fingers on his desk, Kian regarded her for a few seconds before letting out a breath. "Fine. Just be careful."

Carol wanted to pump her fist in victory. "I know what I'm doing, Kian. Besides, those days of carefree living are over. I did some growing up since then."

"That is true. What about the café, though, and your self-defense class?"

"If I get Wonder some help, she can handle the café without me. I can ask Callie to do that. And I can cancel the class for a week or two. It won't take me longer than that to get what I need out of Lokan."

When he nodded, Carol's heart did a somersault. He was actually agreeing.

"We don't have a spare apartment in the keep for you. You'll have to room with the Guardians, or I can give you one of the nicer cells in the dungeon."

"I need a kitchen, and I don't mind rooming with the guys. I'll feed them too." Which would ensure their cooperation.

"I'll call Arwel and let him know that you're coming. I hope he can get a bedroom for you."

She waved a dismissive hand. "I can sleep on the couch."

Besides, if her plan worked, she wouldn't need a bed upstairs because she would be sleeping in Lokan's.

17

TURNER

The reaction Kian and the brothers got when they entered the restaurant amused Turner. The women glanced their way and then gave them their full attention, while the men pretended not to notice the three, or their companions' reactions.

See no handsome guys, hear no female gasps, and speak no comments.

Wise monkeys.

He shook his head. If Bridget were there and heard his thoughts, she would have had something to say about them.

Even before his transition, Turner had felt superior to most people and often thought of them as monkeys. Immortality had made it worse. Now that he had limitless time to learn all that there was to learn, his superiority complex was turning into a god complex, and even he knew that it wasn't a good thing.

"Thanks for meeting me for lunch," Kian said as he joined him in the booth.

Anandur sat next to his boss, and Brundar next to Turner. Usually, having anyone other than Bridget sit so close would have bothered him, but knowing that the proximity made the Guardian just as uncomfortable helped.

Sitting next to Anandur would have been worse. The guy was much less reserved than his somber brother, and he liked touching people.

Still, since this wasn't a social call and they were there as Kian's bodyguards, the brothers tried to act as unobtrusively as possible.

"Are you heading to your old headquarters later?" he asked Kian.

The restaurant's other patrons were all human, but Turner liked to be safe. Mentioning terms like 'the keep' and 'prisoner' might pique someone's interest.

"Not today. I have a meeting with a developer in one of my alternative offices. I'm letting my other business associate stew for a little bit. I'm going to see him tomorrow about that tour I've promised him. Hopefully, by then he'll be ready to talk. If not, I will do what I've wanted to do from the start and beat it out of him."

"Patience, Kian. The reason I advised you to treat him well was so he could see the vast difference between his camp and ours. The idea is to make him talk because he believes it's the right thing to do for his people. I don't think you'll be able to get it out of him any other way."

"I just might. Carol proposed to try and coax him into opening up to her. She will go in as the meal server and use her feminine wiles on him."

Carol was a born seductress, and if any female had a chance of manipulating Lokan it was her. Except, the Doomer was a master manipulator himself. "He would see right through her, and he even might get her to reveal things she shouldn't. The guy is smart. Don't underestimate him."

Kian's smile was chilling. "If Carol fails, I can always employ more rigorous negotiation tactics."

"Your associate is old and experienced, and he didn't grow up surrounded by warm and fuzzy. He'll keep his mouth shut no matter what you do to him."

Sighing, Kian pushed away the empty breadbasket. "As usual, you're right. Perhaps I should get Dalhu to talk to him."

"It won't help. Your associate is not going to believe him either."

They had to pause their conversation when the waiter came to take their order.

Looking over the menu, Kian shook his head. "I don't see anything here that I can eat. Can the cook make me something vegan?"

This was embarrassing. He should have remembered Kian's dietary preferences and chosen a different restaurant.

How was that for a humbling reminder that he was far from omnipotent?

"Would you like a fettuccine primavera?" the waiter asked. "We can make a vegan option for you by omitting the butter and using olive oil instead."

"Sounds good. I'll have that." Kian handed the waiter his menu.

When the guy finished collecting the orders and left, Turner felt that he needed to apologize. "It slipped my mind that you're a vegan. I chose this place because the food is good and it's close to my office."

Kian waved a dismissive hand. "Most places can whip something up for me." He pulled the breadbasket toward him. "And if not, I can always fill up on this."

Reaching for a slice, Turner still felt a smidgen of guilt, a reminder of his pre-transition days of avoiding carbs to stay fit. Now he could indulge in as much of it as he wished and even spread butter over the freshly baked goodness.

"What do you think about my associate's claim regarding special talents?" Kian asked. "Do you think the government is collecting them?"

Turner snorted. "Not against their wishes." He lowered his voice so only the immortals could hear him. "Your associate is thinking in terms of what his leadership does. Recruiting talent, though, that I believe. Although where would they search? I don't suppose they put out want ads, or go scouring psychic conventions."

"Yeah, I see your point." Kian raked his fingers through his hair. "Amanda tested hundreds of people and found only two strong talents. She says that many people have some small ability, but that's not enough to be useful to anyone."

"What about William's game? Bridget told me that it flags players who do exceptionally well, which indicates they have precognition."

"The results were so dismal that we stopped collecting data. It was a waste of time, but at least not of resources. The game keeps making decent money."

As the waiter arrived with their order, Turner leaned back and waited until the guy was done before continuing.

"Trial and error, that's how we find out things. If we don't try, solutions are not going to materialize from thin air."

Kian nodded. "That's why I keep investing the clan's money in Amanda's research. What about the military? Are there any tests performed on soldiers?"

"Not that I know of."

Kian smirked. "I thought you knew everything."

"Unfortunately, I don't. But I'll look into it. See what I can find out without attracting too much attention."

"Speaking of attention. I learned some disturbing news

from my new associate. Apparently, the Russian found out about the ring, bought it back, and resumed his search for Ella. He's convinced that she's alive."

"Damn. I knew that guy was going to talk. What I want to find out is whether Sandoval brought a Russian appraiser to do it on purpose or was it an oversight on his part. If he did it to fuck me over, he's going to regret it."

Kian paused with the twirl of fettuccine on his fork. "I'm sure it wasn't malicious. He owed you for his nephew, right?"

"And he repaid me by endangering my family. Ella is my future daughter-in-law."

Until voicing it, Turner hadn't realized why he'd gotten so atypically angry. This was personal for him.

"But Sandoval didn't know that," Kian said. "You told him that you were aiding a friend."

It was doubly irritating that hotheaded Kian was suddenly the voice of reason, while Turner was trying to extinguish the rage boiling in his gut. "True." He shook his head. "I need to eliminate the threat."

"Ella is not going to like it," Anandur said.

"She doesn't need to find out. I can make it look as if one of his rivals did it."

"Don't do anything rash, Turner," Kian warned. "Ella's premonition that we will need him for something might be true. Besides, my associate hinted about having dirt on the Russian that would get him off Ella's back."

"I'm never rash. Not even when I'm angry. But what kind of dirt could scare someone like that? Did he steal Putin's memoirs?"

Kian laughed. "Now, that's one book I would love to get my hands on."

18

CAROL

"*D*o you know Ewan and Camden?" Arwel asked as he opened the door for Carol.

"Of course, I do. I know everyone in the village. At one time or another, they all show up at the café."

She followed him inside. "I just didn't know that they were a couple of piggies."

Glancing at the messy living room, Arwel shrugged. "I told them to clean up. I guess throwing out the empty delivery boxes and beer bottles was as far as they were willing to go."

She waved a dismissive hand. "Don't worry about it. I'll whip them into shape. You can put the grocery bags on the counter. Thank you for carrying them up for me."

"I'll go down to get the rest. What are you planning on cooking that you bought so much?"

"I don't want to have to go out grocery shopping. I got enough to last me a week."

He chuckled. "You brought enough for a month."

"I'm not cooking only for Lokan. You and I need to eat too, and I don't want to neglect my new roommates either."

"There are plenty of restaurants around here that deliver.

It's not like in the village, where the café is the only place to grab something to eat."

"Well, I like to be prepared. I'm going to start on lunch right away." She winked. "I can't wait to meet Lokan."

Arwel's expression turned serious. "A few words of warning before that. He's charming and manipulative and a liar. Don't ever let your guard down or believe anything he says."

He pulled out a small remote from his pocket. "Kian had William put four cuffs on him. I have a separate remote for each one. The buttons are marked, so there is no way to confuse them. The one with the syringe symbol delivers a neural poison. It won't kill him, and it will take a couple of seconds for the pain to disable him. His body will process the poison in half an hour or so. The buttons with the grenade symbol will detonate the explosives. Whatever limb the cuff is attached to will be blown to pieces. This will take him months to regenerate, so use it as a last resort."

Bile rising in her throat, Carol shook her head. "I don't want it."

"Don't worry. I'm in the cell next door to his. If he overpowers you and takes it away from you, I have three more I can use on him."

"That's why I don't need it. If he does anything to me, you will feel it, right? You will sense my distress."

He nodded. "What if he takes you as a hostage and threatens to snap your neck?"

She shrugged. "Let him. It won't kill me. It will hurt like hell, and I'll probably pass out, but that's better than having this awful thing with me. I'd be terrified of pressing a button accidentally."

"It has a safety feature built in." He lifted the small device so she could see it from both sides. "You have to slide this up before you press a button."

Carol shook her head again. "You have cameras in his cell, right?"

"Of course."

"Then they should do. Watch the feed and if he misbehaves, come in."

Rubbing his hand over the back of his neck, Arwel looked away. "What if you want privacy with him?"

"I'm not shy, Arwel. I don't mind if you watch."

"I mind."

That was a problem she wasn't sure how to solve. "I don't know what to tell you. But having that remote with me is not an option. First of all, because it's not going to do me any good. In the two seconds it will take for the poison to affect him, Lokan will take the remote away from me. Secondly, if he knows what it does, he can hold his wrist to my chest and threaten to kill me if you don't let him out. An explosion that is strong enough to blow his wrist to pieces might do the same to my heart."

Cringing, Arwel rubbed his neck again. "You're right. I didn't think of that. I don't think it can kill you, but I won't take the risk."

"So, what do we do?"

"Either I watch the feed, or I rely on my senses. I don't see any other option."

"Both are fine with me. Besides, this is all worst-case scenario and hypothetical. He has no way out of here, and I'm more valuable to him as a source of information than a hostage." She smirked. "Not to mention my other assets."

"About that. Don't tell him anything valuable."

Carol waved a hand. "Don't worry about it. He is going to think of me as the ditsy blonde who serves his meals and makes his bed. He is going to try to get me talking, and I will, just not about anything he can use. In the meantime, I'm going to pump him for information without him even realizing what I'm doing. No offense to your gender, Arwel, but men are so easy to manipulate that it's laughable."

"I'm not sure this one is. Being a manipulator himself, he might be onto you."

"We will see. First, though, I need to get cooking, and then I need to shower and change into something flirty."

"I hope you're not thinking about putting on a French maid uniform."

Heading to the kitchen, she sighed. "I wish. Those are so sexy. Regrettably, I can't be that obvious. Part of the game is having him believe that he's seducing me and not the other way around."

Arwel stashed the remote back in his pocket. "Too much information, Carol. I'm going to get the rest of the stuff from the car." He turned on his heel and headed toward the door.

"I didn't know you were such a prude," she called after him.

"Yeah, yeah." He paused with the door open and looked at her over his shoulder. "By the way, you can't take your phone when you go to see him. He can take it away from you and dial his people before I can blow his hand up. You'll need to use the landline to communicate with me. Until I let you out, you will be stuck with him."

"Got it." She saluted the Guardian.

Being stuck with Lokan wasn't going to be a hardship, and she'd figured out about the phone on her own.

Even her own people still underestimated her, but that was going to change.

19

VIVIAN

"*I* don't want to sit in the back between you and Magnus." Parker stood outside Julian's car and refused to enter. "Can we borrow the limousine from Kian?"

Vivian shook her head. Getting the entire family to go wedding-clothes shopping together, including Ella and Julian, had sounded like fun, a bonding experience, but it seemed her plan was hitting a snag even before they left the parking lot.

"We can take two cars," Magnus offered.

"I have a better idea," Ella said. "Magnus and Vivian will sit up front, and we will take the backseat with me in the middle. I don't mind being squeezed. What do you say, Parker, can you suffer quietly for the forty-five-minute drive to the mall?"

"Can I go to the gaming store once we get there?"

Magnus chuckled. "Is there still a game that you don't have?"

Vivian ruffled Parker's hair. "Today is about getting clothes for the wedding. You're going with the guys to the tux shop while Ella and I go to the bridal store."

He grimaced. "Can't wait."

An hour later, Vivian and Ella stepped into the dressing room, both carrying an armload of dresses.

"It's good that they make them big." Ella started hanging up the dresses. "Imagine trying to do this in an ordinary department store fitting room."

"Do you need help in there?" the sales lady chirped.

"No, thank you. We've got it," Ella answered, then glanced up to look at the ceiling. "Do you think we can take the glasses off in here? I can't see any cameras."

Vivian followed her daughter's eyes, but there was nothing mounted on the ceiling. "They don't need cameras in here. It's not like anyone can walk out of here with a dress without paying. They are huge. Besides, I'm not going to try on my wedding dress with the wig and glasses on. I need to know how I'm going to look in it as me, and not the Mata Hari version of me."

Ella pushed her glasses up her nose. "Just in case, I'm keeping them on."

Kian had told them about Gorchenco buying the ring back and renewing his search for Ella, warning them not to ease up on the disguises. Supposedly, Lokan had some dirt on the Russian that could potentially get him to back off for good, but Vivian doubted that. Lokan would say anything to gain an advantage, including some made-up story about Gorchenco and a transgression big enough that it could get a major mafia boss in trouble.

Right. For that to happen in Russia, Gorchenco would have to kidnap one of Putin's daughters and treat her like he had Ella.

Was this ever going to end, so Ella could finally be free?

"I believe that we are safe here." Vivian took her wig off and hung it on the hook. "Let's do it. Hand me the first one."

They got into the rhythm, with Vivian trying on one dress

after the other, and Ella putting them back on the hangers and dividing them into two sections—the no ways and the maybes.

"They all look good on you, Mom. You have the perfect body for a wedding dress. Skinny with no curves. If you were taller, you would have been a perfect model."

"Thanks." Vivian grimaced. "That's not much of a compliment. I would have loved having curves like yours."

"Yeah. Wait until I start trying on dresses. They are not going to fit as well."

"Nonsense." Vivian examined her reflection in the mirror. "You're perfectly proportioned."

Ella shrugged. "I like this dress the best on you."

"Me too. Should I just get it? I'm tired."

"Up to you. But I think you should try them all before deciding."

The dress wasn't as overly ornate as the others, and the skirts were not as puffy. Except, wearing a white dress to her second wedding felt somewhat inappropriate. She hadn't been a virgin her first time around as a bride and yet had no qualms about wearing white. But now she was a widow, and wearing it again felt like disrespecting Josh's memory.

"Why are you frowning? Did you change your mind about the dress?"

"It's not that. The dress is pretty, but I'm reconsidering the color. Maybe a pale yellow or blue is more appropriate?"

Ella waved a dismissive hand. "You'll look like a ghost in those colors. What's your problem with white?"

"It's not my first wedding."

"So what?"

"I loved your father very much." A tear slid down her cheek, and she wiped it with the back of her hand. "I feel like I shouldn't wear white again."

"Oh, Mom." Ella pushed up from the bench and wrapped her arms around her.

With a sigh, Vivian rested her cheek on her daughter's shoulder. "I'm sorry. This was supposed to be fun."

"If wearing white makes you feel bad, we can look for something else. But I don't think you should feel guilty about getting another chance at love."

It was just like Ella to go straight to the point without dancing circles around it.

"I know. But I'm also not a young girl anymore. I'll feel like an imposter in a virginal wedding gown."

Ella snorted. "The white no longer represents virginity, Mom. It represents a new beginning, which is more than appropriate in your case. A new husband is just one part of it."

"Don't say that. It's all about Magnus. None of this would be happening without him."

"Not true. None of this would be happening without Julian and your chance meeting with him. What if another Guardian had been assigned to keep you and Parker safe? You might have fallen for someone else."

Pushing out of Ella's arms, Vivian huffed. "I would not. Magnus is one of a kind. He is not interchangeable with any other Guardian."

Ella smiled. "Precisely. Don't you think he deserves a bride in a white dress?"

"He couldn't care less what I wear."

"I don't know about that. This is his first and only wedding."

Ella was right. Magnus might not care what she wore, but he might be disappointed if she treated their wedding as less important than her first one, which a nontraditional colored dress might imply.

"You are a very wise young woman. Let's try the rest of these dresses and choose the best one."

20

CAROL

"*R*eady?" Arwel asked as Carol stepped out into the living room.

"How do I look?" She turned in a circle. "I rock the casual yet sexy look if I say so myself."

Not to be too obvious, she'd put on a simple pair of black leggings and a loose, off-the-shoulder pink sweater with a white camisole underneath. Her cleavage wasn't showing, but the soft sweater draped nicely over her breasts, outlining their shape, and its droopy neckline left one soft shoulder exposed. Low-heeled black boots completed the look.

"You always look good," Arwel said.

A very safe response to a dangerous question that most men weren't smart enough to dodge. Except, he wasn't her boyfriend, and she needed an honest opinion.

"That's not an answer. You've spent some time with the Doomer. Do you think he's going to drool, or should I change into something more revealing?"

Arwel shook his head. "I meant what I said. You look good even in the apron that you wear in the café. I don't know about the Doomer, though. My impression of him is that he is a snob and that he likes the sophisticated type, but I might be wrong. He's one hell of an actor."

"I can't pretend to be the cook or the maid and wear a suit. So, this will have to do. Let's go."

Lifting the covered tray off the counter, Arwel inhaled the aroma. "The smell makes me hungry."

Carol opened the door for him. "You ate two servings already. You should be full."

He followed her out. "But this is so good. It's a shame to waste it on the Doomer."

She patted his shoulder. "It's for a good cause. Besides, I put some away in the fridge. You can have it later."

He looked down at the tray sadly. "By the time I'm back upstairs, there will be nothing left. Your roommates are going to finish it."

"Then I'll make more. Stop fretting."

As they made their way down to the basement, Carol could barely contain her excitement, and as they stopped in front of Lokan's cell, and Arwel transferred the tray to her, she waited impatiently for him to punch in the code.

"Why aren't you using your phone to open it?"

He cast her a sidelong glance. "I'm an old dog who's used to the keypad."

When the door started moving, Carol took in a deep breath and plastered a smile on her face.

She was anxious, but not afraid. After surviving Sebastian, there wasn't much that could scare her. She'd been through the worst. Besides, she wasn't expecting trouble from Lokan.

This was going to be fun.

"Wait here," Arwel told her as he entered.

"Good afternoon, Arwel. I was wondering when you'd come to visit me."

The smooth, cultured voice matched the image she held in

her mind. As her excitement rose a notch or two or a hundred, Carol was glad of the strong perfume she'd sprayed herself with, and the aroma wafting off the beef stroganoff.

She was supposed to play coy and let Lokan do the seducing. Powerful men didn't appreciate prey just falling into their laps. They were conquerors, not scavengers.

"I have a special treat for you, Lokan. Today's lunch is not going to be sandwiches. Sit on the couch and don't make any sudden moves."

"My curiosity is piqued. What's that delicious smell?"

"You'll find out in a moment." Arwel stepped out of the room. "Do you want me to carry the tray in?"

"No, I got it."

She'd prepared a script for the initial interaction, and it didn't include Arwel.

"Very well." He motioned for her to enter.

With a smile on her face and a slight swaying of her hips, Carol sauntered into the room.

Oh boy, Lokan. Talk about sexy.

The man sitting on the couch was so much more than his picture had hinted at.

She loved everything, from his elegant clothes to the confident way he sat with one arm draped over the sofa's back and his legs crossed at the knee.

The sleeves of his white dress shirt were folded up, revealing muscular forearms with a smattering of dark hair, and through the parted collar she could get a peek at his chest, which was likewise covered with lean muscles and sparse black hair.

He was tall but not huge, muscled but not bulky, cocky but not conceited. And that sly smirk that had been curling his lush lips when she entered had faltered for a split second.

She'd had an effect on him.

Recovering quickly, he dipped his head in greeting. "What a lovely surprise. I would've gotten that heavy tray from you, but I've been instructed not to move from this couch."

"That's okay. I'm stronger than I look." She put the tray down on the coffee table and uncovered the plate. "Dig in before it gets cold."

He looked down at what she served him and then back up at her. "We haven't been formally introduced. I'm Lokan, son of Navuh." He extended his hand. "Again, my apologies for not getting up."

She cast a quick glance at Arwel, who nodded his approval.

Her palm was sweaty, and she discreetly wiped it on her leggings before coming around to sit next to him. "I'm Carol, daughter of Moira and an unknown sperm donor."

Smiling, he took her hand in his, but as soon as the contact was made, a powerful current sizzled between them, and his smile turned into a perplexed frown.

"You're an immortal."

"Last I checked, yes, I am."

LOKAN

*C*arol.

The first immortal female Lokan had ever met, and she was exquisite.

A Marilyn Monroe style bombshell, Carol was petite, shorter than the actress by several inches, and with more delicate facial features. What made the comparison apt, though, were her blonde curls and pouty lips, not to mention the sexy, curvy body, and sultry attitude.

If he had any artistic talent to draw a picture of his ideal woman, she wouldn't come close to Carol's perfection.

"Did you make this for me?" he asked.

She nodded. "Yes, and it's getting cold."

"How can I eat?" He rubbed a hand over his heart. "You take my breath away, and I want to keep looking at you."

Across the room at the dinette, Arwel snorted. "I should take notes."

As a growl started deep in Lokan's throat, Carol put a hand on his bicep. "Relax. Arwel meant no offense, and he is my cousin."

Damn. Where had that growl come from?

He'd just met the woman, and he had no claim to her.

Lokan had never experienced jealousy before. Hell, other than his father, every male living on the island was used to sharing the selection of beauties working in the whorehouse. The only other option was seducing one of the housekeeping staff, which Lokan had done on occasion.

"Why are you serving my meal, Carol? Don't you have humans to do that?"

"No, we don't." She looked down her cute nose at him. "As I'm sure you are aware, the clan promotes democracy and human rights, which means that we don't have conscripted or thralled humans working for us."

"What about Vivian and Ella? They are both human."

She waved a hand. "It's a temporary state. They are both mated to clan members and are about to transition. Now eat what I made for you. I'm not going to answer any more questions until you do. This is a difficult dish to make."

He liked her spunk and the fact that she didn't fear him. Not even a little, which was somewhat offensive because he should be feared.

Picking up the plastic fork and knife, he cut a piece off, but then paused with it an inch away from his mouth. "Are you going to be bringing all my meals from now on?"

She nodded.

"Then I must insist that you eat with me. I feel uncomfortable about dining alone and having you watch me."

"Who do you eat with on the island? Your father and brothers?"

So that was why Carol was there.

Smart move on Kian's part. A beautiful woman had a much better chance of getting him to talk. Especially an immortal one, which was sure to throw him off guard since it was his first time in the presence of one.

"Rarely. When I'm there, I eat with the soldiers. When I'm in Washington, I have lunch and dinner meetings in restaurants."

She waved a hand at his plate. "Eat, or I'm going to bring all your meals in cold from now on."

He had a feeling that she meant it. Which implied that it was important to her that he liked what she'd made for him. Not what he expected from a spy.

"I'm eating." He put the piece he'd cut off in his mouth.

As the flavor exploded over his taste buds, Lokan's eyes rolled back with pleasure. He'd eaten beef stroganoff prepared by famous chefs in fancy restaurants, but Carol's was the best one yet, despite it being served on a paper plate.

The disposables were probably a safety measure, and not a reflection of her lack of finesse.

"It's exquisite," he said after he was done chewing. "The best I've ever had, and I've had this dish many times before. You have a gift, Carol."

The smile she flashed him could not have been brighter if he'd told her that she'd won first prize in a worldwide championship.

"Thank you. A while back, I entertained the thought of becoming a chef, but then I realized that working in a commercial kitchen is not the same as cooking at home for fun. I'd rather keep enjoying it as a hobby and choose something else for a job."

Not to piss her off, he took several more bites before asking his next question. "What is your job? Since I'm the only one here, and Arwel was feeding me up until now, I'm sure it's not cooking for prisoners."

"Very astute observation. My day job is running a café. I serve cappuccinos and sandwiches."

"Do you enjoy it?"

She pointed at his plate, and he obligingly cut another piece.

"I do. I'm in the center of things, hearing all the latest gossip as soon as it comes out." She shrugged. "What can I say. I'm a people person."

Eager to ask her more questions, Lokan rushed to finish every last bit on his plate while still keeping his good table manners. When he was done, he wiped his mouth with the paper napkin she'd thoughtfully provided for him and took a long sip from the water bottle.

"How did you end up cooking for me? Is it penance for some transgression?"

"Not at all. I volunteered."

"And why is that?"

She shrugged, lifting one exposed creamy shoulder that made his mouth water. "Someone had to do it, and I was curious. Besides, I'm an awesome cook."

"That you are." He glanced at Arwel before reaching for her hand, but the guy was reading on his phone and not looking at them.

He brought it to his lips for a quick kiss. "Thank you for the meal, which was made even more exquisite by your presence. You are an incredibly beautiful woman."

"Thank you." She flashed him a bright smile. "You are quite handsome yourself. Do you take after your father or your mother?"

He chuckled. "Just as you don't know your father, I don't know my mother. We have this in common. Except, I wouldn't call my mother an egg donor. After all, she carried me in her womb for nine months and then nurtured me for as long as my father allowed it."

"That's sad. Are you close to your father?"

"No one is close to Navuh. He wouldn't give anyone that kind of power."

CAROL

*L*okan was flirty, but Carol knew his interest wasn't feigned. He could fool Ella, but not her.

The question was whether he knew that.

Despite being unfamiliar with immortal females, he seemed intelligent enough to figure out that they weren't so different from their male counterparts and possessed the same enhanced senses. On the other hand, though, he'd been brainwashed to believe that females were inferior, so he might think that other than their immortality, they had no other enhanced abilities.

"I've seen your father's picture. He looks intimidating."

He arched a brow. "Did the same artist who drew mine draw his as well?"

So, he knew about that. Good. For a moment Carol was afraid she'd let something slip. She should've grilled Arwel about what Lokan already knew. In fact, she was going to do that as soon as they left here. The other thing she needed to discuss with the Guardian was the arrangements for the next meal she was going to deliver.

Not much seducing or luring could take place with him sitting a few feet away.

"It's not like we have a bunch of defectors from your camp who can draw." She turned to look at Amanda's portrait that was hanging over the couch. "This is his work, too. You can see how talented he is."

"Arwel told me she's Dalhu's mate. Why is it hanging in this prison cell, though?" He pinned her with a penetrating stare. "Is it to tempt others to cross over by showing them the possibilities?"

What a suspicious guy. But then, she couldn't fault him for that. Not only had he grown up in a vipers' nest, but he was also in enemy territory that he knew nothing about.

She smiled coyly. "Are you tempted, Lokan?"

His black eyes flashed a red glimmer for a moment, making him look demonic.

Sexy demon.

It was a most unusual glow—one she hadn't seen on any other immortal.

He reached for her hand again. "You are temptation personified, Carol. There is a lot I'm willing to do to gain your favor."

As he kissed the back of her hand, his lips felt like a hot brand on her skin, sending shivers down her spine. The good kind.

"Even defect?"

He smirked. "That depends."

"On what?"

"Tell me why this picture is here, and I'll consider it."

The guy was a decent negotiator. If she hadn't been listening so carefully to his wording, she might have thought that he'd just promised to defect in exchange for the story behind Amanda's picture, but all he'd said was that he would consider it.

Could she tell him, though?

If she omitted any details that could identify who Amanda was, it should be okay.

"Some would say it's a very romantic story, while others would say it's creepy."

"You got my full attention."

"It was a chance meeting in a store. Somehow, Dalhu figured out that she was an immortal female and decided to kidnap her. He took her to the mountains, broke into a cabin, and kept her imprisoned there. Long story short, he worked very hard to win her heart and against all odds succeeded."

"So, what happened next? Did she bring him home to her family and they put him in a prison cell?"

"Not exactly. Without going into details of how they found where he was keeping her, a rescue team arrived to free her. Imagine their surprise and disgust when she attacked them to defend him."

He grimaced. "I can definitely imagine that. Consorting with the enemy was probably viewed as worse than defecting."

"You got it. So, they brought him here, not to this nice cell, but to one of the small ones. She tried very hard to forget about him but couldn't. When the Fates give you your true-love mate, you don't question their choice because you are not going to get another."

Lokan smirked. "Is this the romantic part? Because it sounds like a fairytale."

Carol cast him a sad smile. "It's tragic how little you know about immortal mates. This is not a fairytale. Very few get to find their one and only, and the Fates only grant this boon to the most deserving. Those who've made a huge sacrifice for others or who've suffered greatly."

"Then I'm never getting my one and only for sure. What did Dalhu do to get so lucky?"

Lokan was mocking her and not making any effort to hide it.

"In Dalhu's case, the sacrifice came later. His mate, however, had suffered greatly in the past, so the boon was hers. It took her a while to realize this, and when she did, she fought for her right to choose her mate and eventually won. But while the battle was going on, she had him moved to this nicer cell and joined him here."

Carol waved her hand around. "These walls are imbued with great love. Because of his love for his mate, Dalhu pledged his loyalty to the clan, and to prove it he offered to draw portraits of the Brotherhood's leadership. Once he was done with that, he used the art supplies to make countless portraits of his mate. For some reason, they left this one behind when he was let out and allowed to live with her as a free man."

"No offense, Carol, but this is the most unbelievable story I've ever heard. Your clan has been hiding from us for thousands of years, and rightfully so. This is the only reason you have survived. I can't imagine Kian allowing a security risk like this just because one of his people fell in love with the enemy."

"I didn't say it was easy. She had to wage one hell of a battle, and Dalhu had to prove himself in a trial by fire. But in the end, love won."

23

LOKAN

*I*t hadn't escaped Lokan's notice that neither Carol nor Arwel had mentioned the female's name.

He had his suspicions, though.

First of all, she had to be someone important in the clan to wage battle against the mighty Kian. Their leader's hatred for the Brotherhood ran deep.

Secondly, her stunning beauty marked Dalhu's mate as a close descendant of the goddess. Could she be Annani's daughter? Kian's sister?

There was some familial resemblance between them, but then all clan members were descended from the same goddess, so that could be true for any of them.

Not in this case, though.

Lokan was willing to bet that the woman in the portrait was Kian's sister, and the fact that she'd mated an ex-Brother was astounding in its implications.

Perhaps she possessed the power to compel other immortals?

Otherwise, he couldn't conceive of a scenario in which her brother or her mother would allow that.

"Was it love, though, that won the battle? Or was it something else? Did this exceptionally beautiful lady use her special powers to influence your leaders into accepting her chosen mate into the clan?"

Across the room, Arwel snorted. "Her special power is the personality of a bulldozer who doesn't take no for an answer."

Carol pouted. "Do you have a thing for brunettes?"

Was she really peeved because he'd called another woman beautiful? Or was it her way of changing the subject?

"I'm a connoisseur of every kind of female beauty, but I have a preference for petite blondes with a face that angels would envy."

As he'd expected, Carol rewarded him with one of her bright smiles. "How many of those petite blondes have you encountered?"

"Just one." He winked.

Arwel snickered. "Smooth. I'm taking notes."

"I have to admit that she's gorgeous. And she's tall, which I envy. But as far as I know, she really doesn't have any special talents. Not like yours, anyway, which are pretty scary. I'm just glad that you can't compel immortals or invade my dreams."

"How do you know that I can't?"

"Because if you could, you would have been out of here already."

Since he'd never tried to dream-share with an immortal, Lokan didn't know whether he could or not. Compulsion, on the other hand, he'd tried many times. It only worked on humans and not on all of them. Gorchenco was immune, and so were many of the politicians he dealt with.

He often wondered if it had anything to do with corrupt minds, or maybe just suspicious ones. Then again, Vivian and Ella had plenty of reasons to suspect him, and they'd been very easy to compel.

He smiled at her. "That was true before you came. Now that I have your visits to look forward to, I might stay voluntarily."

"Oh, Lokan." She slapped his arm playfully. "You are such a charmer. No wonder you had Ella wrapped around your finger. But I'm onto you."

Except, she didn't seem to mind.

They were playing a game, which he was starting to realize Carol was as masterful at as he was, and upping the ante just made it more fun.

"Ella is a young girl, and although beautiful, she can't hold a candle to you. I would much rather have you wrapped around my little finger than her."

That earned him another slap on his arm. "Not going to happen. Many have tried and failed."

There was nothing like a challenge to get him excited. "But none of them were me." He waggled his brows. "I am incomparable."

"I'm getting sick," Arwel murmured.

The Guardian's presence was a necessary evil, but he was starting to grate on Lokan's nerves.

And apparently on Carol's as well.

Turning to her cousin, she waved her hand at the door. "You don't have to sit here and offer unsolicited commentary. You can go back to your place and turn the volume down on the surveillance equipment."

To Lokan's utter astonishment, Arwel got up and stretched. "I'll do that. When you want out, pick up the house phone and dial zero. I'll come to get you."

"Thank you."

Arwel pointed a finger at Lokan. "Behave." He lifted it up and pointed at the camera mounted near the ceiling. "I'm watching you."

"Carol has nothing to fear from me. She's perfectly safe here."

The funny thing was that he actually meant it, which the empath must have picked up on, and that was why he felt it was okay to leave Carol alone with the enemy.

"She is safe because I got her back," Arwel said as he opened the door using an app on his phone.

That was the one weakness Lokan had discovered so far. If he could take Arwel's phone, he could get out of the cell. Not that he was going to get very far. Arwel wasn't the only one guarding him, and the cuffs they had attached to his limbs contained location trackers that would sound the alarm as soon as he crossed the threshold.

"Finally." Carol tucked a leg under her. "I love Arwel, but he was starting to be annoying.'"

"Do you think I can get up from the damn sofa now that he is gone?"

She waved a hand. "Sure. Do you need to use the bathroom?"

"No, but I want to get a drink from the fridge. Can I offer you a beer?"

She scrunched her nose. "I bet all that's in there is Snake's Venom."

"It's a very good beer."

"Not for me, thank you."

"There are also water bottles."

"I'll take one. I'll bring a fresh supply of drinks when I come back with your dinner."

His heart did a very unfamiliar thing—it skipped a beat. And if he weren't an immortal, Lokan would have feared that something was wrong with it.

"I'm glad you're coming back."

"Of course, I am. This is not a one-time arrangement. I'm here to see to your needs."

He almost tripped over his feet.

But then she continued. "Do you need fresh towels? A change of sheets?"

Pulling out a beer and a water bottle, he chuckled. "For a moment there, I thought you meant something else."

When Carol didn't answer, he turned around and looked at her with an arched brow. But the only answer he got was a coy smile.

The female was a temptress, and she wasn't shy, but she was obviously waiting for him to make the first move.

Except, it might be a trap, and the moment he tried anything, Arwel might storm in with a bunch of his fellow Guardians and beat him up. It didn't make much sense, but neither did letting this gorgeous woman with her fantastic beef stroganoff into his cell.

Was it some kind of mind game? Was Carol Kian's version of a carrot, and the Guardians of the stick?

More information was needed before he dared anything, which meant that he would have to coax those tempting lips of hers into more talking, not kissing. At least for now.

24

CAROL

*C*arol enjoyed watching Lokan's cocky façade starting to show cracks. She was getting to him, and it was beyond satisfying.

Without breaking a sweat, she was manipulating the master manipulator and charming the charmer. It was good to know that even though she hadn't had much practice lately, she'd still got it.

"I don't need my sheets changed. But I would appreciate some fresh towels." He handed her the bottle. "At some point, I'll also need my clothes dry cleaned."

Talk about dialing the thermostat all the way down.

Well, serving his needs was the excuse she'd used for being there, so she couldn't get all huffy about it.

"I'll take care of it."

He sat next to her and popped the lid off the beer. "I'm really sorry about asking you to do such demeaning chores, but it's not as if I can do that myself, and you don't employ humans, which I still find strange."

"Even if we did, no one in their right mind would have allowed them in here."

"Because of my compulsion ability. Although I'm not sure what I could have made them do."

"Compel them to call your father for help."

He snorted. "Not likely. If he didn't execute me on the spot for letting myself get captured, he would have demoted me to toilet cleaning or trash collecting for the rest of my immortal life."

"Ouch. That's harsh. But if he is so mean, why do his people follow him so blindly? Is it out of fear?"

"In large part, yes. But Navuh is also incredibly charismatic. He inspires a religious-type fervor. People are willing to suffer for him, to lose their lives for him, or rather for the cause he promotes."

"Like a cult leader."

"That's a good analogy."

It had taken careful maneuvering, but finally Carol had Lokan where she wanted him. Except, if she hoped to learn from him whether his father was controlling his people by using compulsion, she needed to proceed with caution.

"But if you don't buy into his propaganda, I'm sure there are others who don't either."

Draping his arm over the sofa back, Lokan took a sip of his beer, probably to buy himself a moment to think.

From experience, Carol knew that the best strategy was not to keep pushing but to wait patiently for the answer. Silence was like a void that required filling; if she did it first, the demand would be satisfied, and Lokan would feel less pressured to answer.

"That was what I used to think when I was much younger. Now I'm not so sure. It could very well be that no one admits dissatisfaction with the way things are out of fear, and most definitely not to his son. But my brothers are the same. The few times I dared engage them in conversation on the topic of our father's rulership and suggested that change was needed, I was looked at as a traitor. Then again, my brothers are afraid of him as well."

It seemed that she would have no choice but to ask him point blank. "Do you think your father uses mass compulsion on his people?"

He narrowed his eyes at her. "Why would you think that? Did the two defectors say something to that effect?"

"If they did, it wasn't to me. Dalhu never comes to the café, and whenever Robert does, he reads his newspaper."

This wasn't a good time to mention that she and the other defector had a history. Maybe that time would never come because her week would be up and she'd get all she needed out of Lokan, and that would be it.

Why did that thought fill her with such sadness, though?

They hadn't even kissed yet, and she definitely was not allowed to fall for the Doomer prince.

"Robert? That's not a Brother's name."

She waved a hand. "He adopted an American one. Like you did with Logan. Not very imaginative, by the way."

He shrugged. "It was easy to remember."

"Are you that old, Lokan, that you have trouble with memory?"

"I'm old. But not that old. So, if you haven't heard it from anyone, why would you think my father compels our people?"

"It just makes sense. You must've inherited your compulsion ability from him, but yours is less powerful, which is why you can only compel humans. And because you have the ability to some extent, you are immune to it, and that's why he can't compel your blind loyalty like he can with the others."

He nodded. "You're a smart woman, Carol. I had the same thoughts, but even though I was there and exposed to the effects of it throughout my life, it took a long time to come to this conclusion. You figured it out just from talking with me."

It was nice to hear that he thought her smart, and she was, but not that smart. If not for her talk with Kian, it would have never occurred to her that Navuh might be using compulsion on his people. Not even Kian was that clever.

Turner was.

She waved a dismissive hand. "Sometimes, it's easier to detect a pattern when you are outside looking in. It's like living in a stinky house. You don't smell it until you go on a vacation and then come back. But if guests come over, they smell it right away."

Lokan laughed. "I love your analogies."

Gazing into his dark eyes, she thought that he looked like a different man when he laughed. Or maybe that was the chameleon quality Ella had warned her against. Lokan adapted his behavior to what suited him best at the moment.

A survival mechanism, no doubt. Still, she needed to remember that when he was melting her heart with his smile. Besides, he'd just put the last nail in the coffin of her mission. She wasn't going to the island because there wasn't going to be a revolution no matter how brilliant a job she did.

"I wish it wasn't true, though, because if your father has such absolute control over your people, there is no hope for them."

He frowned. "What do you mean?"

"You said it yourself. If no one opposes him, or rather can't oppose him, nothing is going to change. You will keep on fighting his insane war and try to help him achieve his goal of world domination while sacrificing your lives and any joy you might have had living them."

Lokan wasn't smiling anymore. "You have a way of putting things into perspective. That sounds depressing."

"It is. The only way to change it is to assassinate Navuh, but that's impossible too. He is surrounded by people who are willing to die for him."

The look he gave her was absolutely chilling. "Is that who you really are, Carol? Are you an assassin?"

Her hand flew to her heart. "Me? Are you nuts? I can't even hunt because I can't think of killing an innocent animal."

"Ah, but there are those who would spare an animal but not another person. People are strange."

"I'm not an assassin, Lokan. Why would you think that? I get it that you are suspicious, but that's one hell of a leap."

He shrugged. "Beautiful women don't come to visit enemy prisoners unless they want to get information out of them. I'm not that naive, Carol."

Damn, he was onto her. But she could still turn it around.

"Okay, fine. I wanted to find out whether Navuh was compelling his people's loyalty or not. But nobody sent me. It was my idea, and I used it to convince Kian to let me see you. I'm good friends with Ella, and her stories about you made me curious. And then I saw your portrait, and I just had to see you with my own eyes."

A cocky grin brightening his handsome face, Lokan reached for his beer bottle. "And? What's your verdict?"

"That you are much more handsome in person. The portrait can't show your devilish charm. And your voice, oh my." She fanned herself with her hand. "Smooth as silk. I bet you can talk a girl into an orgasm."

The snort that escaped his mouth was accompanied by a spray of beer, but he was quick enough to turn his head sideways, so none of it landed on her.

"Are you always so outspoken?" He wiped his mouth with the back of his hand.

"Pretty much. Sorry about that."

He waved a hand. "No. That's fine, I like it. I just wasn't ready."

"So, do you believe me that I'm not an assassin?"

"I'm not sure yet. But in case you are, you should be aware of the consequences. Or rather your superiors should be. Without Navuh at the helm, the Brotherhood will fracture into many small militias. To begin with, they will fight each other, but then they will spread out and start trouble elsewhere. It's like chopping a monster's head off and having ten sprout in its place. It's better to have the original monster contained."

25

LOKAN

*W*ithout Carol, Lokan's plush prison cell felt dark and oppressive. It was as if she'd taken all the light with her, leaving only gloom behind.

It had been a long time since he'd enjoyed anyone's company so much. In fact, he'd never met a person he didn't tire of in short order. With Carol, on the other hand, time flew by too quickly, and he hadn't wanted her to leave.

She was witty, flirty, and fearless, her free-spirited personality shining brightly through her smiling eyes. Not to mention beautiful and sexy, but he'd seen his share of gorgeous women, so that wasn't the allure.

Even her immortality couldn't explain his instant draw to her.

Maybe it was the intrigue? The challenge of deciphering who she was?

Pacing the twenty feet or so that was the entire length of the living room, he replayed every moment of the past two hours in his head, searching for clues, glitches, anything that would give him a better insight into this intriguing woman.

One thing he was sure of, though; unless she was the best

actress on the planet, there was no way Carol was an assassin. She was too soft-hearted for that. But she wasn't just a café manager who volunteered to cook his meals and tidy up his place either. She was still hiding who she really was.

Maybe a spy?

That made sense. With her flirty attitude and angelic looks, she would fool most guys into spilling their guts to her. It was also possible that she had a unique talent. After all, she was an immortal female, so there was a good chance of that.

Lokan chuckled. Carol's paranormal talent must be seduction. Were all immortal females so irresistible?

An immortal female.

Damn.

He still had a hard time processing the fact that he'd just spent an entire afternoon in the presence of one.

Stopping in front of the gorgeous brunette's portrait, he thought about the male named Dalhu. To escape Navuh's compulsion, the guy had to have an extremely strong personality. Or maybe he was immune?

Was the other one who called himself Robert immune as well?

Or had they both done it because of their love for an immortal female?

He didn't believe Carol's story about the chance encounter between Dalhu and the brunette who he suspected was Kian's sister. Things like that just didn't happen. Was it something the clan did actively? Trap warriors with honey instead of fishing nets?

If it was working on him, and he had to admit that he felt the temptation, it made sense that it had worked on simple warriors. In their case, love had managed to overpower their leader's compulsion, which was truly remarkable.

Could love free his brothers from his father's hold as well?

It was a fanciful and romantic idea that Lokan allowed himself to indulge in for about two seconds.

He didn't believe one word of the crap about true-love mates, or about the fictional Fates doing the matchmaking to reward those who sacrificed or suffered greatly.

Except, it seemed that Carol truly believed in that nonsense, so he wasn't going to offend her by voicing his opinion on the subject.

His father was right about females' soft hearts affecting their thinking.

Contrary to what Kian and the rest of the clan thought of him, Navuh wasn't insane. His father had an agenda, and he had stuck to it throughout the millennia. Everything Navuh did was with that goal in mind, and his methods, although sometimes abhorrent, worked remarkably well.

Besides, compared to the astounding cruelty and disregard for life of some of the human leaders, Navuh seemed compassionate. He certainly wasn't needlessly cruel, just pragmatic. To him, there was no question whether the goal justified the means.

It always did.

Except, Lokan couldn't care less about Navuh's agenda.

What he cared about were his people, who deserved better than sacrificing everything worth living for on the altar of his father's world-domination ambitions.

The question was what was best for them, and by that Lokan meant the warriors and everyone else living on the island, including the humans.

But whoever thought the answer to that was as simple as eliminating Navuh was naive. Things could get much worse without his father holding everything together.

If only Navuh were more flexible and open to new ideas,

Lokan could suggest a few changes that would make life much better for the island's residents.

First of all, female Dormants should be allowed to transition, and warriors should be allowed to take mates and form family units. Fewer children would be born, but that would be a good thing.

The island was big enough for its current population, but it couldn't support much more than that, and Lokan doubted a new bigger island that was unpopulated and up for sale could be found in today's world.

The truth was that the breeding program was obsolete.

They didn't need more warriors because the Brotherhood was gradually phasing out from the business of war, for the simple reason that demand was dwindling, and instigating new conflicts wasn't as easy as it used to be.

And as far as the human females living on the island were concerned, they shouldn't be forced into prostitution, and only willing ones should be recruited and hired to work in the brothel. He could compel their silence the same way he compelled the pilots', so they could leave when they were too old to work or stay if they wished to.

Except, his father would never agree to make these changes, and there was no way Lokan could achieve any of it on his own in the event the clan sent an assassin to kill Navuh and succeeded. He wasn't powerful enough to hold the Brotherhood together.

Perhaps if his brothers were willing to cooperate, the infighting could be prevented, but he wasn't naive or optimistic enough to believe such cooperation could last. Each of them would try to seize power from the others, and the results would be catastrophic for the island's population as well as for the rest of the planet's occupants.

Stopping again in front of the portrait, he shook his head.

His musings were no longer relevant. He was a prisoner of the clan and powerless to effect any change.

Except, what if he could convince Kian that his plans were aligned with the clan's?

In fact, it was crucial that he succeed.

The way he saw it, Navuh couldn't be disposed of or overthrown without it resulting in the Hydra effect. When Kian realized that, he might decide that his only option was to destroy the island and everyone on it.

Lokan couldn't allow that, which meant that he would have to withstand unimaginable torture.

He chuckled. Perhaps that was the great sacrifice Carol's Fates would exact from him in exchange for gifting him with a true-love mate.

Looking into the brunette's secretive eyes, he murmured, "Do you have the answers?"

Warning Carol against assassinating Navuh had been a necessity. She would obviously report it to Kian, and the guy seemed intelligent enough to understand the reason for it.

The question was how to convince him that there was another way to effect change that didn't involve bombing the island or killing its leader.

When Kian had asked him what he needed Vivian and Ella for, Lokan's answer had been the truth, just not all of it.

Getting them to report who Navuh was hiding in the harem hadn't been about satisfying Lokan's curiosity. Well, in part it was. If his mother was an immortal, she could still be there.

But that hadn't been the main reason.

Whoever Navuh was hiding from everyone, including his own sons, must be either incredibly precious or dangerous to him.

Gaining access to that female and her secrets might open a new way to influence Navuh into accepting change.

Right.

It had been a long shot before, but now it was a pipe dream. Kian would never trust Lokan enough to agree to collaborate on any mission, let alone one that was based on pure speculation.

ELLA

"You actually cooked." Julian kissed Bridget's cheek. "I'm impressed."

"Thank you for inviting us," Ella said and gave her future mother-in-law a hug.

"It's my pleasure. And ignore my son's remarks. I know my way around the kitchen."

"I'm sure you do. Can I help with anything?"

"You can toss the salad and help me carry things to the table. Everything else is done."

"I can help carry things," Julian offered.

"Six hands are better than two." Bridget waved a hand motioning for them to follow her into the kitchen.

Ella had a feeling that Bridget wanted to talk with her alone, and that Julian had spoiled her plans. She wondered what that was about.

A warning not to hurt her son, or else?

Bridget wasn't that type of a mother-in-law. Ella didn't know the woman well, but usually she was all business. It was probably something about the use of contraceptives and how she should toss them if she wanted to transition.

Except, Ella already knew all that, and so did Julian. Perhaps Bridget thought she would be embarrassed to talk about it in front of him?

In the kitchen, Turner was crouching next to the oven and watching a roast through the window.

"Good evening," Ella said. "I didn't know you cooked, Turner."

He waved at her. "I don't. I got it pre-made, but the guy in the store said to watch it when I heat it up, so it doesn't dry up. A meat thermometer would have been a much better solution, but we don't have one."

"That's because we usually don't eat it," Bridget said. "But what you are doing is silly. I think I hear Vivian and Magnus. Can you go open the door for them?"

"I'll do it," Ella said.

For some reason, hearing Bridget call Turner silly had irked her. He was anything but. She owed the guy her life, her future, her happiness, everything. He'd saved her twice. Once from the Russian and then from Lokan.

A shiver ran through her as she imagined what could have happened if the clan didn't have Turner to lead the rescue missions. The Fates had done a double good deed by bringing him into the fold.

The doorbell rang just as she reached for the handle.

"What smells so good?" Parker asked in lieu of greeting and headed for the kitchen as if this was his house.

"There is a roast in the oven," Turner said. "Hello, Vivian." He offered his hand to her mother first, and then to Magnus.

When everyone was done with the hellos and how-are-yous, and Turner deemed the roast ready, Bridget called everyone to the table.

"Let's start with a toast. We have so many things to be thankful for."

"Indeed." Vivian nodded.

Turner uncorked a bottle of wine and poured some for everyone, even letting Parker have a few drops. "You earned it, buddy. Our own compulsion removal master."

Ella snorted. "We should be so lucky. Unfortunately, he is not only good at removing compulsion, he's good at using it too. I can't wait to transition so he'll stop tormenting me."

"It's not my fault that you and Mom are the only ones I can practice on. And because the two of you are going to transition soon, I have to do it a lot."

Vivian ruffled his hair. "Ella is just teasing, sweetie. You can practice on us as much as you want."

Clearing her throat, Bridget raised her glass. "Let's toast Ella and Vivian's safe return."

After the round of glass clinking was done, Bridget continued. "Next toast goes to Parker. The first clan member to ever possess the ability to compel humans. Your rare talent opens up new possibilities for the clan. Once you have full command of it, we might consider bringing humans into the village on occasion, without fear of them revealing our location."

"I'll drink to that." Parker lifted his glass.

"To Parker," Magnus said.

When that round was done, Turner refilled their glasses.

"The next toast is to capturing Navuh's son." Bridget turned to her mate. "And to my brilliant man who made it happen."

As they all clinked glasses, Turner looked uncomfortable and murmured something about just doing his job.

"The next toast goes to Ella and Julian." Bridget smiled. "Congratulations on finding each other and starting your life together. We wish you an eternity of happiness."

"Thank you," Julian said as he clinked his glass with Ella's. "My new mission in life is to make my mate happy."

Bridget nodded and then turned to Vivian and Magnus. "And to you, congratulations on your upcoming nuptials."

As Ella finished her glass, her head started spinning. "Perhaps you should combine the rest of your toasts into one because I'm already getting dizzy."

Bridget chuckled. "I keep forgetting about your human metabolism, but this is the last one anyway. Let's toast to our new and expanded family. May we have many joyous occasions to celebrate together and toast to."

"Amen," Turner said. "Now let's eat before this roast gets cold."

When the meal was done, and everyone had moved into the living room, Bridget pulled out a large box from the hallway closet and brought it over to the coffee table, putting it in front of Ella and Julian. "A little something from Turner and me to celebrate your moving in together."

"What's in it?" Julian asked. "It's a big box."

"Open it." Bridget waved at it.

Together, Ella and Julian tore through the wrapping paper and then opened the box.

"It's a quilt." Julian pulled it out and stood up to unfurl it.

It was big enough to cover their king-sized bed but way too beautiful to serve as a blanket.

"It's gorgeous. Thank you so much." Ella pushed up and rushed to give Bridget a crushing hug, and a perfunctory one to Turner. "We should hang it on the wall instead of putting it over the bed."

"You can do whatever you want with it," Bridget said. "Turner and I bought it in Miami. We went to see a quilting competition, or rather exhibition because most of the quilts were for sale. When I saw this one, I knew that I had to get it for you two."

Ella frowned. "You bought it before the mission. How did you know we would move in together?"

Smiling, Bridget tapped her nose. "A mother's intuition."

CAROL

*A*s Carol watched Arwel input the code into the keypad, she memorized the numbers. Perhaps, if everything went well, she could pay Lokan a surprise visit later tonight without involving Arwel.

The problem would be leaving later. The door had a sensor and would close behind her, but to open it, she would have to call Arwel. It didn't make much sense to sneak in if she couldn't sneak out.

Not a big deal. She had no qualms about what she was doing, and Arwel had no illusions as to what this was about either.

Maybe another woman would have handled it differently, dangling sex as a possibility but never going that far, but it wasn't Carol's style. And besides, she wanted Lokan. For her, having him was going to be a reward for great spying work, not a chore.

The male was gorgeous, intelligent, had a decent sense of humor, and surprisingly for a Doomer, knew how to treat a woman. His current situation had dimmed Lokan's powerful personality a notch, but he was still a formidable male.

She sighed. If only he weren't a Doomer…

Heck, who was she kidding? She didn't give a damn. A Doomer had saved her from the sadist, and another one had chopped the monster's head off. She, more than any other clan member, should know that not all Doomers were bad.

"You should just let me in," she said as the door finally started moving. "You don't need to come in."

His brows forming an upside-down triangle, Arwel looked at her and then shook his head. "I don't like it, but you're right. I'm just hindering your progress, which by the way is impressive."

"Thank you."

"I'll just drop off the stuff you had me schlep down here."

"That would be great."

She had been busy that afternoon, making another grocery run to equip Lokan's cell with all that she considered necessities, and then cooking another gourmet meal for five.

In gratitude, her new roommates had not only serenaded her, but had also donated an entire case of Snake's Venom for her to bring to Lokan's cell. Which was awesome since the stuff wasn't readily available. There was only one store selling it locally, and because it often ran out of stock, the guys were now ordering the beer directly from the brewery in Scotland.

As they entered, Lokan was sitting on the couch the way he'd been instructed to do. "Can I get up and help you with that tray?"

"Yes, please. You can put it on the dining table."

It wasn't too heavy for her, but it was big. This time she was dining with Lokan, and she'd brought several containers in addition to the plates.

Casting a quick glance at Arwel, Lokan got up slowly, avoiding making any sudden moves, took the tray from her hands, and carried it to the dinette.

"I wish I had a nice tablecloth. Given the smells, this meal calls for a formal setting."

She chuckled. "We are still using paper plates and plastic cutlery. Not formal at all."

"Do you want me to put things away?" Arwel asked.

"No, that's okay. Lokan is going to help me do that later."

The Guardian nodded. "Call me when you're ready to leave." He pulled out his phone and activated the door mechanism.

"*Bon appetit,*" Arwel said as he walked out.

Watching the door close behind the Guardian, Lokan waited until the mechanism went silent before turning to Carol. "By the heft of that tray, I was sure Arwel was going to join us for dinner and call the other guys in as well."

"I already fed the others." She started taking lids off the containers. "This is just for you and me."

"Thank you for joining me this time. It will make the experience that much more exquisite."

She chuckled. "You use that word a lot."

"That's because it keeps popping into my head whenever I look at you."

"Oh, Lokan. You're such a smooth talker." She pointed at the chair. "Sit down and let's eat."

"Ladies first."

Stubborn man.

"In a moment. What would you like to drink with dinner? I have wine, whiskey, or Snake's Venom beer."

"Whatever you think goes well with the meal."

"Wine."

"Then wine it is."

So agreeable. Carol wondered if it was an act, and if the Doomer prince would have been as accommodating under different circumstances.

131

Taking the bottle out of one of the bags that Arwel had brought in for her, she handed it to Lokan. "You can pull the cork and pour the wine." Arwel refused to let her bring in a corkscrew, so she'd had to uncork it before bringing it down.

Lokan dipped his head. "My pleasure."

Everything he did was a bit exaggerated, and again she wondered whether he was adding flourish to impress her with his good manners or was he like that all the time.

Navuh's son was Doomer royalty. Perhaps his father insisted on proper etiquette?

For some reason, she doubted it.

"You are very gentlemanly, which surprises me. I was under the impression that Doomers don't have the best of manners, that it's not part of the curriculum in your training camp."

He pulled the cork out and poured the wine into the two clear plastic wine glasses she'd bought. At least they looked like the real thing, which made the table she'd set up a little nicer.

"I don't like this nickname you have for the Brotherhood. It sounds derogatory."

"It's not a nickname. It's an acronym."

He arched a brow. "Not in the old language. It only works in English."

"Well, it kind of fits, and it's easier than saying the entire name. Besides, you should be thankful that it's not Dumbers. The Devout Order of Mortdh Brotherhood could have been the Devout Universal Mortdh Brotherhood or something like that."

Lokan didn't find it funny. "Let's change the subject. What's in all of those bags Arwel brought in?"

"Supplies. I got you a whole case of Snake's Venom beer, compliments of the Guardians. If you knew how hard it was to get this beer, you would appreciate how great their sacrifice was."

"If they believe in the nonsense about the Fates favoring those who sacrifice or suffer greatly, then they might be doing it to increase their chances of getting rewarded with a true-love mate."

"It's not nonsense."

LOKAN

*D*amn.

Lokan shook his head. It had been an uninten-
tional slip. After making a mental note not to offend Carol by
questioning her convictions, he had done it only a few hours
later.

As his father's son, he knew all about the power of belief
and how attached people got to the most absurd ideas.

"I apologize for my comment. It's just that I'm a very old
immortal, and I haven't seen much evidence to support the
existence of true love, or of fate being anything but capricious.
Suffering is random, and self-sacrifice, while admirable, is
rarely rewarded."

Leaning back in her chair, Carol crossed her arms over her
chest and pouted. "I've seen it happen many times. Like Kian
and his wife Syssi, then Dalhu and Amanda, Andrew and
Nathalie, and so on. It only started happening recently, which
leads me to believe that the Fates are planning something big."

Lokan stifled a smirk. Carol had let the brunette's name
slip. Amanda. It was a modern name, so she was either a young

immortal or had adapted it to the times like he'd done with his own.

"What do you think it is that they are planning?"

She shrugged. "You haven't tasted the ossobuco yet." She waved a hand at his plate. "Eat."

"Yes, ma'am."

He cut a piece of the veal and put it in his mouth. He'd expected it to be delicious, and it was. He told her that as soon as he was done chewing.

"Thank you. Don't think I'll keep spoiling you like this, though. Today I was just showing off. I won't be making you beef stroganoff and ossobuco every day. But it paid off in an unexpected way. That's how I got a case of Snake's Venom from the Guardians. It was their thanks for the ossobuco."

"Aha, so it wasn't sacrifice on their part. It was a payment."

Carol lifted her wine glass and took a sip. "Their original thanks was singing for me, but when I asked about where I can get the beer, they gave me half of their stash. I think that qualifies as a sacrifice. Not a huge one, but still."

Without him planning it, the direction the conversation had taken led to where Lokan could ask Carol about the Brother who he suspected had snagged Kian's sister. Who was he? And what made him so special that a goddess's daughter had fallen for him?

"What did Dalhu sacrifice for Amanda?"

"His life in the Brotherhood, to start with. That was the only home he'd known, and since he was most likely under your father's compulsion, it must have been very difficult to do."

It still didn't tell him much about the man himself. "Was he one of Sharim's soldiers? I know that the clan either captured or killed that entire unit."

"No. It happened much earlier than that." Carol lifted the wine glass to her lips and drank all that was left in it.

Something about his comment must have upset her.

Carol's angelic expression had turned so vicious that Lokan was inclined to reconsider his opinion about her not being an assassin. The way she looked now, he could envision her holding a gun and pulling the trigger.

His curiosity prompted him to get to the bottom of this, but given how distraught Carol appeared, he decided it would be wise to drop the subject and move to a more agreeable topic.

"Would you like me to pour you more wine?"

"Yes, please."

For the next several moments, they ate in silence that was disturbed only by the occasional sounds of delight he was making. He did it to please her, but he didn't have to feign his enjoyment. The ossobuco Carol had made was superb.

Leaving her plate half full, Carol pushed it away and wiped her mouth with a napkin. "What I find hard to believe is your claim that you weren't attracted to Ella. I might not be as old as you, but I'm not young either and I know men. No male can stay indifferent to that kind of beauty. And the fact that she is so young and innocent only enhances her appeal."

Carol seemed to be in a combative mood, and he wondered how to appease her. She wouldn't believe him if he denied his attraction to Ella flat out, and compliments weren't going to work either.

After pouring himself another glass of wine, Lokan leaned back in his chair. "There is a difference between appreciating beauty and physical attraction. Ella's face is like a work of art. She is beautiful to look at, I would have to be blind not to see that, but that doesn't mean she stirs desire in me. I like her strong personality, and I find her fun to talk to, and if for some reason I was forced to mate her, it would not have been a hardship. But my preference leans towards more mature and experienced bed partners. I don't have the patience to coax and convince and teach. I like women who are confident in their sexuality and know exactly what they want."

She arched a brow. "Could it be that you prefer what is easily available? I know men like you—successful, busy, and demanding. Lack of patience is not your only problem; lack of time and exacting tastes are big factors too. Paid company is often the answer. I doubt you've done much courting in your long life."

Regrettably, she wasn't wrong. But that was the reality for immortal males under Navuh's rule. There were no immortal females for them to join with, and humans could only be temporary bed warmers.

"There is something to what you're saying. I can, or rather could, pay for the best and get exactly what I want without having to go through the process of trial and error most human males are forced to go through in their search for suitable mates. Perhaps if a mate was my goal, I would have put more effort into it. But since there were no immortal prospects for me, all I was interested in were suitable bed partners."

He took another sip of wine. "Hypothetically speaking, though, if I had my pick of immortal females, I would have gone for the older and more experienced. What on earth could a nearly one-thousand-year-old immortal male have in common with an eighteen-year-old human girl?"

His lengthy answer seemed to mollify Carol, and as he talked, the dark cloud hovering over her delicate features gradually dissipated.

Lifting her wine glass, she smirked. "Then you're in luck because I'm much older than any of the humans you've been with, and vastly more experienced."

He waved a dismissive hand. "I doubt it. Not the age, but the experience. I've been with many pros."

She put the glass down. "Don't forget the age factor. While human females who engage in sex professionally have twenty years at most to practice their craft, their immortal counterparts have centuries."

"That's true. But I can't imagine an immortal female engaging in sex professionally. The only immortal females I know of are clan members. My father might have several in his harem, but since they are his property and not free to offer their bodies to anyone else, they are irrelevant to this discussion. The clan females are free to do as they please, but since the clan is rich, they have no need to degrade themselves like that."

Frowning, Carol crossed her arms over her chest. "What if a female chooses to do it for fun? We are just as lustful as immortal males."

"I can't imagine anyone selling her body for fun unless she is mentally unstable or perverted."

If the blaze in an immortal female's eyes could kill, he would have been incinerated on the spot.

"Do I seem mentally unstable to you? And for your information, only a Doomer could accuse a female of being perverted just because she enjoys sex and is not shy about it."

Why was she getting so huffy?

"I'm not talking about enjoying sex or even promiscuity. I have nothing against a female with a healthy sex drive. I'm talking about selling her body for money. That's the degrading part."

Pushing to her feet, Carol threw the napkin on the table, strode to the bar, and picked up the phone. "Get me out of here," she barked into the receiver before slamming it back down.

"Why are you so angry?" Lokan got up and walked up to her. "It can't possibly apply to you." He reached for her waist.

"That's where you are wrong." Turning faster than he'd expected, she moved out of his reach and headed toward the door.

He knew better than to follow. The mechanism had already engaged, and the door was starting to move. After that phone call, if he chased Carol to the door, Arwel was going to shoot first and ask questions later.

Pushing through the opening before the door completed its swing, Carol disappeared from view, and a moment later the door started closing again.

In the silence that followed her stormy departure, Lokan remained rooted to the spot, bewildered and perplexed.

Carol engaging in prostitution was inconceivable. She must have been offended by him looking down at sex workers in general.

The world was changing, especially in the West. Everyone was so touchy, and things that had been perfectly okay to say only a few years ago were now anathema. Had prostitution been added to the list of those taboo subjects?

If she'd stayed a moment longer, Lokan would have apologized, even though he felt justified in his sentiment that selling one's body for sexual use was degrading.

Lokan thought of himself as a progressive male, and his views weren't chauvinistic or misogynistic in the least. As long as a woman wasn't pledged to one male by matrimony or other contractual agreement that demanded exclusivity, it was her prerogative to do with her body as she pleased.

But selling it?

And the same was true for men. Some males sold their bodies for money as well.

On the other hand, as a user of such services, it was hypo-critical of him to sneer at the people offering them.

Maybe that was what had pissed off Carol so much?

Was she ever coming back so he could apologize profusely and get his only ally and source of information back?

Perhaps he could ask Arwel to communicate his apology to her. After all, the Guardian had an interest in her staying around and not going back to her job at the café. With Carol gone, it would be back to the sandwiches from the vending machines.

Lokan was sure that Arwel was just as sick of them as he was.

29

CAROL

Don't cry. Don't you dare cry.

Not waiting for the door to finish its swing, Carol squeezed out through the narrow opening. "Close it."

Arwel punched the close button, and the door started its reverse track. "What happened?" he asked.

"Weren't you listening?"

Carol started toward the elevators in a brisk walk.

"The audio was muted all the way down. I was just glancing at the video feed from time to time to check that you were okay. You seemed fine, just sitting and talking while eating. Then he said something that pissed you off. I felt your anger, but since you weren't anxious or distressed, I ignored it."

"It's my fault. I've been fooled by his pretend sophistication and charm and have given him too much credit. I should have known better than to expect a Doomer to be truly progressive."

Arwel called up the elevator and then leaned against the wall. "I'm not going to ask what he said and get you upset again. But is this it? Are you quitting?"

"I'm going to sleep on it."

Her disappointment and disillusionment didn't mean she

could abandon her mission. In fact, she'd acted most unprofessionally and was kicking herself for it.

Her biggest mistake hadn't been expecting Lokan to have progressive ideas but allowing herself to believe that something real was happening between them.

Subconsciously.

Consciously, she'd convinced herself that she was playing a game, and doing it well, too. Lokan seemed to be infatuated with her, but then he was playing a game as well.

Except, in her stupidity, she'd bought it.

When they got up to her temporary apartment, Arwel stopped outside her door. "Do you want me to get the tray and the food containers from Lokan's cell?"

"Yes. Thank you. I'm going to grab a shower, so you can just let yourself in and leave everything on the counter."

"No problem. Anything else I can help you with?"

"You can kick Lokan in the butt for me."

He smirked. "I'll happily oblige."

"Just kidding. Good night, Arwel." She leaned and kissed his cheek.

"It's too early for good nights, but same to you."

Opening the door, Carol hoped her roommates weren't there. She didn't feel like talking with anyone. All she wanted to do was to get into the shower and scrub herself clean.

Damn Lokan for making her feel dirty.

Especially since she'd never felt like that before, not even when she'd been an active courtesan. Her clients had been carefully chosen, and she hadn't invited into her bed anyone she hadn't been interested in. Not all of them had been handsome, but that wasn't what she'd been after.

Power excited her much more than good looks.

Regrettably, damn Lokan had both and much more, and it had messed with her head. Suddenly, she wanted more than just great sex or what it could get her, money wise or information wise.

Carol had always enjoyed the game and had prided herself for being exceptionally good at it. In modern terms, it was like turning a hobby into a job.

None of her relatives had sneered at her chosen occupation, not even when she'd been active. They might not have thought highly of it, but there was a big difference between that and calling it degrading.

The only time she'd ever felt degraded had been listening to Lokan and looking into his eyes when he'd pissed all over her life choices.

But what the hell did she expect from a freaking Doomer?

He was such a hypocrite. If he thought selling sex was degrading, then he should feel degraded for buying it.

After the shower, Carol made herself tea and took the mug to her bedroom, then lay awake staring at the ceiling.

Now what?

Could she go back into Lokan's cell tomorrow and pretend that nothing had happened?

That was what she should do. The question was whether she could hold on to the act while keeping her heart out of it. Right now, she was too emotional to make a rational decision. The best thing she could do was to sleep on it and wait until tomorrow.

The truth was that she didn't need to seduce Lokan to keep him talking. She could just dangle it as a possible reward and never deliver. She could bring his breakfast in, chat a little bit, and leave. Then repeat the same thing at lunch and dinner.

No more eating with him. Instead, she was going to leave him hanging and go hunting for a hookup. It had been way too long since she'd had some fun.

But wait. The celebration party for Ella and Vivian's safe

return was happening tomorrow, and there was no way she was missing out on that to serve a meal to the freaking Doomer.

He would have to heat up his freaking lunch in the microwave and eat alone. In fact, she wasn't planning on coming back for dinner either. She would bring him all three meals in the morning, and then let him stew in his own juices for the rest of the day.

Or, even better. She could have Arwel, or one of the other Guardians who had gotten stuck babysitting Lokan, bring him sandwiches from the vending machine. That would teach him a lesson.

The problem was that he didn't even understand what she was mad about, so he wouldn't know what she was punishing him for.

Should she tell him?

No way.

It would be too painful having him look at her with disdain.

30

LOKAN

*T*here wasn't much to do in a cell, even a spacious one. After Carol had left, Lokan emptied the containers she'd left behind, eating every last morsel. If she wasn't coming back, this could be his last decent meal, and he wasn't going to waste any of it.

When that was done, he took the tray to the counter and did the inconceivable, wiping the table clean.

Quite domestic of him.

In his Washington apartment, one of his bodyguards usually did the honors. Not that there had been much to clean because Lokan had been eating mostly in restaurants, but still. Wiping tables or rinsing up mugs had been beneath him.

As he heard the door mechanism engage, Lokan watched it swing open, hoping it was Carol coming back to either explain what had angered her so much, or yell at him, or just pick up the tray.

But it was only Arwel.

"I came for the dishes." He walked in.

"Did Carol tell you what got her so upset?"

The Guardian shrugged. "You must have said something

chauvinistic. She told me to kick your butt, which I would have gladly done, but then she said she was kidding, so your backside is safe."

He'd figured that much himself. Maybe he should ask Arwel if mentioning prostitution or looking down on it was the newest politically incorrect thing?

If that was it, then it was another proof that the Western world was losing its collective mind. His father was probably loving it because it reinforced what he'd been claiming all along, that humans were like sheep who need a strong shepherd to lead them.

Except, Navuh's idea of shepherding wasn't benevolent. If his father had his way, he would have the whole of humanity enslaved, with immortals as its masters, and him as the absolute ruler of them all.

Talk about a dystopian future.

Lifting the tray, Arwel turned around and headed for the door. "I'll see you tomorrow."

"Good night, Arwel."

The Guardian glanced at him over his shoulder. "I suggest you try really hard to come up with the most sniveling apology you can think of. I like having good food for breakfast, lunch, and dinner."

Arwel had just confirmed what Lokan had suspected. Carol might not be coming back.

Damn, how had he messed things up so badly?

And more importantly, how was he going to fix it?

The best way was to admit that he'd been a hypocrite, retract his comment about prostitution being degrading, and then talk about how vital the service was to society, and especially to immortal males. As far as he could tell, her clansmen were in no better situation than the Brothers. Only a few had been lucky enough to secure mates, and the rest had to either use paid services or go out hunting for sex in clubs and bars.

The question was whether she was going to buy it. Perhaps a better way to approach it was to admit that it was just as degrading for the client?

At least it would be closer to the truth.

Except, paying for sex had never made him feel degraded. It was just the way things were. Where there was demand, supply would follow, and it had been this way forever.

So maybe Carol was right, and as long as the service was provided voluntarily, there was nothing degrading about it for either party.

Could he say it with conviction, though?

Because Carol would see right through him.

She'd seen through his game to charm her, but she hadn't minded that because she'd been playing the same game.

Perhaps once she cooled down a little, she would be more reasonable. After all, prostitution was illegal in most of the world. And as long as a person could get arrested for offering sex for money, there was no way the occupation could be regarded as respectable.

Surely, he wasn't the only one who thought like that.

With nothing better to do, Lokan reached for the remote and flicked the television on. It wasn't connected to the outside world, so he couldn't listen to the news and find out if there were any new developments that he should be aware of. There was, however, an extensive selection of movies and shows he could watch.

Scrolling through the offerings, he wasn't paying particular attention to the display. He was still thinking about Carol and how much he missed her company.

Should he attempt dream-sharing with her?

Since he'd discovered the ability by chance several centuries ago, he'd only succeeded in dream-sharing with a handful of human females. Other than with Ella, it had always been about dream sex.

He'd attempted to invade the dreams of several human generals in an attempt to uncover their war plans, but it had never worked. Then he'd tried to invade the dreams of less prominent human males, but that hadn't worked either, so he'd figured he could only dream-share with females.

Visiting immortals in dreamworld had always been out of the question because whoever he dream-shared with would talk, and he wanted to keep it a secret.

Humans he could either thrall or compel to forget the dream encounter, but he had no such power over immortals.

Carol provided a unique opportunity to test his talent on an immortal. If he were successful in entering her dream, he could try entering Kian's or Arwel's.

For what purpose, though?

Ella had taught him a valuable lesson. Gaining access to her dreams didn't mean barrier-free access to her mind. If an eighteen-year-old managed to keep secrets from him, it wasn't hard to do. Besides, entering Kian or Arwel's mind was as good as signing his own death warrant. Fearing the intrusion, Kian would no doubt order his immediate execution, or if he was feeling merciful, stasis.

CAROL

*I*t was after midnight when Carol's eyelids finally started drooping. She'd watched two movies, but the love stories had only depressed her more, so as a last resort she'd turned the comedy channel on and had a few good laughs while watching *South Park*.

With a sigh, she clicked the television off and snuggled under the blanket, hugging a pillow.

Fates, she missed her old, carefree life. But after her capture and torture, she just couldn't go back to that. Going to clubs, alone or with friends, was always accompanied by a residue of fear.

It didn't matter that she never left the village without a gun in her purse, or that she was one hell of a markswoman and had killer aim with that thing, or that she was now capable of kicking serious butt.

Carol went anyway because she wasn't willing to surrender to fear, and she needed to get her fix at least once in a while, but it wasn't as much fun as it used to be.

It wasn't carefree.

Drifting into sleep, she imagined herself sunbathing on the

shore of a tranquil lake, with a soft breeze caressing her face and birds chirping in the trees. It helped her relax, which most nights translated into peaceful dreams.

Sometimes, though, the nightmares came back. Less and less often, thank the merciful Fates, but it required vigilance with her nightly relaxation ritual before falling asleep.

Thankfully, the lucid dream turned into a real one, and as sleep claimed her, she was still lying on the grass in the meadow abutting her lake.

A soft kiss on her lips had her open her eyes. "Lokan? What are you doing here? Am I dreaming about you?"

He was crouching beside her, gazing at her with those nearly black eyes of his and looking devilishly handsome.

"We are sharing a dream. I wasn't sure I could do it with you, but here I am. I came to apologize."

Propping herself on her forearms, she squinted to get a better look at him. Instead of the slacks and dress shirt he'd had on before, he was now dressed in a plain black T-shirt and jeans, looking more like someone she could've bumped into at a store and not the prince of an evil empire.

"You look good in jeans."

"Thank you. Can I sit next to you?"

She moved to the side, making room on the blanket she had spread over the grass. "You can lie down. I don't mind sharing my lake with you."

He did as she'd instructed, lying on his side with his head propped on his hand. "Is it a real lake, or did you make it up?"

"I call it my tranquility lake. It exists only in my mind."

He lifted his head and looked around. "You must spend a lot of time here. The scenery is very detailed for a made-up dreamscape."

"I do. I imagine it before falling asleep to ensure peaceful dreams."

He frowned. "Do you suffer from nightmares?"

"I do. But I don't want to talk about it. You said that you came to apologize."

"Yes, I did. I mean, I do. I realized how hypocritical it was of me to look down on the providers of a service I use, or rather used, on a regular basis. If there is anything degrading about it, it goes both ways, and since I didn't feel degraded by it, my partners in crime shouldn't either."

"Partners in crime, eh?"

"Prostitution is still illegal in most countries."

"Not yours, though."

He chuckled. "The entire island revolves around it. It's the main attraction and a major source of income for us. I don't approve of it because it is not consensual. But if it were, I wouldn't have a problem with it."

She narrowed her eyes at him. "So, if by some miracle you became the king of the island, you wouldn't shut down the brothel?"

"That would be a sure way to cause a riot. Not even my father's compulsion could prevent it. Since it's an island and there is nowhere for the warriors to go, the brothel is essential for them. But I would make sure that the ladies were recruited and not kidnapped, and that they got a decent cut of the proceeds."

"I guess that's pretty progressive thinking for a Doomer."

Turning to lie on his back, Lokan crossed his arms under his head. "I have many more progressive ideas for the island, but at this point, they are just pipe dreams."

"Because you are imprisoned?"

"Even before that. I wasn't powerful enough to effect changes on my own, and my brothers were not about to cooperate with me because they are under my father's influence."

He sounded sincere, but Lokan was a master manipulator

and an exceptional liar. He might have been telling her things he thought she wanted to hear.

"What other changes would you enact?"

"My vision for the island is to make it a real community that provides a good life for my people. First of all, I would allow the dormant females to transition, and the warriors to take them as mates and form family units. Over the years, the need for the brothel would subside."

"With our miserable fertility rate, it would take many centuries. That's why our clan is so small, while your father has tens of thousands of warriors."

Unless Merlin's intervention worked, but she didn't hold out much hope for that.

He turned to look at her and smiled. "We are immortals. We have time. And the low fertility rate is a blessing. Imagine the world overrun with our kind. Humanity would eventually become an endangered species."

"Why do you care? Doomers have little regard for humans."

Riling Lokan on purpose to make him slip, Carol expected him to get angry.

Instead, he sighed. "We are superior to humans in almost every way, except for our brains and our emotional makeup. We are not smarter, and we are ruled by the same primitive impulses of love and hate, loyalty and competition. The fact is that there are billions of humans on this earth, and the future of this planet depends on their best and brightest combining their brain power and making it a better place for everyone, including us. Bottom line, we need them, but they don't need us."

She waved a dismissive hand. "Speak for yourself. The clan has been helping humanity along since the beginning, providing it with technological knowhow and promoting democracy and equality for all. You guys, on the other hand, have been doing everything in your power to hinder its progress."

"That is true. But just as you were not personally responsible for all that good work, I wasn't personally responsible for all the hindering. We are just two cogs in two different machines."

"Yes, but I'm a tiny insignificant cog, while you are a prince. I'm sure you could have done more."

He chuckled. "I assure you that I couldn't. I followed orders like everyone else, and all the careful scheming I've done over the years has borne very little fruit."

He was good. She had to give him that. Listening to Lokan, one could think that he was a pure soul who'd been secretly laboring to improve his people's lives.

Perhaps his intentions had been indeed good, but Carol would believe it if he could support his claims by actions.

"Talk is cheap."

"What would you have done differently if you were the queen of the island?" Lokan asked.

LOKAN

"*I* haven't given it much thought. Your ideas aren't bad, just incomplete."

He liked listening to her talk, not because of what she had to say, but how she said it. She could be talking about the most boring subject, and still sound as if she was trying to seduce him. Everything about her was tempting, from the way she moved those lush lips of hers, to the slight raspiness of her voice, and the stubborn tilt of her chin.

"Give it a try."

"I'm a café manager, not a politician. I'm not even leadership material. All I know is that people should be free but still held in check by laws that protect the community from those who seek to take advantage by unfair means. As for the outside world, the Brotherhood needs to find a different goal for its existence than global domination, and it needs to stop instigating wars. The trafficking needs to stop too, and all those women you force into prostitution should be set free. Just don't ask me how to achieve that because I wouldn't know where to start. I thought that seeding new and better ideas in the minds of the soldiers might lead to change from the inside, but if Navuh is compelling their loyalty, it's not going to happen."

"Not right away."

"Why, do you have a long-term plan?"

"I'm still working on it."

She waved a dismissive hand. "It's hopeless. Unless…" she smirked, "you find a way to eliminate the brothel. You said that even the compulsion wasn't going to help Navuh if that happened. The warriors would revolt."

He leaned closer. "Sex makes the world go around, not money. Money is just the means to get sex."

She focused on his lips. "Is that so?"

"Indeed." He cupped her cheek and kissed her softly, just a brush of his lips over hers.

Her eyes fluttering closed, she wrapped her arm around his neck and kissed him back, her small tongue seeking entry, which he allowed.

If only this was happening in reality and not in dream world. The sensations were all there, but they were somewhat muted.

Carol went deeper, lifting up and pressing herself against his body. The feel of her soft breasts on his chest aroused him, but he still couldn't help thinking how much better it would be to really hold her in his arms.

Leaning away, she sighed. "It's not the same. I want to kiss you for real, to feel your hard body against mine and your strong hands touching me everywhere."

Even in the dream, he felt his eyes blaze fire. "Then come to me."

"You're a very tempting devil." She smoothed a finger over his brows. "I've never seen an immortal's eyes glow red."

"I'm one of a kind." He put his hand on the small of her back and pressed her tighter against him, letting her feel his dream erection.

"Oh, wow. That feels real enough. Have you ever had dream sex?"

"I did. But she was a human. I don't want my first time with an immortal to be in dream world. But I'll take it if that's the only way I can get it." He cupped her bottom and gave it a squeeze. "I know it's going to be mind-blowing with you and not just because you are an immortal. You are exquisite, Carol. The sexiest, most tempting female I have ever met."

Worrying her bottom lip, she took a moment to contemplate his offer. "I like it when you call me exquisite."

"Does it mean that you'll come?"

"Arwel is not going to like it, but I don't care."

He hadn't considered that it might get her in trouble. Sleeping with the enemy was going to be frowned upon at best. She wouldn't be the first though. After all, Kian's sister had set a precedent. Then again, what Amanda could get away with, Carol might not.

"Are you going to get hell for this? I don't want you to get in trouble."

Smiling, she cupped his cheek. "It's so sweet of you to worry about me. But I'm a big girl, and no one can tell me who I can or cannot have sex with. Not even Kian."

"How soon can you be here?"

"Give me fifteen minutes. I need to force myself to wake up."

"You're going to suffer a headache, but only for a few moments."

The last thing he wanted was for her to change her mind about coming because of that. Now that it was on the table, the prospect of losing it for any reason was intolerable.

He couldn't wait to experience no-holds-barred sex with an

immortal female. And not just any female, Carol. Even without exposure to the rest of the clan's fairer sex population, he had no doubt that she was incomparable.

"I've forced myself to wake up before, so I know what to expect. See you soon, lover boy." She waggled her brows before winking out of the dream.

The speed with which she departed indicated practice. Carol must have woken herself often. The question was, why?

She'd admitted that she'd been suffering from nightmares, and he had a feeling it was a frequent occurrence. What was the source, though?

Had something happened to her?

Despite her diminutive size, Carol projected strength and resilience. Whatever she'd gone through must have been traumatic.

The thought of anyone hurting her was enough to wake him up without him even trying, and the moment he opened his eyes, two glowing red circles appeared on the ceiling.

If whoever had harmed her hadn't been punished already, he would find a way to make it happen.

CAROL

*N*ervous butterflies buzzing in her stomach, Carol got out of bed and rushed into the closet. She hadn't brought a lot of clothes with her, so the selection was limited, but she'd packed some sexy lingerie.

Nothing over the top, just lace and satin in her favorite shades of pink. Well, the panties were a skimpy thong, with a little bow in the back, but from the front it wasn't too revealing. The bra, however, was lacy and completely see-through, showcasing her nipples as if she was wearing nothing.

Carol's signature look was all about blending the sweet and seemingly innocent with the sultry. Men found the combination irresistible, and she was sure Lokan would too.

The button-down silk blouse she shrugged on looked modest, but was great for stripping slowly, and since Arwel was going to let her in, she pulled on simple black leggings instead of the skirt she would've normally paired with that blouse.

A little eyeliner and mascara to accentuate her eyes, lip gloss, and she was ready to go.

But first, she had to shoot Arwel a text.

Sorry to bother you so late, but I'm coming down, and I need you to let me into Lokan's cell.

His return text came right away. *No problem. I'm awake.*

Good. She'd been afraid he would make some snide remarks. Except, he was probably saving them for later.

When she got to the dungeon level, Arwel was waiting for her next to Lokan's cell, leaning against the wall and smirking.

"I didn't think you'd forgive him so soon."

"He apologized."

"When?"

"He dream-shared with me."

That wiped the smile off Arwel's face really fast. "That's bad. If he can dream-share with immortals, no one is safe."

"That's why I'm here," she lied. "I need to find out who he can dream-share with. If it's only people he meets face to face first, then we need to limit who's allowed to visit him. But in any case, I don't think it's a big deal. If Ella could keep him from reading her thoughts, then it is not so difficult to do."

"I disagree. Ella had trained herself from a young age to block her mother. She knows how to protect her mind. When I was waiting outside the interview building in Washington, I couldn't feel her."

"That's interesting. Even so, if an eighteen-year-old human can do it, I'm sure adult immortals would have no problem."

"I hope you are right." The smirk was back. "Should I turn the volume down again?"

She shrugged. "Suit yourself."

"I think I'll do that. I'll also lower the resolution and dim the display."

"You can turn the thing off completely. I don't expect any trouble, but if anything happens, and I get scared, you'll feel it." Which brought another thought. "Are you going to feel my other emotions as well?"

He grimaced. "And his. But don't worry about it. It's my curse, and I've learned to live with it."

"You don't have to stay so close. Can you feel us from upstairs?"

"It's too far, and there are too many other people in between. But as I said, don't worry about it." His finger hovering over the keypad, he looked at her. "Does it bother you? Knowing that in a way, I'm sharing your experience?"

"A little. But not enough to dissuade me from going in there."

"I'm glad that you're not shy." He punched in the numbers.

"You are a good sport, Arwel. I was expecting some snide remarks or comments about how wrong this is."

He arched a brow. "Why? You're just doing your job."

Not really. But she didn't mind him thinking that.

The truth was that she was using her spying mission as an excuse to be with Lokan and not the other way around.

When the door swung open, she waved Arwel goodbye and sauntered in. Except, Lokan wasn't in the living room, waiting for her with a glass of wine as she'd been expecting.

The door to the bedroom was open, and the lights inside were off, but the dimmed light from the living room was enough for her to see the front of the room.

Could it be that he hadn't woken up yet?

"Are you still asleep?" Carol crossed the threshold, realizing immediately that he wasn't. Two glowing red eyes zeroed in on her like a couple of lasers from twin shooters.

Oh, boy. Her prince was aroused.

He chuckled. "Do you think I could sleep with all that anticipation raging inside of me?"

"I hope not."

"Come here." Lokan patted the bed.

With her pupils finally fully dilated, she saw that he was

bare-chested, but his lower half was covered by a blanket. Was he naked all the way below the covers?

Giving him an appreciative once-over, Carol followed the beautiful contours of his lean muscles, starting with his shoulders, moving down to his six-pack stomach, and following the trail of sparse dark hair to where her view was terminated by the duvet.

She assumed he was aroused, but it was impossible to tell because he had one knee up, effectively hiding anything that might have given him away.

As befitting the direct grandson of a god, the male was beautifully made, and she was sure that what was hidden under the blanket was just as scrumptious as what he allowed her to see.

When she just kept looking, he smirked. "Do you want me to come to you?"

"Stay where you are. I like looking at you."

"Same here. Can you admire me while stripping so I can enjoy the view as well?"

Could she ever…

He didn't know it, but he was dealing with a pro. If only there was a pole she could use, she would have given him a performance to remember.

Perhaps the bedpost would do?

It was a lovely four-poster, her favorite type. There were so many naughty things one could do with such a bed.

Sauntering over to the nearest bedpost, she smiled coyly. "Grab on to the headboard slats and don't let go no matter what."

He frowned, his eyes blazing red. "That's not how I like to play."

She had no doubt of that. Lokan was an immortal male, which made him naturally dominant, but he was also very close to the godly source, which made him doubly so. He was used to issuing commands, not following them.

"Humor me. I'll make it worth your while."

Reluctantly, he did as she asked, at the same time lowering his knee and letting her see what she'd suspected he'd been hiding under the blanket.

It was quite an impressive tent.

"What are you going to do?" The slur in his voice sent a trickle of desire straight to her straining nipples.

When she started on the buttons of her blouse, he smiled, revealing a pair of fangs that were long and sharp.

As a shiver rocked Carol's body, her fingers faltered over the small button.

Misinterpreting her reaction, he tried to cover those beauties with his lips. "Don't be afraid of my fangs. They are big, but I know how to use them to deliver pure pleasure."

Carol chuckled at the double entendre. "I'm not afraid of your fangs, I crave them." She was about to add that she'd missed an immortal male's bite and the unimaginable bliss the venom delivered, but then she would have to explain how she knew it.

It wasn't that she was ashamed of her relationship with Robert, it just wasn't the time or place to mention it.

LOKAN

*C*arol's admission that she craved his fangs ramped up Lokan's arousal to fever pitch.

He hadn't expected it. Throughout his long life, women had reacted with horrified expressions and shrieks of terror whenever he'd gotten carried away and forgotten to compel their silence or thrall them to ignore his fangs and glowing eyes.

By now, Lokan knew the words for demon and devil in nearly every human language. Modern women were a little better, some of them mistaking his fangs for prosthetics and the red glow in his eyes for specialty contact lenses.

In recent years, there had been fewer shrieks.

As Carol went back to slowly unbuttoning her blouse, he itched to let go of the headboard and go to her. He could rid her of her clothes so much faster. But she'd promised to make it worth his while, and he was curious.

Everything about the situation was a novelty to him. Starting with the extraordinary immortal female stripping for him, to the self-restraint she'd demanded from him, to his compliance. It wasn't in his nature to be on the receiving end.

He wasn't the type of male who enjoyed things being done to him. Typically, he was the one in charge.

But here he was, obeying commands from a tiny female, and enjoying it to his great surprise. If only she would do it faster, though. Not that it wasn't exciting, but he was having a really hard time holding on to that headboard.

"How many buttons does that damn blouse have?"

She paused. "Would you rather I hurried?"

It was a trap. If he admitted that he wanted her to go faster, she would get offended because he didn't appreciate her slow striptease. With an emphasis on the tease. But if he said no, it would imply that he wasn't eager to see her naked.

Women liked to play these games, perhaps even subconsciously, but Lokan was too old and experienced to stumble over such a minor obstacle.

"I'm conflicted. The slow reveal is incredibly alluring, but in my heightened arousal, I might tear this headboard apart."

"Patience, my prince." She turned around and hooked her thumbs in the elastic of her pants.

Lifting up for a better viewing angle, Lokan watched mesmerized as she bent down and slowly shimmied out of them, then lifted them in the air and twirled them a few times before tossing them across the room.

Regrettably, the damn blouse was long, covering that delectable bottom, and at the same time outlining it so perfectly that it looked like Carol wasn't wearing panties.

Glancing at him over her shoulder, she smiled and shrugged the blouse off, first revealing her creamy shoulders, then the enticing curve of her back, and finally letting it drop to the floor.

She was wearing panties after all, provided a string with a bow on top qualified as such. That bow was his undoing. He just had to tug on it and watch it unravel.

As Lokan sucked in a breath, a cracking sound preceded the slats breaking away from the headboard.

Looking at him over her shoulder, Carol pretended fright. "Oh, my. Don't break the furniture, my prince. And please grab the next slats over."

"I'm done with this game." He lowered his arms.

"Patience, darling. The best is still to come."

With a groan, he reached for the slats again. She was killing him. "Tug on that string for me."

Carol reached behind her and touched the little bow. "This one?"

"Is there another one?"

She held his gaze as she pulled on the bow and let the panties flutter down to the floor.

Dear gods. That ass was a work of art.

"Now, the bra."

Reaching for the clasp, she pinched it with two fingers, and as the back strap parted, she took pity on him and removed the garment with one pull, twirling it over her head and then tossing it down to the floor.

Looking at him over her shoulder, she fluttered her eyelashes. "Should I turn around?"

He was about to shout yes, when he remembered that the damn camera was pointed straight at her. "Hold on. I need to take care of this."

He bent down and picked up her bra, then stood on top of the bed and draped it over the camera, covering the lens as best he could with the semi-sheer lace. "Now you can turn."

As she did, they both sucked in a breath.

Her eyes riveted to his straining shaft, Carol mouthed, "Wow."

"Wow, indeed." He leaped off the bed and took her into his arms. "Exquisite."

"Wait." She pushed on his chest. "I wasn't done. I wanted to pole dance for you."

"Not this time, babydoll."

35

CAROL

*I*t had been ages since anyone had called Carol babydoll. She'd always liked the endearment, but coming from Lokan's lips in that smooth, deep voice of his, it was the best one yet.

She pouted as he laid her down on the bed and loomed over her. "I wanted to dance for you and then kiss your body all over, tormenting you with the sweetest of pleasures."

His smirk was evil as he looked at her with hungry eyes. "Tonight, I'll be the one doing the pleasuring." Dipping his head, he flicked his tongue over her nipple, and then over the other. "I've never seen a female as beautifully built as you." He ran his hand over the side of her breast and down the dip of her waist. "I thought that such a perfect hourglass figure existed only in paintings."

She ran her fingers through his short hair. "You say all the right things."

"I mean them. Those are not just lines I drop every day."

"How about once in a century?"

"Not even." His hand closed over her nape, and he took her lips, his tongue slipping into her mouth without preamble.

He wasn't hesitant, and he wasn't gentle. He was taking what he wanted, thrusting his tongue into her mouth as if he was conquering it, claiming it as his.

Just the way she liked it.

It wasn't that he was brutal, not at all. Just confident, and rightly so. This was a very experienced male who knew precisely what to do with a woman.

Finally.

After thousands of lovers, she'd found the right one for her. What a pity that Lokan was a prisoner. Him being the enemy didn't even factor into it. She could have him cross over the same way Dalhu and Robert had.

But first, she had to convince him that she was the one for him. When he accepted her as his true-love mate, there would be no going back for him.

As he lifted his head, his dark eyes were glowing with that peculiar red inner light, but as he trailed his gaze over her body, they no longer looked demonic to her, just appreciative.

Her prince loved what he saw.

His muscles were tensed, but his fingers feathered over her in a barely there touch, gentle, exploring. He started with the undersides of her breasts, brushed over her belly, and then hovered over her center.

In a blatant invitation, she let her legs fall apart.

"So soft," he said, trailing those fingers along the inner curve of her thigh. "I can feel the heat of your desire calling to me. And your scent, it is maddening, so different. If I didn't know you were an immortal female before, this scent would have given you away."

Her original plan of starting a revolution on the island had been terminated because of Navuh's compulsory hold over his people, and now Lokan's comment had pounded the last nail into its coffin. She would've been discovered despite the heavy perfume she'd used. Lokan could smell her natural scent despite it.

Then again, Lokan's sense of smell was probably more acute than Robert's because he was a more direct descendant of the gods. She could have probably fooled the noses of the rank and file warriors. But that was neither here nor there. That plan was dead.

He lifted his eyes to look at her face. "Did my comment bother you? I can feel you drifting away from me."

"Not at all." She reached for his neck and tugged his head down. "Kiss me again like you did before."

As he did as she'd asked, his fingers dipped between her wet folds, teasing, caressing, and when he worked one inside her, she moaned into his mouth. Intensifying the kiss, he retracted the finger and came back with two.

Fates, this was good. But she wanted more. Needed it.

Lifting her bottom off the mattress, she took his long fingers deeper inside her. Lokan could make her climax like this, but for her first orgasm with her prince, Carol wanted him inside her, joining them. Nothing less was going to satisfy her.

He must have read her mind.

His mouth never leaving hers, he mounted her and then aligned his erection with her entrance.

"Yes," she murmured against his lips.

As he entered her, the groan that escaped his throat was the only indication of the restraint he'd exercised. But he didn't just ram into her, although she would have been fine with that. Holding himself still, he waited for her to adjust to him.

Compared to her, Lokan was a big guy, but the penetration wasn't painful. All she felt was an incredible fullness in the part he'd already claimed, and just as incredible emptiness in the part he still hadn't.

Letting go of her mouth, he lifted his head and gazed into her eyes as he drove the rest of the way in, burying himself to the hilt.

"Yes." She clutched his shoulders.

His expression, usually so guarded, was a mix of wonder and possessiveness. If she could read his mind, Carol was sure she would hear him say, "Mine."

Instead of uttering the word, though, he said it with his body. His chest pressing into hers, his hips retreated and surged forward in an incremental increase of tempo and power.

It was as if he was testing how much she could take, and upon discovering that she had no limits, he finally let go, ramming into her again and again and driving her up and up to the edge of the cliff.

His tongue flicking over her neck was what drove her over, and as the climax washed over her like a tsunami, he hissed and sank his fangs in the spot he'd marked. Another thunderous wave rocked her body, and then another as Lokan's hot seed jetted into her.

But even before the venom hit her system, Carol nearly passed out from the intensity of it, and a dim thought flitted through her head that she might not survive this.

Was it possible to expire from too much pleasure?

The thought evaporated as soon as the euphoria spread throughout her body, and the convulsions finally eased up, relaxing her muscles and leaving her boneless.

"Lokan," she whispered before drifting off on a cloud.

36

LOKAN

*A*fter licking the twin incision points closed, Lokan collapsed over Carol and buried his face in the crook of her neck, where he could keep breathing in her scent.

Nearly one thousand years of existence hadn't prepared him for this night, and for this extraordinary experience with this exquisite woman.

Lokan could now understand why and how Dalhu could overcome his father's compulsion and forsake his only home to be with Amanda.

Except, he doubted that even Kian's sister, the daughter of a goddess, could compare to Carol. There was no one like her on the face of this planet.

Perhaps he was exaggerating, and maybe for another male a different female would be such a unique treasure, but for him, there was just one.

Even though he barely knew her, wasn't in love with her, Carol was his one and only. He was as certain of it as he was certain of the sun rising the next day.

What she'd told him about true-love mates was not a fantasy. It was as real as the unmistakable connection he felt with her. This hadn't been just sex, or even lovemaking; this had been a joining. Not only of bodies, but of souls.

Was that the real reason his father didn't allow dormant females to transition? Because immortal unions were so powerful that they provided mates with immunity against his compulsion?

And was it the reason he kept his harem in complete isolation? Did Navuh have a true-love mate in there?

If he had, she was his Achilles heel, and that was why he kept her hidden. What about the other females in his harem, though?

How could he have sex with anyone other than his true-love mate?

Lifting his head, Lokan gazed at Carol and was filled with immense satisfaction for putting that blissed-out expression on her gorgeous face.

Planting a soft kiss on her parted lips, he knew with absolute conviction that he would never desire another female again. Which meant that Carol had to become his.

Exclusively, officially, and irrevocably.

The question was how it was done. Did the clan have marriage ceremonies? Did the goddess bless the unions? What made them official and indisputable?

How was he going to keep his treasure from slipping away?

This was insanity. Or chemicals.

How the hell was he feeling such an overwhelming sense of rightness and possessiveness toward a female he wasn't even in love with?

But then what did he know about love?

Absolutely nothing.

He hadn't loved a mother because he'd been deprived of her. He didn't love his father because Navuh had never acted as one. And he didn't love his half-brothers because they were his rivals, and none of them would hesitate to get rid of him if given half a chance.

The closest Lokan had come to loving anyone had been the Dormant into whose care he had been given after his father had taken him away from his mother. But that woman had been dead for a very long time, and he could barely remember what she'd looked or sounded like.

Was that the reason he was so overwhelmed right now?

His deadened emotions had gotten resurrected, probably by some weird chemicals released during the joining with an immortal female. Apparently, immortals and humans were different in more ways than he'd known or suspected.

When Carol tried to shift under him, Lokan realized that he was still squashing her with his weight. Holding on to her because he wasn't willing to separate from her yet, he turned them both sideways and tucked her head under his chin.

"This is nice," she murmured. "I like you holding me like that."

"Good. Because I'm never letting go."

She chuckled softly. "We can't stay like this forever."

"Says who?"

"I need to use the bathroom."

"No, you don't. You're staying right here."

Burying her nose in the crease between his pectorals, she sighed. "You smell amazing, and I don't want to go anywhere either."

Caressing her hair, he kissed the top of her head. "Is this what it's like for all immortal couples?"

"Just the very lucky ones. Not everyone gets their true-love mate."

"Is that what it is? Because I've never felt anything like this. I can't let you go. Ever."

Lifting her head, she looked into his eyes. "I'm not letting you go either." She chuckled. "Lucky for me, you have nowhere to run."

"I wouldn't even if I could. The other true-love mates couples, did it happen so fast for them?"

She smirked. "Oh, so now you believe me."

"I do, but I might have lost my mind because this cannot be happening. We barely know each other, and we are not in love because we can't be after less than twenty-four hours."

"I have to admit that this is unusual. As far as I know, it didn't happen so fast for any of the other couples. Ella and Julian struggled for a long time, but that was because of you and your compulsion. She might have realized that he was the one for her weeks earlier. He knew it right away, by the way. In fact, he fell in love with her picture before ever meeting her."

"That ruins my theory about this being a chemical reaction."

"It's the Fates, Lokan. I told you that."

"Sorry, but I don't buy it. There must be a rational explanation, like rare genetic compatibility, or pheromones. I'm not a scientist, so I don't know what else it could be. But it must be something other than some imaginary beings pulling the strings."

"I don't care what it is." Cupping his cheek, Carol gazed into his eyes with so much adoration that his heart felt like it was going to explode. No one had ever looked at him like that. "I'm just grateful beyond words for being granted this boon, and I'm offering my thanks to the Fates. You can thank genes or Lady Luck if you want."

"You're calling being paired with an imprisoned enemy luck? I think your Fates could have done better for you."

"Are you kidding me? I got myself a bona fide prince. I'm lucky beyond measure."

37

CAROL

*A*s Carol opened her eyes, it took her a split second to realize that the pair of glowing red embers hovering over her face belonged to Lokan. He was close, and the light he was emitting was so intense that her pupils must have contracted protectively, and that was why everything else looked dark in comparison.

"Good morning, babydoll."

"How do you know it's morning?" The only indication she was getting that it was time to get up was coming from her bladder.

He lifted her hand. "Your watch."

"Oh." She'd forgotten to take it off. Not that it mattered. Keeping Lokan in the dark, so to speak, didn't apply to the time of day. "I should get up and make you breakfast."

"Don't." He put a warm hand on her shoulder. "Stay in bed with me."

"I can't." She lifted her wrist and glanced at the time. "I need to go."

"Where?"

Flinging the comforter off, she swung her legs over the

other side of the bed. "First, to visit the bathroom, then to make breakfast and lunch for you and Arwel because I need to be somewhere this afternoon."

"Can't you cancel?"

Rounding the bed, she leaned over him and kissed his lips. "I can't. We'll talk after I'm done in the bathroom."

As she padded toward the door, Carol was acutely aware of Lokan's eyes on her bare bottom, and she gave it a little swing.

"Gorgeous," she heard him murmur.

In the bathroom, Carol counted back from ten as she quickly used the toilet, washed her hands, and brushed her teeth with the new toothbrush she found in the vanity drawer. The door opened as she counted down to zero and then to minus one. Lokan sauntered in, a pair of silk pajama pants hanging low on his hips.

Scrumptious male.

Tall, lean, every muscle perfectly defined as if it was sculptured by a loving hand. And that smattering of dark hair marking a trail from his navel to the top of his pants…

Yum.

Her appraisal hadn't gone unnoticed, and as his shaft rose to attention, tenting his pants, Carol's core tightened and tingled in response.

They hadn't even scratched the surface of what they could share in bed, but regrettably, she was pressed for time.

Cupping himself over his pants, Lokan smirked. "You keep staring at me like that, I'm going to take you straight back to bed."

Still staring, she licked her lips. "I wish I could, but I need to shower and get ready."

He pulled on the string holding his pants up and let them drop down his muscular thighs. "We can shower together. I promise to be quick."

That was an offer she couldn't refuse.

"How quick?"

"Let me show you."

In a blink of an eye, she was in his arms, pressed against that incredible hard body of his while he carried her into the shower.

As he'd promised, twenty minutes later, Lokan carried her out into the bedroom, wrapped in a towel, squeaky clean and thoroughly satisfied.

"Room service in this hotel is unbelievable," she said as he put her down on the bed. "I feel obligated to leave a generous gratuity. I'll do it later, though. After dinner."

"I'll await it with bated breath." He padded back to the bathroom and returned a moment later wearing his sexy, black silk pajama pants. "Where are you going to be at lunch?"

There was a note of jealousy in his voice that she didn't like. Not because she found it objectionable, but because she wanted him to have good thoughts about her while she was gone, the kind that brought him pleasure and not irritation.

Carol lifted her panties and pants off the floor. "The clan is having a big barbecue to celebrate Vivian and Ella's safe return. And since Ella is my friend, I need to be there."

He grimaced. "I'm sure my capture is a big part of the celebration."

She glanced up at the camera which Lokan had draped her bra over last night. "Can you get it for me?"

"Stand over there." He pointed to a dead spot in the camera's view angle.

When she obliged, he leaped on the bed, bouncing up and snatching her bra on the fly.

"Impressive." Carol clapped her hands. "Do you play basketball?"

He tossed her the bra. "When I'm on the island. The

warriors play soccer and basketball in their free time."

"Your father allows it?" She closed the clasp and reached for the blouse. "I thought that he sucked all the fun out of his people's lives."

"Not all of it. Just most. After the training is done for the day, the men can do as they please. They can't hang out in the resort, because they might intimidate the guests, and other than that there isn't much to do. They can visit the brothel, but they have to pay for the services, and it's not cheap, or play sports games, or take a swim in the ocean."

"Doesn't sound too bad." Carol finished buttoning her blouse.

"The simple soldiers see nothing wrong with any of it. They count themselves lucky for having such a great leader who provides them with everything they need. Between the compulsion and having to recite it in a devotion five times a day on their knees, they can't help but believe it."

She arched a brow. "Were you required to do it too?"

"Of course."

"What does it say?"

"Do you really want to hear it?"

"I'm curious."

"Do you speak the old language?"

She shook her head. "I understand a little of it. But I can't say even the most basic things. It's so different than all the languages I know that I think it's based on entirely different principles."

"It is. None of the modern languages have their roots in it." He rubbed his hand over the back of his neck. "The translation is not going to sound as impactful, but here it goes. Glory to Lord Navuh, the wise and the just, with his bounty we thrive, by his will we live or die, we are all brothers in the Devout Order of Mortdh, in his name we wage this holy war."

"Short but to the point. It sums everything up."

"Now imagine nearly twenty thousand warriors saying it in unison five times a day."

"Only twenty? I thought there were more."

"That's what my father wants everyone to believe. He never says the exact number, and most people don't bother to count."

Carol shrugged, acting as if the information he'd let slip was inconsequential. "Twenty thousand is plenty. No wonder Navuh has a god complex."

"Does your goddess demand anything like that?"

Carol laughed. "No way. Annani is a diva, and she likes being the center of attention, but she doesn't require anyone to recite devotions or pray to her."

"How do you address her, then? By her given name?"

He seemed almost disgusted by the lack of respect it implied.

"We address her as Clan Mother and try to be very polite, but we do it out of respect, not out of fear."

"Did the goddess choose Clan Mother as her title?"

"I think so. Why?"

"No reason. I was just curious."

She had a feeling there was more to it than that, but this was a talk for another time.

"I'm going to make something quick and simple for breakfast and lunch." She glanced at her watch. "I'll be back in about half an hour. Do you know how to operate the coffee machine?"

"I'm sure I can figure it out."

Pampered prince.

It seemed that Lokan had never made coffee before. Great. "Let me show you how it is done, so next time you can do it yourself."

38

LOKAN

*W*hile Carol was gone, Lokan got dressed, made a pot of coffee and drank a cup, then another, and then emptied the carafe and brewed a fresh one.

It really wasn't complicated, and it came out tasting decent enough. He was learning. From now on, he could make it every morning and bring a cup to Carol in bed.

One less excuse for her to get out of it. If he had his way, they would be making love every night and every morning and sometimes after lunch too.

Good times.

He chuckled. It was ridiculous to refer to his capture and imprisonment as good anything, and yet, he couldn't help the buoyant feeling that was all about Carol.

The difference the right woman could make.

She was the difference between a life of meh and a life of joy, between apathy and energy, between despair and hope.

She was everything, and the prospect of losing her was more terrifying than facing a battalion of Guardians in a life and death fight.

Damn. If his father was hiding his true-love mate in the

harem, Lokan could now understand why he was guarding the place with such zeal. It wasn't about jealousy or control; it was about fear of anything happening to her.

Navuh had always been paranoid, searching for shadows of conspiracy and dissent even though neither was likely because of his compulsory hold over his people.

Lokan hoped he would never get as crazed.

Except, Navuh having a true-love mate didn't make sense. His many sons couldn't have been born to one mother, which meant that Navuh had several immortal females in his harem and was dividing his attentions between them. That wouldn't have been possible if he'd bonded with his one and only like Lokan had with Carol.

Exclusivity wasn't a matter of choice. Lokan just knew that no other female would ever appeal to him.

Dear Mortdh, he was losing his mind.

What was taking Carol so long?

He didn't have a watch to check the time, but it seemed like much longer than half an hour. He wondered whether preparing the meals for the day was taking her longer than she'd estimated, or if his perception of time had been altered by her absence.

It was strange how a woman he hadn't known even existed twenty-four hours ago had become so vital to him so quickly.

Were the imprisonment and loneliness getting to him?

That combined with the incredible first-time sex with an immortal female must have been the reason he'd let himself get swept away on the wings of fancy.

The Fates were a myth, and there was no such thing as true-love mates.

So why was he rubbing his chest to alleviate the ache that had settled there as soon as Carol had left him?

Lokan had thought himself a loner before, but the truth was

that he'd always been surrounded by people. Not friends or family, but he'd shared the Washington accommodation with his small contingent of soldiers, and he'd met with politicians and lobbyists and other influential humans at least twice a day. During his visits to the island, he'd been even busier.

Never before had he been so completely isolated and with nothing to do.

That was the most logical explanation.

Soft-hearted women could entertain such mystical beliefs as Fates and true-love mates, but hardened warriors who'd lived for as long as he had should know better.

Except, this hardened warrior's heart leaped like a teenage boy's when the door's mechanism engaged, and the gloom that had shrouded him during Carol's absence dissipated as if waved away with a magic wand.

"Bye, Arwel. I can take it from here," he heard Carol say, and a moment later she walked in holding two large plastic containers in her arms, and a plastic shopping bag hanging from the crook of her elbow.

He rushed to take them from her, stopping to plant a quick kiss on her lips before carrying them to the dining table.

"I missed you," he admitted almost despite himself. "What took you so long?"

She cast him a bemused glance. "Ten minutes longer is not that long."

"It felt like an eternity." He took her hand and pulled her into his arms. "I need to kiss you."

Wrapping her arms around his neck, she stretched up on her toes and pulled him down at the same time. "Then kiss me, big boy. I missed you too."

Kissing alone wasn't going to cut it, though. His hands roaming over her back soon found their way to her bottom, lifting her up and pressing her against his erection.

Breathless, she pushed on his chest. "Save it for later, lover boy. I want to eat breakfast with you before I have to run."

"Can't you skip it? If the entire clan is going to be there, maybe Ella is not going to miss you."

She cupped his cheek. "You can survive a couple of hours without me."

"Is it far? How long is it going to take you to come back?"

Hearing himself sounding needy and whiny irritated the hell out of Lokan. Where the hell were his damned balls?

In Carol's pocket. That's where.

"It's not far, and no, I'm not going to tell you where it is." Turning away from him, Carol opened the top plastic container. "I didn't have time to make anything elaborate. Do you know what a shakshuka is?"

"It's a Mediterranean dish. I've had it before."

"Not like I make it." She took two paper plates out of her shopping bag and loaded them with poached eggs in tomato and pepper sauce. "What I love about it is that it's an entire meal made in one skillet. The fewer dishes I have to wash, the better." She pointed at the fridge. "Can you get me a soda? And get one for yourself too. This is spicy."

Why did he like it so much when she bossed him around?

Was it the novelty of it?

Or maybe because it implied a familiarity that had been missing from his life?

As he handed her the soda can and joined her at the table, Carol popped the lid and took a long sip. "I see that you made coffee while I was gone."

"It wasn't hard." He lifted the fork and scooped an egg with some sauce on it. "If there was a kitchen here, you could have taught me how to make the shakshuka. It seems simple enough to make."

She arched a brow. "Have you ever cooked anything in your life?"

"No, but I can learn. I would love to serve you a meal once in a while." More like every day.

He really needed to pull his balls out of Carol's pocket. What was happening to him?

"That's so sweet of you, and so uncharacteristic, not only for a Doomer, but for any male from your part of the world." She chuckled. "What am I talking about? That's uncharacteristic of most males period. Guys like to get served, not to do the serving."

"I wouldn't know. It's not like I grew up in a normal family unit or have been exposed to one."

"Where did you grow up?"

"In the Dormants' enclosure. I was taken away from my birth mother when I was still a baby and given into the care of a Dormant. All of Navuh's sons are raised like this."

"Why? That's so cruel, for the mothers as well as for the children."

"Harem politics. That's the answer he gave me. None of us knows who his mother is. I can be the son of the chief wife, or that of the lowliest concubine, but it doesn't determine my position in the Brotherhood. Navuh decides who does what based on merit, or whatever he feels like toward that son at a particular point in time. Some of his sons never make it to the top, and they are either low-level commanders or even rank and file. It also eliminates some of the rivalry between the sons. Killing one another is not going to advance anyone's agenda."

She nodded. "In an odd way, it makes sense. It also explains why he shows no love to either one of you. He might think that he's protecting you from one another."

Lokan finished chewing and forked another egg. "You're giving him too much credit. I think he is a self-centered megalomaniac who doesn't care about anyone but himself and his world-domination agenda."

"You're probably right. You know him personally, while I only have hearsay and speculation to base my opinion on."

"It's impossible to know him because he doesn't let anyone get close to him. Perhaps the females in his harem know more, but he keeps them completely isolated, so they won't reveal his secrets. That's why I wanted to get Vivian and Ella. If I could have snuck one of them in, she could have communicated what she'd learned to the other, and the mystery would have been finally solved."

"Doesn't he isolate them because he doesn't want his sons to know who their mothers are?"

"That's the official explanation. But I don't buy it. Not entirely."

"Do you know if your mother is still alive? Did he tell you at least that much?"

Lokan shook his head. "I'm not allowed to ask. The few times I did, I was punished. I learned to keep my mouth shut and search for answers on my own. Regrettably, he is incredibly smart and designed an impenetrable system."

"You told me that you could've snuck Ella or Vivian into the harem."

"Getting a human female in is doable. Risky, but with my compulsion ability possible. The problem is getting information out. Once they are assigned work in the harem, they don't get out, not with their memories intact. Vivian and Ella's telepathic communication was the only way."

In reality, the only way out of the harem was in a coffin, but he wasn't ready to admit that to Carol. He'd had a vague plan of having the one he'd snuck into the harem fake her own death so he could get her out that way, but he hadn't worked out the details, and the truth was that he would have done it even if he had to leave her there.

Lokan had never claimed to be a good man, and it hadn't bothered him before. But it did now. He wanted to be a better male for Carol.

She shook her head, her large blonde curls bouncing around her perfect face. "No wonder you worked so hard on luring them into a trap. It really wasn't about Ella's beauty."

CAROL

"*C*arol." Kian waved her over. "I need to talk to you."

She was on her way to the car, eager to get back to Lokan, but when the boss called, telling him she was in a rush wasn't an option.

"Can you wait a moment? I want to put this bag in my car."

After the barbecue was over, she'd gone to her house and collected a few more items of clothing and accessories. She'd even put in a board game and a pack of cards to play with Lokan.

The way things were going, it looked like she was in it for the long haul. The three hours away from him had been hard to endure. She felt as if there was an invisible tether connecting them. It was elastic, capable of getting stretched, but only to a certain point. After a while, the pull to get back had gotten too strong to resist.

"If you're heading to the keep, we are going there as well." Kian waved her over again. "You can hitch a ride with us, and we can talk on the way."

As usual, Kian had Anandur and Brundar with him, but

bringing Andrew along indicated that he was on his way to interrogate Lokan.

It was an inconvenience to leave her car in the village, which would necessitate hitching a ride when she had to get back, but she needed to talk to Kian before he went to see Lokan, and unless she did it over the phone, the only way to do it in time was sharing the ride with him.

Regrettably, it was going to be with an audience.

Not a big deal. It wasn't as if she'd intended to keep her relationship with Lokan a secret. In fact, she was quite sure that most of the village population already knew what she was doing.

What they didn't know, however, was that she and Lokan had been fated for each other. She was supposed to get him to talk by any means available to her, not to fall for him.

"I'm coming."

Anandur was already closing the distance between them and reaching for her bag. "Let me carry this for you."

"Thank you."

Kian's Lexus was spacious, and with Anandur driving and Brundar sitting next to him, and Andrew taking the back seat, she and Kian got in the middle row.

"Should I put my ear buds in?" Andrew asked.

Kian looked at Carol.

She shrugged. "What's the point? Whatever Anandur hears is not going to stay a secret for long. You'd better hear it straight from the source."

Looking at her through the rearview mirror, Anandur made a face. "I don't talk when I'm not supposed to. All you have to do is tell me that you don't want anything said in here to get out."

"It's okay. I meant no offense, and I have nothing to hide.

But this is so new, and I'd rather it stayed between us for the time being."

As Anandur pulled out of the parking spot, Kian turned to her. "I'm taking Lokan on a tour of the catacombs. Anything I should know before I talk to him?"

"There is plenty. First of all, you should know that he and I are mates." When Kian's eyes widened, she lifted a hand and kept talking. "I might be a little biased in his favor, so I'm just putting it out there to make you aware of that. But you should also know that my loyalty is first and foremost to the clan, and I'll never do anything to betray or endanger it, not even for my fated mate."

With a groan, Kian raked his fingers through his hair. "How did that happen? And are you sure?"

Carol nodded. "I know it happened incredibly fast, but I know it's real." She chuckled. "I'm old and experienced enough to know that what I feel for Lokan is unlike anything I have felt before. And since I've had an immortal lover already, I also know that it's not because the sex is out of this world."

"Can it be that he's just incredibly charming and you're infatuated with him?"

"He is. But that's not it. The three hours I spent away from Lokan right now made me feel as if I was fighting a tether that was pulling me back to him. I've never experienced this with anyone else and in no other situation."

In the front, she could see both Anandur and Brundar nodding their heads.

She waved a hand in their direction. "You see? They know what I'm talking about. And I'm sure you do too." She then glanced back at Andrew. "Do you agree? You're mated too."

"That's how it felt in the beginning," Andrew said. "It got easier later on. Otherwise, none of us could get any work done."

That was good to know because she'd started to worry. Being joined at the hip with Lokan could get tiring fast. She was too independent to enjoy such an attachment even if it was otherwise wonderful.

Looking resigned, Kian nodded. "Now that we have that established, what else can you tell me about him?"

"Did he tell you about what he needed Vivian and Ella for?"

"He wanted to find out what, or rather who, Navuh is hiding in his harem."

"Did he tell you why it was so important for him to find out?"

"He thinks that Navuh has someone special in there, and that this someone has influence over him. Since the only way to change the Brotherhood seems to be changing Navuh, Lokan thinks that this female might be the only one who can do that."

She smiled. Of course, that was how Lokan had presented it to Kian. To admit that he wished to find out who his mother was and whether she was still alive would have made him look weak.

Not macho enough.

"In my opinion, it's an excuse to cover his real reason, and he might be even telling himself the same lie. Lokan wants to find out who his mother is or was. She might have been a Dormant who died a long time ago, but she could also be an immortal. He didn't tell you that because that would have made him look less manly, and we all know how important that macho nonsense is to you guys."

"That's a powerful motivator." Kian nodded. "The question is, what am I going to do with this information?"

"There is more. Lokan has some pretty progressive ideas for the island, but even before his capture, he felt powerless to implement any of them. Apparently, he is the only one of his brothers who is immune to Navuh's compulsion, and he can't get them to back him up."

"Yeah, I got that from him. Tell me about his ideas."

40

KIAN

"What are you going to do about it?" Anandur asked as the four of them parted ways with Carol at the elevators.

Kian was glad she hadn't insisted on coming with them to Lokan and had gone upstairs to prepare dinner instead. Having her there would have made things awkward for everyone, even without the revelations she'd shared with them during the drive.

"About what?" Kian asked.

There was a lot to choose from. Starting with Carol's megaton bomb about Lokan being her mate, to the real reason behind his ambitious plan to infiltrate Navuh's harem, and to Lokan's surprisingly progressive ideas for the island's population.

Naturally, he was going to verify those claims with Andrew's help. Lokan might have been selling Carol a load of crap to get her on his side.

"About Carol's claim that she and the Doomer are mates."

"I'm not sure they are. Lokan is charming and manipulative, and Carol has been lonely since breaking things off with

Robert. She can't possibly know that Lokan is her one after spending one day with him."

After having an immortal lover, even one she hadn't been in love with, going back to humans must have been underwhelming, to put it mildly. It would be like drinking watered-down whiskey after sampling the best of Macallan scotch.

Stepping into the elevator, Anandur scratched his beard. "If it were anyone else, I would have agreed with you. But not Carol. Having an immortal lover is not a novelty for her, and I've never heard her mention any human male she developed feelings for. I don't think she would mistake infatuation or great sex for a true-love fated bond."

Kian arched a brow. "If memory serves me right, she didn't mention the word love. She only said that they were mates."

Anandur shrugged. "Sex often precedes love. The incredible attraction is the first sign."

"Which can be easily mistaken for more," Andrew said. "Before I met Nathalie, I thought that Amanda was the hottest female to walk the planet." He glanced at Kian. "I hope you don't mind me saying that."

"Not at all. At the time, I would have been overjoyed if she'd chosen you instead of Dalhu. But that would have been a mistake. Amanda and Dalhu proved that they were true-love mates beyond a shadow of a doubt."

Andrew nodded. "Until I met Nathalie, I didn't know how much stronger the connection between true-love mates was, and I might have settled for less."

"Time will tell," Brundar said, summing up the discussion.

It was good advice, especially since they'd reached the dungeon level and were heading toward Lokan's cell.

Arwel was waiting for them by the door. "Do you need me with you, or can I take a break?" He handed Kian the remote to Lokan's cuffs.

"I think that between the four of us we can handle one Doomer. Did you change the setting on all of them?"

"Yes. They will explode only if you take Lokan out of the building. He is safe as long as he is inside."

"You sure? Taking him to the catacombs is supposed to demonstrate how benevolent we are. Blowing up his wrists and ankles would be counterproductive to that."

Arwel shrugged. "I did everything that William told me to do and then had him double check it. If the cuffs explode, you know who to blame, and it's not me."

"Noted. Is there anything you want to report before we go in? Any unusual behavior that you've noticed?"

Arwel smirked. "Carol has him wrapped around her little finger. After she left this morning, he kept pacing the cell like a caged animal, looking distraught. He hasn't done that before. I think our Doomer prince is in love."

"Or he's an exceptional actor," Kian murmured.

He was not buying the insta-matehood. It hadn't happened this fast for any of the other couples. Not even Syssi and him.

Except, a small voice in the back of his head called him a liar, reminding him of his first reaction to Syssi. Kian remembered it as vividly as if it had happened yesterday. If not for his self-doubt and skepticism, he might have realized immediately that she was the one for him.

In fact, he'd known that from the very first moment their hands had touched and their eyes had met. After that, he'd spent several days trying to deny it, and then several more days trying to justify the instinctive response with logical explanations.

Maybe if he hadn't been so stubborn and cynical, he would have declared them true-love mates from day one, just as Carol had done.

Now that Kian was more familiar with what Amanda and

Syssi referred to as the Fates' matchmaking process, he couldn't even get angry at Carol or Lokan for their unexpected mating.

It hadn't been their choice.

He was sad for Carol, however, and disappointed at the Fates for saddling her with Lokan as a mate. The woman had definitely suffered enough to merit a better pairing. She deserved a prince, but not the son of their arch-nemesis, who was a prisoner with no future prospects.

Lokan's case was different than Dalhu and Robert's. He wasn't an ordinary Doomer, or even an ordinary immortal. Despite him mating Carol, the man was too dangerous to ever entrust with the clan's location.

Unlike the other two ex-Doomers, Kian could see Lokan overriding the natural devotion to his fated mate in favor of his wider agenda.

That agenda, however, was still an enigma.

Was he his father's puppet like Navuh's other sons?

Or was he indeed the progressive thinker who wanted a better future for his people?

There was also a third option. What if Lokan had sought to overthrow his father and seize control of the island to become the next despot?

Did it matter?

Lokan wasn't going to leave his cell, so none of his possible agendas were relevant. At some point, he might opt to go into stasis instead of enduring endless imprisonment, and if by that time he'd revealed all that there was to reveal, Kian might grant him his wish.

The only problem with that was Carol.

If Lokan was indeed her fated mate, she would want to follow him and enter stasis as well.

41

LOKAN

*K*ian was on the other side of the thick door. Lokan couldn't hear him, but somehow, he sensed him.

It wasn't the prickling sensation in the back of his neck like he'd felt the first time Kian and his bodyguards had entered his cell. That had gradually subsided the longer they'd stayed with him until dissipating entirely by the time they'd left.

Still, he was willing to bet good money that Kian was about to enter. Not Arwel, and regrettably not Carol, but his cousin and probably his bodyguards. For some reason, Lokan couldn't feel the others, only Kian.

It was probably his imagination.

Arwel had called him earlier, telling him to get ready for Kian's visit, and his inner clock must have calculated the time elapsed, signaling his subconscious that his guest should have arrived.

This was a much preferable explanation to some nonsense spiritual mumbo jumbo.

Still, when the door mechanism engaged and the taller of

the bodyguards entered, followed by the somber blond, Lokan had to wonder.

"Good afternoon, gentlemen." He dipped his head. "Did you enjoy your celebratory barbecue?"

"Very much so," Kian answered as he entered together with the lie detector.

Did he go everywhere with the guy?

Made sense. If Lokan had someone like that, he would have taken him to every meeting. Except, that would have been superfluous since he'd solved the problem of reliability by assuming everyone was lying all the time.

Life was much less disappointing when that was the standard expectation.

"Ready for your tour of the catacombs?" Kian asked.

Lokan glanced at his cuffs. "Aren't you going to remove them? I was told an alarm will sound the moment I cross the threshold."

The redhead snorted as if it was a joke.

Treating Lokan with more respect than the bodyguard had, Kian explained, "We can change the setting on the cuffs any way we please. You can leave the cell, and nothing will happen. But if you try to leave the building, that's another story. Not that you'll ever get that far."

The redhead batted his eyelashes. "You can run, but you can never leave because I'll catch you."

Choosing to ignore the remark, Lokan followed Kian outside. "It's a pleasure to leave that cell even for a walk down to the catacombs. I assume they are here since we are not leaving the building."

"That's right."

An elevator took them several levels down, and as they exited into a dark lobby, the motion sensors activated soft lighting.

Four archways led out from the lobby, but since the lights had been activated only in the entry chamber, Lokan couldn't see what was beyond them.

Kian walked toward the opening that was straight across from the elevators. "We seldom visit here, so there is no sense in keeping the lights on."

A glass door sealed the entryway, but the moment Kian got closer it parted open with a hiss and the lights in the tunnel came on. "Someone really wanted to preserve the atmosphere here." Lokan chuckled. "Not only are the lights shaped like wall torches, but they also flicker."

The door closed behind them.

"Maybe it's faulty circuitry," the lie detector said.

Lokan shook his head. "From what I've seen so far, everything in this place is built to the highest and most exacting standards. If the lights flicker, they are supposed to."

"Thank you," Kian said. "And yes, it was designed this way. We have a very talented interior designer."

After a short walk, they reached the first enclaves and the first corpses, or what looked like ones.

Although emaciated, the bodies didn't smell dead. There was no decay, and when he got closer, Lokan could hear the very faint heartbeat Kian told him to listen for.

The walls of the corridor were lined with enclaves three tall on each side in some places, and two in others.

There were so many of them.

Lokan stopped next to nearly every one and listened for the elusive heartbeat, and each time it was there, just as Kian had told him it would be.

When they reached a fork, Lokan stopped. "I don't need to see any more. I believe you."

"Do you wish to pay respects to your dead? They are in a different section of the catacombs. We keep this one optimally regulated for the preservation of the bodies in stasis. Just don't ask me what that optimum is because I have no clue. Our doctor reassures me that this is it."

Lokan dipped his head. "You've shown our warriors unexpected mercy. I want to express my deepest gratitude for your kindness." He bowed his head even lower.

Not even his father had ever gotten that from him voluntarily.

"Truth," the lie detector said.

"Don't thank me. Thank my mother. I'm not kind to my enemies."

Lokan ignored the vehemence in his cousin's voice. "Then please convey my gratitude to the goddess."

"You can thank her in person. She is coming to see you."

Lokan's gut clenched and then surged with excitement. "When?"

"Sometime tomorrow." Kian seemed amused by Lokan's shock. "No need to panic. As long as you are as polite and as well-spoken as you've been so far, you'll do fine with Annani."

"I'll do my best. And even though I'm sure you'll take every precaution available to you, I want to assure you that even if I wasn't shackled with these cuffs, the goddess would have nothing to fear from me. I'm forever in her debt for persuading you to spare my people."

"Truth," the lie detector said.

Despite the guy's reassurances, Kian didn't look convinced. "Words are cheap, Lokan. I believe in actions. If you want to express your gratitude in a meaningful way, do it by giving me the island's location."

Despite the evidence he'd been shown, this was still an extremely tough decision to make. There was no going back from that.

"Give me your most solemn oath that you're not going to attack the island."

Kian shook his head. "I can't do that because at some point in the future it may become necessary. But I can vow never to attempt to destroy it or seek the annihilation of its population."

Kian's unwillingness to give him a blanket oath was actually reassuring because it meant he was going to abide by his word.

"Let me rephrase it then. I want you to swear that if for any reason you ever attack the island, it's not going to be with indiscriminate bombing, conventional or unconventional, and that you and your men will do your absolute best to preserve as many lives as possible."

His hand over his heart, Kian nodded. "I give you my oath that I will never use the information you give me to destroy the island or its inhabitants. If at any point an attack becomes unavoidable because we need to free one of our own or prevent a major catastrophe, I will do everything in my power to minimize casualties on both sides."

That was the best vow he was going to get. "If you show me a map of the region, I'll mark the island's location for you."

"Don't you have the coordinates?"

"I don't. But I know where the island is."

"How did you fly in and out of there without having the exact coordinates?"

"I didn't. I flew to a nearby private airport, where I stored my plane, and an island transport picked me up from there. No one flies in or out of the island other than the compelled human pilots. But since I was the one doing the compelling, I knew where the island was. I just never bothered to ask for the flight coordinates."

CAROL

*A*s the spatula slipped from Carol's hand and landed on the floor, she cursed under her breath. Nerves of steel were required to wait patiently for Kian to be done with Lokan.

She'd thought she had them, but apparently, hers were only iron strong. If Lokan refused to cooperate, Kian might resort to torture to get the island's location out of him.

What was she going to do if that happened?

For better or worse, Lokan was her mate; should she plead for leniency? Would Kian listen to her?

Not a chance.

If showing Lokan the catacombs wasn't enough to reassure him that the clan had no intention of annihilating his people, she would have to convince him of that somehow.

After rinsing the spatula, she flipped the chicken breasts in one pan and loaded the second one with another batch. Given her stress level, she'd chosen a simple recipe, but since she needed to pass the time, she'd made enough chicken Milanese to feed every Guardian in the building in addition to her roommates, Arwel, and Lokan.

The side dishes were simple too. White rice and green beans.

When the last batch was done, she pulled out her phone and texted Arwel. *Are they done yet?*

He answered right away. *We are on our way back.*

Did it work?

Yes.

Thank the merciful Fates.

The wave of relief that swept through her was so powerful that Carol's knees went weak, and she had to lean against the counter.

There would be no torture.

Her mate wouldn't be harmed.

Taking several fortifying breaths, she went back to work. After dividing the enormous pile of cutlets into portions, she loaded everything into several containers and packed a big insulated bag with all that was needed for her and Lokan's dinner.

Arwel could handle the distribution of the rest between the Guardians. She still needed to freshen up and pack a few personal necessities.

The guys weren't back yet when Carol got to the dungeon level, and after a few moments of standing next to Lokan's door, she put her bags on the floor and leaned against the wall.

The ping of the elevator stopping on her level preceded the murmur of male voices.

"Something smells delicious," she heard Andrew say.

"It seems Carol is back with dinner." That was Anandur's voice, and a moment later the five men rounded the corner.

Walking between the brothers, Lokan seemed as confident and nonchalant as he usually did, but she could sense his stress even from a hundred feet away.

Was that a mate thing? Was she more attuned to him now that they had formed the bond?

Because his expression was the same one that he fooled everyone else with, smug and slightly bored, and revealing nothing of what was going on inside of him.

"Hi, guys. I made enough to feed all of you," she said as they stopped in front of Lokan's cell. "I put the containers on the counter in my apartment. If you hurry, you can still eat it warm." Hopefully, this would get them out of there faster.

Her eyes searched Lokan's, but his expression remained impassive.

"Thank you," Andrew said. "But Nathalie and Phoenix are waiting for me to come home."

Kian and the brothers thanked her and said much the same. Except for Arwel, each was eager to get back to his mate.

Lokan's expression didn't change, but she caught the red flash in his eyes.

Was he excited about being alone with her? Or was it in response to the exchange he'd just witnessed? Immortal males eager to get home to their mates was a novelty for him. Did he find the prospect of joining that exclusive club tempting?

Punching the code into the keypad, Arwel opened the door. "As soon as you get inside, I'm going to restore the previous settings on your cuffs."

Lokan nodded. "I expected as much." He glanced at Kian. "Don't I deserve some perks for my cooperation?"

Kian slapped him on the back. "You've already gotten the biggest perk there is. I'm allowing Carol to stay with you in your cell and serve you gourmet meals three times a day."

"That's true." Lokan dipped his head. "And greatly appreciated. I'm grateful for that and for your merciful treatment of my people. You are a good man, cousin." When Kian opened his mouth to protest, he lifted a hand to stop him. "I know that as far as the warriors go, you are just following your mother's orders, but did she also order leniency toward me?"

Kian shook his head.

"That's what I thought. Thank you for allowing Carol to stay."

"You are welcome." Kian lifted a finger. "But if you harm a hair on her head, you'll see the other side of me, and let's just say that it's far from lenient."

The vehemence in Kian's voice sent a wave of dread down Carol's spine, but Lokan only smiled. "I like your attitude. Since I am a powerless prisoner, I'm glad that my mate has such a fierce protector."

43

LOKAN

*F*inally alone with Carol, Lokan pulled her into his arms. "I couldn't wait for them to leave so I could do this." He smashed his lips over hers.

She returned the kiss with just as much fervor, her hands running over his back and then cupping his ass to pull him closer against her.

Her strength still surprised him, especially given her petite size and delicate features, as did her boldness. Lokan was well aware of how intimidating he was to most people, humans and immortals, males and females alike. On a visceral level, they sensed what he was, and their instinctive fear of him was the right response.

Lokan was powerful, physically and mentally, and he wasn't a nice guy. He was decent, or as decent as he could afford to be given his station in the Brotherhood, but that didn't mean that he was even remotely good or harmless. He was dangerous to whoever stood in his way or the way of his ambitions, and he had very few qualms about eliminating those who did, sometimes with extreme prejudice.

"Your dinner is getting cold," Carol said when he let go of her.

"Fuck the food. Let's go to bed." He lifted her and started toward the bedroom.

"No way." She pushed on his chest. "We can do that after we eat and you tell me everything."

Reluctantly, he let her down. "As you wish."

She smiled at him sweetly. "Get us drinks from the fridge while I set the table."

Getting told what to do by a woman was still a novelty for him, but surprisingly Lokan didn't find it offensive.

Where he came from, women were supposed to obey rather than issue orders. On the island, as well as in some of the more extreme patriarchal societies, this was not only expected but also enforced.

Still, he'd always suspected that the reality was different inside the homes of loving partners.

How was it possible to care for a woman and not provide for her needs? And how was a man supposed to know how to do that without her sharing her dreams and wants as well as her displeasures and dissatisfactions openly with him?

Except, most of the men he'd interacted with truly believed that women were meant to serve men, and that their own needs and wants were inconsequential. It was even true of some of the Westerners he'd dealt with, but more so in places where the belief was backed by religion and ideology.

Mortdh's teachings weren't even the most extreme in that regard. In fact, even though females were held in low esteem by Mortdh's followers, their lives were at least protected.

The god the Brotherhood worshiped had never advocated physical abuse as a way to control women, and killing females was prohibited because it was considered a waste of a valuable resource. It wasn't a particularly noble sentiment, but it was better than the right some societies gave men to execute their wives, daughters, and sisters for *honor* offenses, which often meant that mere suspicion of infidelity or impropriety could be used to justify murder.

"Don't just stand there, dinner is served," Carol interrupted his musings.

He opened the fridge. "What would you like to drink?"

"Water, please."

He pulled out a water bottle for her and a Snake's Venom for himself.

"Thank you for cooking this wonderful meal for me," he said as he sat down.

She grimaced. "I know it's not as fancy as the other ones I've made for you, but I was too stressed out to get into the zone of cooking something elaborate."

"I wasn't being sarcastic. This looks and smells delicious. What did you stress about?"

She made a face. "You and Kian. I was afraid that you'd refuse to cooperate, and he would decide to torture you to get the island's location out of you."

"Would he have done it?"

"I don't know. Kian has a heart of gold, but he can be ruthless. Especially with the clan's enemies, which for the time being you still are, at least in his eyes."

"I am not. But I don't expect Kian to take my word for it. Besides, I'm powerless in here." His lips twisted. "Not that I had much power before. I was a big cog in my father's machine, but still just a cog. I had no say in determining policy or influencing his decisions. The Brotherhood is a monarchy, not a democracy, and Navuh has absolute power over everything and everyone in it."

Before demoting Losham, Navuh had on occasion listened to his brother's advice, but after Losham had been tasked with

I. T. LUCAS

the demeaning jobs of heading the Brotherhood's drug operation and bringing fresh flesh to the island, Navuh hadn't taken
on anyone else as his advisor.

It was a shame. Losham was brilliant and moderate. He'd
been the voice of reason that had kept Navuh's more ambitious
plans in check.

Carol cut a piece of chicken and motioned for his plate. "If
you want me to believe that you like what I make for you, you
have to prove it. Deeds, Lokan, speak louder than words."

As he lifted his fork and knife, Lokan wondered whether
Carol was hinting at something. But what?

He'd already promised Kian the island's location. What else
could he do to prove himself the clan's friend?

Was he their friend?

He wasn't. Except, wasn't the enemy of his enemy a friend?

Regrettably, he couldn't think of his father as anything but.
As long as Navuh had absolute power over the Brotherhood,
no change was possible. Like everyone else on the island,
Lokan was a slave to his father's agenda, or rather had been
before his capture.

In a way, he'd been freed.

At the realization, Lokan's chest expanded. He was no
longer his father's slave, but he wasn't free either.

Right now, he was in limbo.

"Did you like it?" Carol asked.

He glanced at his empty plate. "Is that proof enough?"

"Oh, I don't know. You were thinking so hard that I could
see the cogs in your brain spinning. I doubt you even tasted
anything."

She wasn't wrong. He hadn't been paying attention. "I'll
take another piece, and this time I'll savor the taste."

An angelic smile lit up Carol's face. "Thank you for being
honest." She picked up a cutlet from the container and dropped

it on his plate. "Would you like some rice and green beans as well?"

"Yes, please."

When she was done reloading his plate, Carol leaned back in her chair. "You're not powerless, Lokan, and you never have been. You have two extremely unique powers, one of which your father doesn't even know about."

"The dream-sharing is useless. I tried to dream-share with people I found difficult to compel and failed. You are the first immortal I tried this with, and I was very surprised that it worked. Other than you, I did it with Ella and several other human females, with whom it was all about sex. I think it only works with women I've met in person and that I'm at least somewhat attracted to."

"You should try it with some other immortals."

"I don't dare. I was warned not to try it with Ella, and I'm sure it applies to any other clan member. My people are out of the question, too, because they will talk, and my father will find out. I can only do it with humans whom I can compel into silence."

"We can ask Arwel's permission, and you can try it on him."

"To what end?"

She shrugged. "Just so you know the extent of your power and whether you can dream-share with immortal males or not."

"I'd rather not. If I succeed in dream-sharing with Arwel, Kian will view me as a threat, and he might decide to eliminate me after all."

44

CAROL

*L*okan wasn't wrong. Arwel had been of the same opinion when she'd told him about the dream-sharing.

Had it been a mistake to tell the Guardian?

Whether it was or not, it had been done.

The thing was, so far, Kian had been uncharacteristically reserved in his treatment of Lokan, regarding him as a valued asset rather than an enemy and a threat.

It was easy to forget that the regent would have no qualms about putting Lokan in stasis. As soon as Kian had the island's location, Lokan would be of little further value to him. For the time being, Kian might leave him be because of her, but the moment Lokan posed a threat to the clan, it would be game over.

The only reason Kian didn't view the dream-sharing as a threat from the start was that Lokan had no idea where they were holding him. Even if he dream-shared with some human on the island and asked that person to tell his father or brothers that he'd been captured by the clan, it would do him no good.

Even if Lokan managed to dream-share with a clan member, he wouldn't find the village's location from them either, because the vast majority of them weren't privy to that information, and she very much doubted he could dream-share with Kian or one of the council members who were.

Then again, if Lokan dream-shared with Arwel, Kian might become wary of him.

"It's good that at least one of us thinks things through. It's better not to experiment with your dream-sharing and draw too much attention to it."

He took her hand. "For better or worse, Kian and I think alike because we are both leaders with an extensive military background. If I were in his position, I would not have risked leaving someone with my ability to use it on my people and find out things he shouldn't. You, on the other hand, think with your heart first. That is why females shouldn't be soldiers. You are too compassionate and lack the bloodthirstiness of men."

Carol shook her head. "You can take the Doomer out of the island, but you can't take the island out of the Doomer."

Her comment was offensive, and she was well aware of that, but so had his been. Lokan had earned the insult fair and square.

Except, he just smiled. "I know that you think I'm brain-washed by Mortdh's chauvinistic teaching, but you can't argue with nature or with facts. Regardless of Western propaganda claims, males and females are not exactly the same and are not suited for the same jobs."

Looking smug, he continued. "I'm not a chauvinist. I accept that one gender is not smarter or better than the other, nor is one more or less valuable to society. But they are valuable in different ways."

With a sigh, she pulled her hand out of his. "You are old,

Lokan, and you think in outdated terms, and it's probably impossible to undo nearly a thousand years of thinking in a certain way. But the only difference is physical, and even that is rendered irrelevant by technology. I can squeeze the trigger just as easily as any male, but I happen to be a better markswoman than most. And as for ruthlessness, I won't kill indiscriminately, and neither will my clansmen. But all bets are off when it comes to protecting my people or in self-defense. I haven't killed anyone yet, but if the need arises, I know I can and will."

If she could've killed the sadist, she wouldn't have hesitated for a millisecond, except maybe to prolong his suffering. The monster hadn't deserved the merciful death by beheading Dalhu had granted him.

Frowning, Lokan reached for her hand again. "Who hurt you, Carol? Give me the name, and I'll find a way to avenge you even from here."

She must've made a face. Something to watch for if she had any aspirations of ever becoming a spy. "Was I that obvious? How did you know?"

He lifted her hand to his lips and kissed the back of it. "Your angelic expression turned murderous for a moment. It happened only once before, when I mentioned Sharim and his men. What's the connection?"

Impressive. She hadn't expected him to pay such close attention. Apparently, Lokan had been listening to every word she'd said and watching every facial expression.

Carol just hoped it was because he was so enamored with her and not because he was searching for clues to get free.

It wasn't a tale she wanted to share with him or with anyone else, but for better or worse Lokan was her mate. To protect her clan, there were so many things she couldn't share with him yet, or ever, but she could tell him about herself.

Not an easy thing to do. In fact, she dreaded telling him about her past. As attuned as he was to her, Lokan still hadn't made the connection between her response to his views on prostitution and her selling her body for sex.

She might lose any respect he had for her, and that would be a blow she wasn't sure she could recover from.

Torture by a stranger was not as bad as that. It had passed, and she'd survived. That was all that mattered. But to spend her life bonded to a male who didn't respect her was inconceivable.

Then again, hiding it from him for eternity was not an option either. Her past wasn't a secret, and Lokan learning about it from someone else would be even worse.

At some point, she would have to confess, but not today. Telling Lokan about what she'd suffered at Sebastian's hands would be enough for now.

"It was a freakish coincidence for which I paid dearly. About three years ago, I went to smoke outside a club at the same time as a van full of Sharim's men showed up. As an immortal female, I lack the built-in alarm mechanism immortal males have to detect each other. All I saw was a bunch of hunky males get out of that van, and I allowed myself to have naughty thoughts about one of them."

"They smelled you?"

"I'm not sure. A lot of what happened that night is kind of vague." Carol wasn't ready to admit that she'd been drunk and high that night either. That too would have to wait for another time. "They might have thought that I was a human and wanted to have their fun with me, but when I started struggling, they figured out that I was too strong for a human."

Lokan's expression turned from irritated to feral, the red glow from his eyes making him look like a gorgeous demon. "Did they rape you?"

"No. They brought me to their leader."

His fangs fully extended, Lokan hissed. "Did he rape you?"

"He did much worse than that."

"What can be worse?"

She pinned him with a hard stare. "Can you imagine what a sadist can do to an indestructible female?"

LOKAN

*N*ever before had Lokan felt like his blood was boiling. The phrase had always seemed figurative to him, an exaggeration used to emphasize the feeling of anger. But now he understood its true meaning.

The meal forgotten, he dropped his napkin on the table, pushed to his feet, rounded the table, lifted Carol off her chair, and sat down, cradling her in his arms.

"I heard rumors of Sharim's inclinations, but I assumed he was choosing partners who were into that crap. I'm so sorry, babydoll." He held her close to his chest and rubbed circles on her back. "I wish I could kill him for you, over and over again."

Carol sighed. "For a long time, I wished that too. I mean, I wished I could have killed him myself. But first I would have subjected him to the same torment he'd inflicted on me."

Her voice had turned into a whisper, but Carol didn't tear up or shudder as she told him her horror story. Such a brave woman.

"Did he torture you for information?"

"In the beginning. I pretended to be a dumb blonde who

knew nothing about anything, and he bought it. But he kept torturing me anyway. He got off on it."

Reining in the fury, Lokan tried to keep his tone calm for Carol's sake. She needed his comfort, not his anger. "How long did you have to suffer before the clan saved you?"

"Long enough to start losing my mind. But the clan didn't save me. One of his men took pity on me. First, he helped me by sneaking in painkillers, so I could at least numb the pain, and eventually, he helped me escape before my people managed to find where Sebastian was holding me."

"Sebastian?"

"That's the name Sharim used while in the States. Anyway, after I got away, I called Kian and told him about the other girls Sebastian had kidnapped and locked up in the basement to serve the other men. Me, he kept for himself."

"Is he in the catacombs? Because a monster like him should never be revived. Although I wouldn't mind doing it temporarily, just to torture him and then to execute him."

Carol's eyes blazed with vengeance. "That would have been awesome. But no, he is not in stasis. He's dead for good."

"Did the man who helped you escape kill Sharim?"

She shook her head. "No. Dalhu did. By then, Kian trusted him enough to take him along on the rescue mission, and he even gave him a sword. Dalhu bested Sebastian in a fencing duel and took off his head while the Guardians watched. I wish I had been there to witness it. I was told that it was an epic duel. I'm not even sure if they brought his corpse for burial in the catacombs. I hope they burned it together with the monastery he'd used as his base."

"I need to thank Dalhu for that. I wish I could do that in person, but since I can't, can you do it for me?"

"Sure."

"And thank the other one who saved you, too. If I'm ever in a position to reward him for his bravery, I will do so lavishly."

Carol chuckled. "The Fates have already seen to that by giving him his true-love mate. Robert counts himself extremely lucky."

"I'm happy for him and even happier that it isn't you."

Looking up at him, Carol scrunched her nose. "About that. For several months, I rewarded Robert in person. But I knew he wasn't the one for me and let him go, so he could find the one he was meant for."

Lokan swallowed. Thinking about Carol with any other male was difficult, but the jealousy was irrational. It wasn't as if he'd been celibate while waiting for her to pop into his life.

"Are you jealous?" she asked.

"Of course, I am. I'm jealous of any male you've ever been with, but I know I have no right. I've been with plenty of females too."

She scrunched her nose again. "Yeah, hearing that makes me jealous too. I think it is best that we don't mention our past partners to each other again. They are inconsequential anyway."

"I agree. And I understand why you felt obligated to reward Robert."

"Yeah. He's a fine male, and he sacrificed everything to help me. At the time, I didn't know about the compulsion, which must have made his decision to help so much harder. Robert didn't hate his life in the Brotherhood. He didn't want to leave the only home he knew, but he did it because he couldn't stand seeing me suffer. I wanted to reward him for that, and at the time, I wished with all my heart that he was the one for me, but he wasn't."

"What did he do when you ended things with him?"

"Sulked." She chuckled. "You should have seen the nasty

looks I got from my own people. I was the ungrateful bitch who kicked out the guy who gave everything away to save her. Never mind that he was drowning his sorrows by bedding most of the clan's single ladies. They only stopped giving me the stink eye after he found his true-love mate."

Lokan couldn't imagine the clan turning against their own over her supposed mistreatment of a Brother.

"How did you know he wasn't the one for you?"

"As I said, Robert is a good man, and he is perfect for Sharon, but not for me. He bored me to death. We had nothing to talk about, and we weren't compatible in bed."

That last statement helped to relieve the jealousy that burned through his veins every time Carol mentioned bedding the guy.

She chuckled again. "Don't get me wrong, even as mediocre as Robert was, he was a thousand times better than any human, and since there were no other immortal males for me to choose from, it wasn't easy to give him up. What all those who looked down on me didn't understand was that I did him a favor by releasing him. He deserved better than being barely tolerated. He deserved to be loved and cherished."

Loved and cherished.

Carol had just put into words Lokan's greatest desire, one that he hadn't been aware of until she'd verbalized it for him.

They weren't there yet. Their bond had snapped into place so quickly that those feelings hadn't had time to solidify, but they were going to.

From what Carol had told him about fated mates, they had to love and cherish each other. Wasn't that what true love implied?

CAROL

"You are so brave," Lokan said. "It takes an incredible resilience to overcome what you did. Ella was so much worse after Gorchenco, and what was done to her was nothing compared to what had been done to you."

"True, but don't forget that Ella was a young, naive girl who had never been exposed to the ugly side of humanity before, and to make it worse, she was a virgin. I was none of those things."

"Still, I'm amazed and grateful that you were able to put this behind you."

"Thank the merciful Fates." Carol wound her arms around his neck. "They've rewarded me with you. Now you just have to prove that you are worth it."

Lokan's normally composed expression turned troubled, and his olive-toned skin paled. "I don't think it's possible. Even if I was perfect, which I'm not, and even if I was free and could shower you with gifts and trips and fulfill all of your heart's desires, I could never compensate you for that. If the damned Fates are responsible for your unimaginable suffering, then all I feel for them is intense hate. I'd rather stick to my conviction that they are a myth and that what happened to you was a random misfortune. I will definitely never offer my thanks to those imaginary bitches."

Gasping, Carol put a finger over his mouth. "Shush. Don't say things like that. The Fates can be vindictive and take back their gifts. Besides, it gives me comfort believing that my ordeal wasn't meaningless. I like thinking that it earned me a big reward. You." She pulled up and kissed him. "I got a prince. I can't imagine a greater gift."

He grimaced. "I can. In my current predicament, I'm worth less than the lowliest of warriors. I wish I could be more for you."

"I have all that I need right here." She kissed him again.

Her grim tale must have disturbed Lokan greatly because it took him a couple of seconds to get into it, but when he did, he did it with gusto, taking charge and setting her body on fire. As he devoured her, his large, strong hands were everywhere, caressing, gripping, kneading.

There was nothing timid about him or the way he touched her, and she loved his intensity and his dominance. That was what an immortal male should be like.

She was one lucky lady.

The Fates had done right by her, and Carol was grateful despite Lokan's misgivings. She would take her imprisoned enemy prince over any other immortal male.

When he finally let her come up for a breath, it was only to push up to his feet and carry her to the bedroom.

"We didn't finish dinner," she tried a weak protest.

"I have a different feast in mind." He put her down on the bed.

Well, she wasn't going to argue with that. Reaching for the hem of her shirt, she started to pull it up, but Lokan stopped her and pointed at the camera.

"I'm not an exhibitionist."

Taking off his own shirt, he climbed on the bed and tossed it over the camera. Unbelievably, the thing stayed on and didn't slide down.

"You are really good at this."

"I'm good at many things." He waggled his brows.

One of his many talents, as she discovered a moment later, was undressing a female in a matter of seconds without tearing her clothes.

Naked before him, Carol felt her arousal flare. Lokan might not be an exhibitionist, but she was.

Her allure was her special talent, and she craved the reactions her nude body elicited from males.

It was a power rush.

The Fates had gifted her with a perfectly curved, extreme hourglass figure. Carol was the archetypical temptress, who males lusted after, coveted, and even fought over.

Lokan's eyes blazed red as they roamed up and down her body. "You are Aphrodite personified."

Bracing on her forearms, she smiled coyly. "If I'm your Aphrodite, then you are my Apollo."

"Why Apollo?"

"Duh, he was the most handsome of gods."

Dropping his pants, Lokan pounced on her, caging her between his outstretched arms and knees. "If I'm Apollo, then I need to make sure you don't run away or trick me. If memory serves me right, Apollo didn't have much luck with the ladies, despite his perfect physique and many godly powers. Daphne ran away and turned into a laurel, Coronis was unfaithful, and Cassandra tricked him into granting her a wish, and when he did, she asked to remain a virgin till the day she died."

Looking up at his gorgeous face, Carol didn't want to talk about Greek mythology. She wanted to feel his weight on top of her, and to bury her nose in his neck, filling her lungs with his intoxicating male musk.

But there was another part of her that enjoyed the banter and the fact that Lokan seemed well-versed in mythology. She knew he was better educated than the other Doomers, but this demonstrated that he was interested in more than the arts of war and politics. Although on second thought, Greek mythology was filled with both.

"Didn't Apollo have the gift of prophecy?" Carol asked.

Lokan dipped his head and nuzzled her neck. "Among his many other talents."

"So, he should have known not to chase the wrong ladies."

Lokan's eyes were smiling as he gazed at her with what looked like adoration. "Maybe he was a glutton for punishment."

Fates, she was falling in love with him, and it seemed like he was falling for her too.

Dear merciful Fates, let it be real and not an act.

"Perhaps Apollo was so confident in his sexual appeal and prowess that he believed he could change the future?"

"That's also possible."

"What about you? You seem pretty damn confident."

"I am. But I'm also smart, proud, and I know a good woman when I see one. I would never chase after a female who wasn't interested in me and hope to change her mind."

"You did with Ella."

"That was different. I wasn't stupid in love with her. I needed her for a mission." Lowering himself slowly on top of her, he positioned his hard shaft at her entrance and cupped her cheeks. "I don't want to talk about Ella or some silly human myths. Right now, in this bed, the only epic story that matters is ours."

LOKAN

"*D*on't go." Lokan wrapped his arm around Carol's middle and pulled her back against his front. "Isn't it Sunday? It's okay to laze in bed."

"I have to go. People are counting on me."

"To do what? Isn't your current job to see to my needs?"

Lifting his arm off her waist, she chuckled. "This is not a job. This is a holiday in paradise."

And didn't that make him feel like the king of the world. Watching her rounded bottom bounce as she rushed into the bathroom, Lokan wanted to follow her and grab it, but he knew she wouldn't appreciate it.

The woman needed a few moments of privacy in there.

He'd lost count of how many times they'd made love. Carol was just as insatiable as he was, and just as lustful and resilient. Finally, after nearly a thousand years of bedding human females, he could let go and unleash his ferocity without fear of causing damage.

Even better, Carol was a hellcat in bed, scratching and biting and squeezing, and he loved every second of it. It was a shame none of the marks she'd made had lasted for longer than a few seconds. He would've liked to look in the mirror and enjoy the sight.

A night with a harem full of human females could not have satisfied him as much as having her alone.

His immortal mate.

How could he be so unlucky and lucky at the same time?

But even after Mortdh knew how many bouts of sex, Lokan was still hungry for his female, and as he heard the water in the shower running, he jumped out of bed, hurried into the bathroom, and stepped into the shower.

If she was leaving soon, he wanted to enjoy these last minutes with her.

"Do you want to wash my hair?" Carol handed him the shampoo. "I bet you've never done that before."

Pretending not to get her meaning, he huffed. "I wash my hair every day."

She batted her eyelashes and fluffed her curls. "It's not the same."

"No, it isn't."

This felt intimate, familiar, something he'd never had the pleasure of doing because he'd never cared about a woman enough to want to do that.

Sitting on the shower bench, Lokan pulled Carol into his lap and took the shampoo bottle from her.

"I love your hair. It mirrors your personality." He poured a handful and rubbed it into her soft curls. "It's playful and bouncy, soft and fragrant, but it's also strong, and the curls always spring back to their original form."

With a sigh, she leaned her head against his chest. "I didn't know you had a poet in you."

He chuckled. "Is that what it was? Poetry?"

"I wouldn't know. I'm not a very literary girl, and poetry bores me. I like action, adventure, sex…"

He nuzzled her neck. "My kind of girl. So, who is counting on you to show up today, and what do you need to do?"

"I'm helping with setting up a wedding party." She turned to look up at him. "Vivian and her mate are making it official today, and a bunch of us volunteered to prepare things for the celebration. They kind of sprung it upon us, and there was no time to hire professionals to do that. Except for the food, that is. Some of it will be catered by a pro."

Taken by surprise, he stopped massaging her scalp for a moment. "Does the clan have a special mating ceremony? Like a human marriage?"

"Not really." She waved a dismissive hand. "We kind of make it up as we go. Former Dormants usually want a wedding-like party, and that's what Vivian is having. Because she is older, her transition can be potentially fatal. Her mate wants them to be married before she attempts it, and he is also adopting her children, so she knows that they will be taken care of if anything happens to her."

It still amazed him how much he didn't know about his own kind. Every day he was learning something new. "I didn't know there was an age limit for transitioning. What is considered safe?"

Carol shrugged. "Every case is different, but it looks like the younger the person, the easier the transition. It's best to do it when puberty hits, but most of the Dormants we have discovered were older, and some had very difficult transitions. Thank the merciful Fates, we haven't lost anyone yet."

"I'm glad Ella is so young. She should have no problem transitioning."

"I hope so. She's my friend."

Reaching for the shower handle, he rinsed the shampoo out, careful not to get any of it into her eyes.

"I was hoping she would come to visit me, even if it was to

gloat. I want to meet the guy who bested me." Lokan was competitive, and it rankled losing to another.

Turning to look at him, Carol pinned him with a hard stare. "You don't sound like someone who had only a professional interest in the girl. What gives, Lokan?"

Damn. He should have been more careful. He'd gotten Carol upset for no reason.

They'd became so close so fast that he felt comfortable letting his guard down around her. That was a mistake.

Lokan knew nothing about relationships and couldn't take anything for granted. The prudent thing was to talk less, listen more, and learn.

"Nothing gives. I'm curious, and I'm damn competitive. I hate losing even when I'm not interested."

She relaxed, once more leaning against him. "I get it. I'm the same way, but it's not a good thing. It means that we are both too full of ourselves and think that we are all that, and that there could be nothing better out there."

He squirted more of the shampoo into his palm. "There isn't. You are every guy's wet dream, the perfect woman, and you even know how to cook. Wars have been waged over less worthy females."

Not expecting a compliment back, he kept massaging her scalp even though her hair was already clean. It just felt good to be taking care of her like that. There wasn't much else he could do for Carol. Washing her, massaging her, and satisfying her sexually was all he could do while locked up in a cell. And even that was dependent on Kian's goodwill and could be taken away from him at any moment.

"What happened?" She turned in his arms. "Why did you get sad all of a sudden?"

"I was just thinking that this could be taken away from us at any moment. We are at Kian's mercy. He has absolute power over us."

Cupping his face, Carol shook her head. "That's true to an extent, but Kian is not the be-all and end-all. Annani is. And the goddess is a staunch romantic. If Kian decided to separate us, as a last resort, I could appeal to her heart."

"Wouldn't that be dangerous to go over his head? Kian might retaliate."

"He won't. The clan doesn't operate like that. The worst I can expect from him are a few stink eyes, and I can live with that."

48

CAROL

"I have an idea," Callie said. "We have this big, beautiful kitchen here in the underground, and we have the banquet hall. What if we make communal meals in here like they do in Scotland? It would be nice for everyone to meet for dinner. It would be like having a party every night."

"Are you volunteering to cook for everyone?" Carol finished with one appetizer platter and started on another.

"The Odus can handle most of it, and we can make a schedule for everyone to come help once or twice a month."

"I like it," Wonder said. "I could close the café earlier. It's not easy handling it mostly by myself. I need more help."

"Why don't you ask Ella?" Callie opened one of the ovens and checked on the salmon.

"She has her hands full with the fundraiser." Wonder glanced at Carol. "When are you coming back?"

"I don't know yet."

So far, no one other than the people directly involved with Lokan knew about the mating. Carol hadn't told anyone else. Not even Ella. She had no doubt most assumed she was having her way with the infamous prisoner—after all, her past wasn't a secret, and she wasn't shy about her sex life—but for some reason, her and Lokan's mating was difficult to announce.

Robert and Dalhu had been accepted because they had left the Brotherhood voluntarily. Lokan had been captured while trying to abscond with Ella and Vivian. Many clan members harbored resentment toward him, and she couldn't even fault them for it. Their reasons were valid.

"Hi, everyone." Ella walked into the kitchen. "Can I help with anything?"

Amanda wrapped her arm around Ella's shoulders. "This is your mother and Magnus's wedding. Today, you are a guest, darling."

"But I have nothing to do until an hour before the party. I can at least help set up the tables."

"The Guardians are doing that. We have everything covered."

"What about decorations?"

"That too. But if you want, you can hang out with us here."

Eying the appetizers, Ella whistled. "Did you make these, Carol? They look amazing."

"I wish. These are compliments of Gerard. He had his assistant chefs work all night and prepare most of the fancier dishes."

"That's so nice of him."

"Not really." Amanda grimaced. "I had to use threats and bribes to get him to do it for us. I love him, but he is such a prick."

Her statement was followed by a general murmur of agreement. Carol knew no one who liked Gerard. The guy was a stuck-up jerk.

Walking up to Carol, Ella bent over the tray. "They are such fancy little things. I would love to learn how to do this."

"You can learn anything you want from YouTube. Just don't

think of apprenticing with Gerard. Amanda was being polite calling him a prick. He is much worse than that, but he is also talented as hell."

Ella shrugged. "All chefs are prima donnas. And the more talented they are, the more temperamental." She turned to Carol. "How are things going with Lokan? Is he behaving, or is he trying to manipulate everyone?"

"He's behaving." Now was a good time to fess up, but Carol didn't want to do it in front of everyone. "I'm going up to the surface to smoke. Do you want to join me?"

Ella lifted a brow. "I didn't know you smoked."

Yeah, she also didn't know about the drugs and the booze, but that had been the old Carol. The new one had been clean for a long time.

"I occasionally do, and right now, I feel like having a few puffs. Are you coming?" Carol grabbed her purse even though she didn't have cigarettes with her. She had one old pack stashed somewhere in her house, but she had no intention of going there.

"Sure. No one wants to let me work anyway."

When they entered the elevator, Carol leaned against the side and crossed her arms over her chest. "I don't really want to smoke. I just wanted to talk to you without everyone listening in."

"Is everything okay? Did Lokan tell you anything about me?"

"It's not about you and Lokan." The elevator doors opened, and they stepped out into the glass pavilion. "It's about Lokan and me."

Ella shrugged. "That's none of my business. I knew that you wanted to sleep with him. You told me so."

"It's more than that. We've bonded. He is my mate."

Ella's hand flew to her chest. "Oh, Carol. I'm so sorry, and I hate telling you this, but he is playing you. Lokan is an amazing actor. He had me completely fooled."

"It's real. I'm not a naive young girl, Ella. He can't fool me."

"Are you sure? Because he is much older than you, and he's smart and cunning. Is there some kind of test you can subject him to?"

Carol snorted. "The only test I can think of is bringing a gorgeous naked woman to his cell and watch his reaction. If he gets a stiffy, then he's not my mate. Amanda says that true-love mates feel desire only for each other and no one else, so that should be a good indicator.

"There are exceptions." Ella looked down at her shoes.

"Not really. In your case, the confusion existed only because of Lokan's compulsion. If not for that, you would have felt no attraction toward him."

"That's true. The moment he removed it, my desire for Julian flared up, and my attraction to Lokan vanished."

Carol waved a hand. "There you go. Case proven."

"Where are you going to find a beautiful woman to come to his cell and strip, though?"

"That's not a problem. I could hire a human stripper, and after her performance have Arwel thrall her to forget. The thing is that Lokan would see right through it and somehow control his reactions."

"Does he know that mates are not attracted to anyone else?"

"I don't think that I told him about it."

"Then how would he know to control his responses? Human males can be happily married and deeply in love with their spouses and still get a hard-on when watching a stripper shake her boobies at them."

"Hmm." Carol tapped a finger over her lips. "Maybe I can have Arwel bring a stripper in. Because if I do it, it would be suspicious. Lokan knows I'm the jealous type."

Arwel could tell him that the stripper was his reward for disclosing the island's location. A Doomer would think nothing of it.

Damn. What was she thinking?

The seed of doubt Ella had planted in her head had immediately grown into a full-sized tree, but it had no roots.

In her heart, Carol knew the truth. Lokan wasn't playing her. He was her mate, and she didn't need any tests to prove it.

49

KIAN

*O*ut on the clan's airstrip, Kian looked out of the limousine's window searching the sky for his mother's plane. She should be arriving at any moment, and as always, his stress level was on the rise.

What would she do this time?

It had been years since she'd done anything outrageous, but the potential for trouble was there, and as much as he tried to calm himself down, he couldn't help worrying.

He should have gotten used to Annani's unpredictability, but it wasn't something Kian could just resign himself to. It drove him nuts.

"I'm excited," Syssi said. "Every time your mother arrives for a visit, it's because something major is happening. By now I'm like those dogs in the Pavlov experiment, getting butterflies in my stomach regardless of the reason for her visit."

Kian pulled her closer to him and kissed the top of her head. "You are an angel. Annani is not the easiest in-law to get along with, and yet you seem genuinely fond of her."

"She's always super nice to me. I couldn't have asked for a better mother-in-law."

It warmed his heart that the most important people in his life were getting along splendidly. Amanda and Syssi were more like real sisters than sisters by marriage, and his mother and Syssi adored each other. The Fates deserved a big thanks for that. They'd gifted him with the best mate in the entire universe.

"Annani is cool," Anandur said. "I don't know why you get so stressed out every time she comes to visit. All she asks for is to spend a little time with her loved ones. That shouldn't be a problem."

Not a problem. Right. That depended on what mood she was in and what crazy shenanigans she had in mind. Kian liked being in control, but since Annani was the ultimate authority and her wishes had to be obeyed no matter how irrational, he had absolutely none over her.

Like sparing the damn Doomers and keeping them in stasis in the keep's catacombs.

Fucking waste of space.

Fates only knew what she would demand of him with regard to Lokan. The bastard was a charming manipulator, and he might get her to release him. Especially since he could claim that he was mated to Carol.

Kian hadn't forgotten or forgiven Annani's intervention on Dalhu and Amanda's behalf. Except, Dalhu had turned out to be a stand-up guy and a perfect mate for his sister.

But that wasn't going to happen with Lokan. Navuh's son could never be trusted.

"The plane is landing, master," Okidu said. "We should assume our positions."

As they filed out of the limousine, Onidu, who had driven Kian's Lexus to the strip, joined them. It was going to be an Odu reunion, and Kian wondered what the seven were going to talk about on the way home. If they were going to talk at all.

He often wondered about that. Did the Odus talk to each other when no one else was around? Or did they have some other method of communication?

They were like black boxes, which no one dared to open because no one could fix them if something got damaged. Still, if not for his mother's adamant refusal, he might have considered taking a chance with one to uncover the secrets of their technology. Life in the village could have been much more comfortable with a bunch of Odus doing all the menial jobs. The alternative was to wait for Parker to grow up and compel human workers to silence.

"Here it is." Syssi pointed to the sky.

Once the jet landed, the stairs were lowered, and the first Odu came out holding two suitcases. Behind him, Oridu carried out two more.

Walking up to the stairs, Kian offered his hand to Alena and then to his mother, helping them down even though they didn't need his help.

"Welcome to Los Angeles." He bowed his head.

Stretching on her toes, Annani kissed his cheek and then rushed toward Syssi. The two embraced for a long moment, and then Annani let go so Alena could hug Syssi as well.

When all the greetings were done, Annani glanced around and frowned. "Where is Amanda? Why did she not come to greet me?"

Syssi threaded her arm through Annani's and led her to the limo. "She is working hard on the wedding preparations. Your daughter should have been a general. No one else could have pulled off a full-blown wedding party in just a few short days. She is amazing."

Annani smiled proudly. "Mindi is like me. When something needs to be done, she does not wait. She does it right away."

Kian stifled a groan.

Alena smiled indulgently. "I'm so excited for the wedding. Is anyone pregnant yet? We desperately need some babies up in the sanctuary."

Casting a quick glance at Syssi, Kian was relieved to see her smiling instead of cringing.

"Not yet. But I have a feeling we will have some good news soon," she said.

His gut twisted. Did Syssi know something she wasn't telling him?

Annani clapped her hands. "Coming from you, it is as good as a promise. I cannot wait."

Once they were seated in the limo, Anandur got behind the wheel, and Brundar joined him up front.

"Do not forget to send Okidu back for my pilot," Annani said.

"One of the Guardians from the keep will pick him up once he is done servicing the jet."

"Good. He can meet us there. I want to go see Lokan right away."

Why wasn't he surprised?

"It's not a good time today. We have a wedding to attend."

She waved a dismissive hand. "The wedding is many hours from now, and I instructed my Odus to help with the preparations in any way they are told to. We have plenty of time to visit with Lokan and be back in the village to get ready."

It was pointless to argue with his mother. Once she made up her mind, it was better to just say 'yes, ma'am' and do what she wanted.

"I'll call Andrew to meet us there."

"Why do we need to bother him on his day off?" Annani asked.

"Lokan is an excellent liar. I don't trust anything coming out of his mouth unless Andrew is there to verify its veracity."

"Very well." She waved magnanimously. "Call Andrew."

He sent a message instead, apologizing for taking the guy away from his family on a Sunday, and then sent another message to Arwel, instructing him to prepare Lokan for the visit and read him the riot act.

Thankfully, Carol was in the village, helping with the wedding preparations. It was better if Annani didn't know about the mating just yet. The longer he managed to keep it from her, the better.

Except, the Doomer was probably going to mention it right away to gain her sympathy.

Perhaps it would be better if he told her first.

"Before you meet Lokan, there are a few things you should know. He is very clever, charming, and manipulative. Don't ever let your guard down."

Annani nodded.

He took a deep breath. "The other thing you should be aware of is that he and Carol believe that they are each other's fated mates. Or at least Carol believes that. I think he is manipulating her, but Anandur disagrees, pointing out that Carol has plenty of experience, including with an immortal male, and it's not likely that she could be fooled by Lokan pretending to be her mate."

"Did you get Edna to probe him?" Annani asked.

"Not yet. I should, though. In the meantime, we can use Andrew's lie-detecting skills."

"I can probably enter Lokan's head, but I would rather not do it without his permission."

"I'm not sure of that. He has two uncommon talents. Compulsion and dream-sharing. He might have more that he hasn't revealed yet. In any case, he is incredibly powerful, and you shouldn't think of him as a regular Doomer."

She waved a hand. "I am well aware of that. Lokan's father

is the most powerful immortal in existence. Navuh's powers are as strong as a god's."

It rankled to hear his own mother admit that her arch-nemesis's son was more powerful than her own, but it was the unfortunate truth. Especially if their suspicion about Navuh's incredible ability to compel his entire island's population was true, and it seemed that it was.

Even Annani didn't possess such an ability, and according to her, before the catastrophe had destroyed the other gods, she had been one of the most powerful.

"Carol says that Lokan's curiosity about the harem is more personal in nature than what he admitted to me. She thinks he wants to find out who his mother is, or was. None of the sons knows whether his mother was a Dormant or an immortal, a wife, a concubine, or a servant."

"They must all be immortal. I can't see Navuh refraining from biting a Dormant just because he doesn't want her to transition. And that's also the reason why he keeps them locked up and under such heavy guard. He is the only one on the island who has access to immortal females."

"What I don't understand," Syssi said, "is how come the immortal females don't thrall their human servants to let them go, or at least to sneak messages out to their children."

Kian took Syssi's hand. "Compulsion is stronger than a thrall. Navuh has all the humans working in the harem under compulsion, so they can easily resist the immortal females. Besides, without proper training, the women wouldn't know how to do it. You still can't thrall, and I've been training you."

Syssi shrugged. "Because I didn't have any use for it, so I wasn't motivated. Those women have all the motivation in the world. I can't imagine not being able to communicate with a child of mine. That's just awful."

50

LOKAN

The door mechanism engaging took Lokan by surprise. Carol wasn't due back until late at night, and she'd left him with enough food to last the rest of the day, so there was no reason for Arwel or any of the other Guardians to come in.

Not that he was complaining about having an unexpected visitor. It was maddening to sit around and do nothing, being completely isolated and not knowing what was going on in the world.

He'd attempted to entertain himself by watching some movies, then he had given a shooting game a try, but those kinds of activities had never appealed to him. Lokan was a doer, not a spectator.

Perhaps he should start writing his memoirs. At least there was some creativity in it. If Dalhu could become a painter, then he could turn into a writer. What else was there to do in a prison cell?

When Arwel walked in though, Lokan didn't have to be empathic to sense the Guardian's nervous excitement.

"In about half an hour, you are getting a very important visitor. Annani is coming to see you."

Lokan swallowed. He wasn't the type who got intimidated easily, but facing a goddess must be ten times worse than facing his father, and Navuh was intimidating as hell.

"Should I put on a suit?"

Arwel shrugged. "I don't think Annani cares one way or another. You're fine the way you are." The Guardian glanced around the room. "Just tidy up a little."

The dishes from his late breakfast were still on the dining table. But since they were all disposable, all he needed to do was to put them in the trash and wipe the table's surface clean. Even he could do that.

"When she comes, you are going to sit on the couch with your hands on your thighs, palms down, and not move. If she asks you to come closer, wait for my okay before responding. Any suspicious twitch, and I'm going to send poison into your veins. It's not going to kill you, but I bet you don't want to be spasming and foaming at the mouth in front of the goddess."

"You have nothing to worry about. I'm not an idiot."

Arwel nodded. "I'm counting on it. Other than that, be polite, don't cuss, and address her as the Clan Mother."

"No problem. I have a lot of experience dealing with my father. I know how to act in front of a ruler."

Arwel seemed offended by the comparison. "Annani is nothing like Navuh. But you'll discover it soon enough. Prepare to be awed."

"Is she very beautiful?"

If she looked anything like the picture of her daughter that was hanging over the couch, then the answer was yes.

"Otherworldly so." Arwel glanced at his watch. "Twenty-five minutes. You'd better get moving."

Once the door closed behind the Guardian, Lokan took

care of cleaning the table first, and then rushed into the bedroom.

A suit was in order. First of all, because he wanted to look dignified, but also out of respect for the goddess. She'd spared his men when she had no reason to do so, and for that, she deserved his gratitude and utmost respect. Even if she was a worse diva than his father, her compassion had earned her the best and most humble attitude he could muster.

Since he was not a humble male by nature, that wasn't much, but he was going to make an effort.

After a quick shower, he put on a white dress shirt, a dark blue suit, a matching tie, and even polished his shoes with a towel.

He'd even gone as far as making the bed, a first for him since he'd always had someone else do it for him. Chances were that she would never go in there, but she might need to use the washroom, and to get there, she would have to go through the bedroom. Annani was a goddess, but she was still a female, and females appreciated tidiness.

He was a prisoner and the son of her sworn enemy. Anything he could do to improve her impression of him, no matter how small and seemingly insignificant, was worth the effort.

51

ANNANI

$\mathcal{E}$xcitement churning in her stomach, Annani waited for Kian and the brothers to enter Lokan's cell first and secure it for her.

It wasn't necessary, she could handle any immortal, except maybe for Navuh, but it eased Kian's mind.

Next to her, Syssi shifted from foot to foot. "It's my first time too. I can't wait to meet Lokan, especially after hearing about him and Carol. Even Kian and I didn't bond so fast."

Annani lifted a brow. "Are you sure?"

Her daughter-in-law blushed. "I was attracted to him immediately. Heck, it was like getting struck by lightning. My legs turned into jelly."

Smiling, Annani patted her arm. "If you were an experienced immortal like Carol, you might have realized right then and there that Kian was your fated mate. But since you were not familiar with the concept, you thought that it was only lust."

Syssi blushed again, her eyes darting in the direction of the elevators. "I hope Andrew is not going to be too late. I wonder what's keeping him. There shouldn't be much traffic on a Sunday."

Annani had forgotten about Andrew coming to join them. Were there enough chairs for everyone to sit on? The brothers would volunteer to stand, but Annani did not like the tall men to hover above her and crowd her space. She preferred for everyone to be seated.

"It is going to be crowded in there," she murmured.

Taking her words the wrong way, Syssi's eyes darted toward the elevators again. "I don't really need to be there. I can wait in the old café, or in Arwel's room."

"Nonsense." Annani reached for Syssi's hand. "I was just stating a fact, not suggesting that you should not come in."

As Kian came out, he regarded them both with a stern expression. "Lokan has been instructed to sit on the couch with his hands on his thighs where the brothers and I can see them. I don't want either of you to come closer or offer him your hand for a handshake." He pinned Annani with a hard stare. "Please don't disregard my instructions because they are crucial for your safety. I don't want to explain why, but I assure you that I'm not being overly cautious."

Poor Kian. Always afraid for her, or rather of what she might do.

"I will do as you ask, my son." She smiled sweetly. "Not because I think these measures are necessary, but because I do not want you to be tense. Let us go in and have a pleasant talk with Lokan, shall we?"

With a slight dip of his head, Kian waved them ahead of him. "Ladies first."

Assuming a reassuring expression, Annani glided into the small living room, her eyes immediately going to the male sitting on the couch in the pose he had been instructed to hold.

His dark eyes widening in awe, he dipped his head. "Greetings, Clan Mother. I apologize for not bowing properly to you, but I was instructed not to move."

"No bowing required." Annani glided to the armchair Kian was standing behind and sat down, arranging the skirt of her gown around her knees.

When she was seated, Kian motioned for Syssi to take the other one. "This is my wife, Syssi."

"Nice to meet you." She smiled at Lokan.

He dipped his head. "The pleasure is all mine."

Grimacing, Kian sat on one of the dinette chairs the brothers had arranged to face the couch and the lone man sitting on it.

Annani had seen the portrait Dalhu had drawn of Lokan, but it had not done him justice because Dalhu had not known him well. The charcoal drawing did not showcase the powerful personality shining through his eyes, or the dangerous vibe that emanated from him like a force field.

There was something about Lokan that tugged at her heart. A feeling of familiarity. Was this the affinity Amanda was talking about?

Except, Annani had not felt this way with Dalhu or Robert. Still, they were both good males, and she was glad that they had joined her clan and proven to Kian that not all Doomers were evil, and that there was hope for them someday living peacefully alongside her clan.

Lokan was definitely his father's son. She could see Navuh in his lean, tall build and in his gorgeous, dark features, but where Navuh's were harsh and angular, Lokan's were softened by what he must have gotten from his mother.

Who was she?

Navuh had inherited his father's harem, which contained several immortal females, but Annani had not known them.

Perhaps some of her people had survived the cataclysm and found dubious refuge in Navuh's camp?

The door opened, and Andrew walked in together with Arwel. "My apologies for the late arrival, Clan Mother." He bowed to her.

"No apologies needed, Andrew. It is I who feel bad about tearing you away from your lovely family on a Sunday. How is sweet little Phoenix doing?"

"Running around and causing havoc. She is a ball of energy."

"I would like to see her. Talk with Nathalie and let me know when is a good time."

He bowed again. "I will."

From the corner of her eye, she caught Lokan observing the conversation with a frown and wondered what it was about. Did he disapprove of the familiarity between her and her people? Or was he impressed by it?

For some reason, his opinion mattered to her.

LOKAN

*O*therworldly.

Arwel had been spot on with that one word. Before his capture, Lokan hadn't dedicated much thought to Annani and what she looked like or who she was as a person.

Unlike his father, Lokan had no interest in the clan. They were a small and insignificant group of immortals, and they posed no real threat to his people. He had no problem with their humanitarian efforts, and he didn't mind the technological knowhow they were drip-feeding to humanity. On the contrary. The Brotherhood benefited from the innovations as much as the humans did.

But that was because he wasn't interested in world domination or enslaving humanity, while his father was obsessed with it.

Lokan's interest in the goddess had been sparked only after he'd discovered that she'd been sparing his men, but the image he'd conjured in his head had been all wrong. For some reason, he had imagined a tall female with blonde hair and fair, gentle features, wearing a compassionate expression that bordered on pained, as if the fate of the world was resting on her shoulders.

Where the hell had he come up with that?

Annani was pale-skinned, but that was the only resemblance to what his imagination had come up with.

For starters, Annani's skin glowed, actually emitting light. He'd never known that the gods had been luminescent. Several human myths mentioned it, and there was even a reference in The Book of Enoch about Noah being born with luminous skin and his father accusing his mother of cheating on him with a god. But myths were not a reliable source of information.

In this case, however, they'd gotten it right. It made sense that if Annani's skin emitted light, so had those of other gods.

Was it true of her size too? Had all the gods been so short? And so perfect?

Annani was tiny, even shorter than Carol, and so beautiful that it was hard to look at her.

What about the hair?

Annani's was flaming red and so long that it reached past her thighs. Had the gods been red-haired?

But those were physical attributes.

The most significant difference between his imagination and reality was the expression. Hers wasn't compassionate or pained, it was determined and commanding. Annani's eyes shone with wisdom and curiosity. She looked regal, but not in the condescending way his father did. Annani just had that aura about her.

Was it also an attribute of the pure-blooded gods? Or was Annani special?

And that voice. If he'd heard it without seeing her, he would have described it as otherworldly as well. Melodious was a poor description, but it was the only one that had popped into his head.

Crossing her legs under her long silk gown, Annani put her

hands on her knee. "I have heard that your father separates his children from their mothers at an early age and has them raised by Dormants."

One tiny foot peeked from under the dress's hem, catching his attention. The goddess was wearing flat-heeled soft shoes that matched the dark-green color of her dress. Apparently, Annani valued comfort and had the confidence to forgo high heels even though everyone in the room towered over her.

Well, the males did. Kian's mate was an average-sized female, but even she looked tall in comparison.

He lifted his head to look at the goddess's impossible eyes. "This is true."

"Do you at least know your mother's name?"

He shook his head. "I don't."

Compassion flitted through her wise eyes, and her voice softened, turning soothing. "Do you know how old you were when you were separated from her?"

"I was told that I was about eighteen months old when I was delivered to the Dormants' enclosure."

The goddess's small foot started swinging back and forth under the long skirt of her dress. "That is young, but it is old enough to remember at least something of your mother."

"Blue eyes. As a kid, I used to dream about blue eyes looking at me lovingly. Back then, before my father started importing women from other ethnicities, the color was uncommon in the Brotherhood. So naturally, I thought that they belonged to my mother. But it might have been just a dream."

"What else do you remember about her?"

He shrugged. "As I said, it wasn't a memory. But in the dreams, she had fair skin and rosy cheeks."

"What about the color of her hair?" Annani sounded almost breathless.

"I don't remember seeing her hair. She might have been

wearing a scarf around her head like the Dormants in the enclosure. Or maybe I just gave her one in my dreams because that was what all the females were wearing back then."

Annani put her hand over her chest as if the next question was going to pain her. "Does the name Areana ring a bell?"

"I'm sorry. It seems important to you, but it does not."

She nodded. "You probably called her mother or mama. Little kids do not call their mothers by their given name." Looking deflated, Annani slumped into the armchair.

"Is Areana someone you knew?"

"She took my place as your grandfather's intended and traveled north to his stronghold. I was hoping that she made it there before Mortdh dropped the bomb and destroyed all the other gods. I thought that maybe you would know if your father was keeping her. Areana was a tall blonde with blue eyes."

Annani chuckled. "Well, compared to me, everyone is tall. So, she might have been average-sized."

The goddess sighed. "I hope she survived, but then thinking of her imprisoned for thousands of years and at your father's mercy breaks my heart. I do not know which is worse. Then again, when I knew Navuh, he was not the monster he later became, and he was quite enamored with Areana, so I dare to hope that other than keeping her isolated he has been kind to her."

The wheels in Lokan's mind went into hyper drive.

If Areana took Annani's place as Mortdh's intended, she must have been a full-blooded goddess. His grandfather would have never accepted a mere immortal as a substitute.

Could Navuh have appropriated her for his own after his father's death?

Was she the big secret he was hiding in his harem?

If Navuh was keeping a pure-blooded goddess imprisoned

in there, it was no wonder that he had the place under such tight lockdown.

A goddess could undermine his position.

Then a sudden thought struck him. Could Areana be his mother?

Could he be the son of a goddess?

He had to find out.

Affecting nonchalance, Lokan phrased his question as a statement. "It sounds like you cared for Areana."

"Of course, I did. Areana was, and hopefully still is my half-sister."

Stunned, Lokan didn't even bother to hide his response.

"I need a drink."

53

KIAN

"I need one too." Kian got up and walked over to the bar fridge. "I see Carol has kept you fully stocked," he said as he opened it and pulled out a bottle of Snake's Venom and handed it to Lokan. "Anyone else wants a drink?"

Not surprisingly, the brothers and Andrew shook their heads. Anandur and Brundar were on duty, and Andrew stayed away from alcohol except for special occasions.

"I would like a bottle of water," Annani said.

He pulled out two and handed one to his mother and the other to his wife, then took another beer for himself.

This afternoon was turning more bizarre than he'd ever imagined. It seemed likely that bloody Lokan was his cousin for real.

Around a thousand years ago when Lokan was born, a blonde, blue-eyed woman was a rarity in Navuh's region. According to Annani, the vast majority of immortal offspring born to the gods had been olive-skinned and dark-haired, taking after the local population. The northerners Mortdh had brought as a present for her hadn't had a chance to intermingle with the local population to affect the coloring. They had been killed by the nuclear blast together with the rest of the people living in the nearby cluster of Sumerian cities.

So, unless Lokan had been dreaming up ghosts, or Mortdh had managed to snag the rare fair-skinned immortal female for his harem before annihilating the south, Areana was probably the only one who could have been Lokan's mother.

"Andrew." Annani turned her head to look at him. "You have a friend who can draw a portrait from a verbal description. I remember the portrait he drew of Eva from just listening to Bhathian. It was very accurate."

"Tim is very talented," Andrew said.

Annani nodded. "We can bring him here and have him draw Areana from Lokan's memory."

"I'm not sure I remember enough of her. I was a kid when I had those dreams. That was a long time ago."

Syssi cleared her throat. "What about reaching into Lokan's mind? Would you recognize her in his memories?"

Annani shook her head. "Those memories are old, and they are buried deep. Tim can probably summon them up with his questions. He must be very good at that to produce such accurate portraits."

Andrew groaned. "Every time I ask him to do me a favor, he demands a more outrageous compensation. I wish we had someone else."

"Do you know anyone?" Syssi asked.

"Unfortunately, not at his skill level, and this job requires the best."

"I will pay whatever he asks for," Annani said.

"Then it is agreed." Kian lifted his beer bottle. "We need to prove or disprove this insane hypothesis one way or another." He took a long swig.

"You could do a DNA test," Syssi suggested. "Today it is as easy as sending a little bit of saliva to a lab."

Kian shook his head. "No offense, but that is a terrible idea. We can't risk our genetic material getting exposed. Bridget claims that standard genetic testing will not reveal any differences, but that is true for today. The technology is advancing, and better ways of testing will no doubt be developed in the future."

"Yeah, you are right. I still don't get how it is possible for our genes to look so similar to that of humans."

"Just one percent difference is responsible for all of the human variety, which means that seven and a half billion people are ninety-nine percent genetically the same," Lokan said. "Maybe we are also different by just one percent, except in our case that's what makes all the difference."

Kian sneered. "I didn't know they taught evolution and biology in the Brotherhood training camp."

"They don't. I read a lot."

"That is commendable," Annani said. "Knowledge is power."

"Kian and your other children were born immortal, right?" Syssi asked.

"Of course. It is only the second generation that needs their genes induced into immortality."

"Then if Lokan is Areana's son, he didn't need to transition." Everyone's eyes turned to the Doomer.

"Did you have a transition ceremony?" Annani asked.

"I did."

"How old were you?"

"About twelve. My father claimed that I was more developed than other boys my age and that I was ready for my transition earlier than most."

Annani nodded. "He might have wanted to hide the fact that you were already an immortal. The fangs and venom glands do not start to grow before puberty, so there would have been no outward signs except for the rapid healing. Do you remember ever getting a scrape or a cut and healing fast?"

Frowning, Lokan shook his head. "I don't. My childhood was spent mostly with my tutors. I didn't get to run around with other boys or get into fights. My father was very strict and demanding of me, more so than of my other brothers. He always said that I was the smart one and that he had high hopes for me, and that I needed to learn as much as I could about as many things as possible. I wanted to please him, so I applied myself to my studies even though I hated my chief tutor."

Kian snorted. "Yeah, I remember your story about telling him to kiss your ass and him actually doing it. That was how you discovered your compulsion ability."

Annani clapped her hands and laughed. "What an amusing anecdote. What did he do?"

"He ran to complain to the head of the Dormants' enclosure, who in turn complained to one of my older brothers, who reported it to my father. I was rewarded by having my transition ceremony moved up and leaving the Dormants' enclosure for the main camp. The best thing about it was no more tutors."

Kian and Annani exchanged glances. The more Lokan revealed about his childhood, the more it seemed like Navuh had been cleverly hiding the fact that Lokan had been born an immortal. His other sons, those who hadn't spent all their time with tutors, were probably born to his immortal concubines.

54

LOKAN

*W*hen the door closed after the last Guardian had left, Lokan let out a breath and dropped his head back.

Annani seemed to believe that he was her sister's son, and even Kian, who was the biggest skeptic of the bunch, seemed to agree with her.

Perhaps he was only pretending out of respect for his mother?

Watching the interaction between Kian and Annani hadn't provided him with clues as to the kind of relationship they shared, but her brief conversation with Andrew, the lie detector guy, had been most illuminating. It had been friendly and familial, as if the goddess considered him a close relative.

When Annani had inquired about his family and expressed her wish to visit them, Andrew had seemed honored but not intimidated, and when she'd asked him to check with his wife for a good time, Lokan had almost choked on his own saliva.

Her attitude toward her people was so different than his father's, so easygoing, and yet it was evident that they revered her, and that included her son.

When the door started opening again, he glanced around to check if anyone had left something behind and was coming back for it, but the only remaining items were empty water and beer bottles.

"You can get off the couch now," Arwel said as he walked in.

"I know. I'm still too stunned to move." He was surprised to hear himself admitting that to the Guardian.

Arwel wasn't his friend. He was his jailer.

Hell, Lokan had no friends. He had acquaintances, and half-brothers, none of whom he could drop his act with even for a moment. Appearing confident and in complete control was a survival necessity.

Or rather had been.

No one here cared if he lost it and started singing obscenities or crying. Not that he was inclined to do any of that, but theoretically he could, and it wouldn't make any difference in his circumstances.

Arwel opened the fridge and pulled out two more beer bottles. "I felt it. That's why I came over. Do you want to talk about it?"

Lokan reached for the bottle. "What are you, my shrink?"

The Guardian popped the lid on his and sat in the same armchair Annani had sat in. "I figured you needed someone to talk to after that revelation. It's not every day that a guy discovers his mother might be a goddess. This is some heavy shit."

"Tell me about it." Lokan took a long swig of the delicious beer. "Can I ask you a favor?"

"That depends."

"I need to restock the fridge with more of these." He lifted the beer bottle. "There was money in the wallet you guys took from me, and much more in my bank accounts, which you can use the debit card to access. Carol said that these are hard to get."

"They are. We need to order them from Scotland, but we found a way to get them here in less than twenty-four hours. We pay a flight attendant on the line between here and Edinburgh to bring us cases of them."

"So, can you get me some?"

The Guardian nodded. "How can I refuse Annani's nephew?"

"Oh, yeah? Get me out of here."

"Except for that."

"I thought so."

"Besides, where would you go? Your mate is here. From what I've seen of the other mated couples, they can't stay away from each other for more than a day or two even after being together for years. It's starting to be a damn problem because they won't go out on missions unless they are local."

It seemed he wasn't the only one who was lowering his guard. Arwel had just let slip something he hadn't known about.

"Missions? I thought the Guardians were protectors of the clan, and as far as I know, there haven't been any altercations between mine and yours lately. What else can you guys be doing?"

Raking his fingers through his hair, Arwel grimaced. "I guess I can tell you. It's not like you can do anything with the information. We rescue girls from traffickers. You know, the guys you Doomers buy women from to fill up your brothel."

"Most of the ones we get are runaways and druggies."

"Same difference. You prey on the weak and the helpless. It's abhorrent."

"I agree."

Arwel pinned him with a hard stare. "And yet I'm sure you

took advantage of their services."

Oh, that was good. As if the clan males hadn't been frequenting whorehouses and paying for sex same as the Brothers. Everyone knew that brothels were the best places to hunt for them.

"Don't get all saintly on me. You want to tell me that you've never paid for sex?"

"I did. But the women did it voluntarily."

"Oh, yeah? Did you ask? A woman doesn't sell her body unless she is forced to by either circumstances or coercion. There are a few exceptions, I will give you that, but I bet the ones you've been with did not belong to that exclusive group. Like it or not, you and your clansmen are just as guilty of supporting the flesh trade as the Brotherhood is."

Cringing, Arwel took a long swig of his beer. "In my case, I'm sure they were willing because I could read their emotions, but you are right about my clansmen. They had no way of knowing unless the women were new to the trade and still distraught over it, emitting strong scents of fear."

"Did it stop them?"

"I hope so. But I'm ashamed to admit that we didn't do much to help them. The rescue missions are a recent thing."

For several moments, they each drank in silence.

"Did you know that Ella was a Dormant when you rescued her?" Lokan asked.

"In the beginning, we didn't know. Vivian didn't tell us about their special ability. We did it just to help her. But then Ella told Vivian telepathically that she had to run, and there was no way for Vivian to explain why except to fess up."

"How did Vivian know to turn to you? Do you advertise in the newspapers?"

Arwel laughed. "No, we don't advertise. It all started with a psychic convention and a picture of a beautiful girl."

55

KIAN

"You've been quiet." Kian looked at Andrew as the door to Lokan's cell locked behind them.

"He didn't lie. It would have been disrupting to yell 'truth' after every sentence."

In the elevators, he noticed how quiet his mother and wife were. Usually, when the two got together, they chatted happily, but now they both looked like someone had died.

"Why the long faces?" he asked.

A tear slid down Annani's face. "Areana's life is one long tragedy. She lost her true-love mate and lived like a celibate hermit for seven decades. Then she selflessly agreed to take my place as Mortdh's bride, only to get sneered at. Then she got taken by Navuh, who must have lost his mind after his father died. Having a child of her own was probably the highlight of her miserable life, but then Navuh took even that away from her. I cannot fathom the misery of such existence."

Syssi sniffled. "It's just horrible. I wish we could whisk her out of there and help her find new love. She is your father's daughter, right?"

"My father met my mother many years after he already had

Areana with another goddess. Regrettably, he did not treat my sister well. Areana was such a weak goddess that he was embarrassed to acknowledge her, and he did so only grudgingly. Our community was too small to hide the fact that she was his. Ahn never invited Areana to the palace or even mentioned her in conversation until he needed her to take my place. I loved my father, but he had his faults. He was a good leader, though."

"None of us is perfect," Kian said.

Annani sighed. "There are degrees, my son. I do not wish to besmirch my father's memory, but long before I was born, when humanity was still in its infancy, he had done some very bad things. I would have never discovered them if not for Khiann. Navohn, his father, had told him some of the less than flattering history of our people."

Kian wondered what Ahn had done that was so terrible, and why he was only hearing about it now. He'd thought that his mother had told him everything she remembered about the gods, but now it seemed like she had not. She'd hidden the ugly from her children, leading them to believe that other than Mortdh, who had been insane, the gods had been entirely benevolent.

At the parking level, Kian and Andrew slapped backs. "Talk with Tim. I don't care how much he charges, I want him here as soon as possible."

Hopefully, the portrait would look nothing like Areana, and they could put this entire unsettling episode behind them.

Except, Annani might claim that Lokan just didn't remember enough. His mother wanted her sister to be alive, and she wanted Lokan to be her nephew. To sustain that belief, Annani was willing to clutch at the weakest of straws for as long as she could.

"I'll let you know what the bastard is demanding for his services."

"Just say yes to whatever and get him here."

"He might ask for your firstborn." Andrew winked. "I'll see you all at the wedding." He clicked his car door open.

When the rest of them were seated in the limo, Syssi turned to Annani. "I truly hope that Areana is indeed Lokan's mother and that she is still alive. Since you were born to two different mothers, Areana and her descendants can mate yours. I wonder whether she had more children. Perhaps Lokan is not her only son."

"What if Lokan's dreams were meaningless?" Kian asked. "We all want to believe that Navuh has Areana, but he might not. We are basing everything on a young boy's dreams of a loving blue-eyed woman. Even the memory of the dreams could be faulty. Lokan was a lonely, motherless boy, and time might have colored his recollection."

"There is also a lot of anecdotal evidence," Annani said. "You cannot deny that Navuh's treatment of Lokan is suspicious. It strongly suggests that Lokan was born immortal. I am more convinced than ever that Navuh has my sister, and he is keeping her locked up in his harem. This is the big secret he has been hiding."

Syssi sniffled. "Poor Lokan. And poor Areana. It's such a cruel thing to separate a child from his mother. Why would he do that? Just to be nasty?"

Kian shrugged. "Harem politics, I guess. Mothers have a great influence on their sons, especially when the father is distant and has many wives or concubines and many children. History is full of rulers who were assassinated by their sons with the encouragement of their mothers. Then there is the rivalry between the mothers and between the sons for preferential positions and for succession."

Crossing her arms over her chest, Syssi shook her head. "I can't believe that you are justifying him."

"I'm just playing devil's advocate. Navuh is saving himself a lot of headaches by keeping the sons separated from their mothers. In fact, he is removing the main incentive for them to murder each other."

"How did you arrive at that conclusion?" Annani asked.

"As long as he doesn't choose an heir, no one knows which son it is going to be. Usually, it's the first born to the chief wife, but since only Navuh knows who was born to whom, and he keeps rotating his sons between positions, he can keep it to himself for as long as he wants and have them all jumping through hoops to please him in hopes of being chosen."

Syssi waved a dismissive hand. "He could have compelled them not to kill each other, and he could have even compelled the mothers to only say nice things about him to their sons. That would have been a much more merciful solution."

"I think he is doing it because he wants to hide Areana's existence," Annani said. "She is a goddess, and she glows. If the sons grew up in the harem, they would have seen that and figured it out, even if she did not tell anyone who and what she was."

"What does he do with the daughters?" Syssi asked. "With so many children, some of them must have been girls."

Another tear slid down Annani's cheek. "My guess is that he sends them off to the Dormant enclosure when they are still babies, same as he does with the boys. But unlike the sons, he does not acknowledge the girls as his."

56

MAGNUS

"Come on, Magnus." Anandur slapped his back. "You can't stay in the house until the wedding. It's bad luck. Besides, as soon as the bridesmaids show up, they are going to kick you out anyway. Wonder says that they are planning a mini bachelorette party for Vivian while she gets ready."

Magnus shook his head. "It's after three o'clock in the afternoon, and the wedding is in six hours."

The guys had been trying to persuade him to have a bachelor party, but he'd declined. For starters because everything had been so rushed that there had been no time, and secondly because he didn't see the point in having one. He could have drinks with the guys whenever he wanted. Except, it seemed that his former partner had disregarded his protests and had organized something anyway.

Anandur grinned. "Plenty of time to smoke a fine cigar and down a bottle of the finest whiskey."

"Where?"

If it was at one of his friends' homes, he had no problem with that, but he wasn't leaving the village. The drive alone would eat up at least an hour of the time remaining until the wedding.

"My house. Grab your tux and whatever else you need and leave your lovely bride to have her pre-wedding fun with her friends."

"Let me check with Vivian."

He found her soaking in a bubble bath with a glass of wine and a hydrating mask smeared over her beautiful face.

"Are you having fun, love?" He crouched next to the bathtub and pressed a careful kiss to her lips, which was the only part of her face not covered in muddy gunk.

"I'm nervous."

He arched a brow. "About the wedding?"

"No, about meeting the goddess."

"Annani is awe-inspiring, but not scary, and she loves presiding over weddings. I'm very honored that she chose to preside over ours. It was a nice surprise."

Vivian smiled. "I think of it as my reward for helping catch Lokan. She wouldn't have come to our wedding if not for him."

"That's true."

"The bubble bath is so relaxing." Vivian closed her eyes and sighed. "But I should get out. The girls are going to be here in less than an hour."

"About that. Anandur is trying to drag me away to his house, saying that I shouldn't be here while you are getting ready."

"He is right. It's bad luck for the groom to see his bride in her wedding gown before the ceremony."

He chuckled. "When were you going to kick me out?"

She reached with a soapy hand and cupped his cheek. "I would never kick you out. I planned on getting all the girls into our bedroom and getting ready in there."

"I would have seen you coming out."

"I was planning on calling Anandur to come get you and escort you to the banquet hall."

"I love you." He leaned and kissed her again. "We can still do that. Are you okay with me going to Anandur's and leaving you alone in here?"

"Of course. I love you, and I always want you near me, but having fun with your friends before the wedding is part of the tradition."

"It's a silly one, but fine." He pushed up to his feet. "I'll see you at the altar then, my love."

"Parker may want to join you guys later. Is it safe to send him to Anandur's?"

He chuckled. "The only travesty he might witness is Anandur doing his stripper act, and the only danger in that is that the kid might pee his pants from laughter."

Vivian smiled. "I'll tell him to take a change of underwear with him. And if you can, record the act for me. It must be hilarious."

It was, but Magnus wasn't about to show his wife a recording of another guy stripping, even as a joke.

"I'll think about it."

In the bedroom, he packed his stuff in an overnight bag, grabbed the suit bag with his tuxedo, and walked out to the front porch to join Anandur.

His friend clapped him on his back. "I told you that she wanted you out of the house."

"Not really. Vivian had something else in mind, but she is okay with me getting ready at your place."

As they took the steps down to the walkway, Ella rounded the corner and frowned. "Where are you going?"

"I was told that it is bad luck for the groom to see the bride in her wedding dress before the ceremony. I'm going to Anandur's."

"Oh, good. I was scared that you and Mom had a fight and that the wedding was off."

He wrapped his arm around her shoulders. "First thing, we never fight. And second thing, even if we did, I would never leave even if she tried to kick me out. I'm not ashamed to admit that I would have groveled and pleaded until she forgave me."

Smiling, Ella stretched up on her toes and kissed his cheek. "I love you, Magnus MacBain. You're awesome."

It wasn't the first time Ella had told him that she loved him, but the words still grabbed his heart and gave it a twist.

"I love you too, Tink."

Since Parker had started calling her Tinkerbell, the nickname stuck.

Anandur pretended to sniffle. "I'm so touched." He swiped his thumbs under his eyes, wiping away imaginary tears. "And jealous."

Ella walked over to the redhead, reached for his neck, and pulled his head down to peck him on the cheek. "I love you too, but not as much as I love Magnus."

He ruffled her hair. "It will do. Are you going to keep the pink?"

"As long as the Russian is still looking for me, I have to. But I might keep it even after that. I like it."

Anandur's expression turned serious. "Lokan claims to have some dirt on Gorchenco. We can have him off your back by threatening to expose it."

"I heard. But did Lokan tell you what it was?"

"Not yet. We were busy getting the island's location out of him, and then Annani arrived and opened a whole new Pandora's Box."

Magnus frowned. "What do you mean?"

"She thinks that Lokan is the son of her half-sister Areana, who Navuh has been hiding in his harem for the past five thousand years."

"What made her think that?" Ella asked. "Does he look like her sister?"

"You've seen him. He looks like a softened version of Navuh. But from what he told us, there is a lot of circumstantial evidence to support that belief. He really might be Areana and Navuh's son."

Magnus rubbed his hand over his goatee. "That's bad news in so many ways."

"Why?" Ella asked. "Do you think Annani would wish to free him because he is her nephew?"

"That's one possibility, and that's a huge problem for obvious reasons. But what I was thinking was that as the son of a pure-blooded goddess and the most powerful immortal ever born, Lokan could be as powerful as Annani."

Anandur shook his head. "If that was true, he would have dethroned his father a long time ago. From what he told Kian, Lokan felt quite powerless in the Brotherhood. Navuh's charisma and his power of compulsion is the glue that holds it together. Lokan thinks that without him, the Brotherhood would fracture into many warring militias, and that would be a disaster. They would wreak havoc on the world."

"Personally, I think that something good is going to come out of this," Ella said. "The Fates have worked long and hard to bring this about. They must have a plan."

Anandur waved a dismissive hand. "The Fates are fickle, and they might be just messing with us for their own amusement."

Ella's eyes widened, and she put a finger on his lips. "Don't say things like that. You might offend them. Say that you're sorry."

Rolling his eyes, Anandur acquiesced. "Okay, I apologize.

The Fates have been wonderful to us lately, gifting many with true-love mates. But what I keep wondering about is why did they wait for so long? Where were they for the past five thousand years?"

Ella shrugged. "Some plans take longer than others. Perhaps they had to wait for certain players to be born, or for the circumstances to be just right, or maybe they've been busy helping others. It is not our place to question them."

VIVIAN

Flanked by her bridesmaids, Vivian trotted out of the house on her high heels, dreading the long walk to the pavilion. She would have worn flats and taken the heels in a bag to change into them later, but the dress was too long for that and would have dragged over the dirt.

Gripping the skirts in both hands, she was about to step off her porch when the sound of an electric motor made her lift her head.

"Surprise!" Ella clapped her hands. "Your chariot has arrived, Mom."

The cart used to deliver groceries and other heavy loads from the parking lot had been decorated with white ribbons and flowers, and a bunch of balloons had been tied to its back. Behind the wheel, Julian looked impressive in a tuxedo and a top hat.

"This is beautiful. Whose idea was it?"

"Mine," Ella smiled smugly. "You kept worrying about having to walk in your high heels and getting blisters by the time you made it to the banquet hall, so I figured you needed a ride. But a bride can't arrive in just any old thing. So, Julian and

I appropriated some of the decorations and used them for the cart."

"Thank you. This is perfect. We should do that for your wedding as well." She looked at her bridesmaids. "Who is riding with me?"

"I think you should ride alone," Ella said. "Julian is going to drive slowly so we can walk behind the cart."

It seemed like a good solution because only two more could fit in the cart, and it wouldn't have been fair to the others.

Which reminded her that the goddess was staying in the next house over and would have to traverse the same distance on foot. "How is the goddess getting to the wedding? Personally, I think she should arrive on a palanquin, carried by four Odus, but since it's too late to get one of those, maybe Julian should come back and offer her a ride?"

"First, we need to get you there." Ella took her elbow and helped her up into the back of the cart. "I'll call Amanda on the way and ask her opinion."

"Ready?" Julian glanced at her over his shoulder.

"Ready."

As the procession snaked along the path, Vivian tried to listen to Ella's conversation with Amanda, but could hear only every other word over the electric motor's hum.

"What did she say?" she asked when Ella hung up.

"She loved the palanquin idea and said she was going to use it for the next wedding. Annani is at Kian's house right now, and the walk from there is short, so it's not a problem."

"Oh. I didn't know that."

"They are heading out right now, so we might meet her at the elevators."

Talk about butterflies.

Vivian preferred to meet the goddess at the altar. She couldn't imagine being stuck with the Clan Mother inside a small space like an elevator and having to come up with clever things to say.

Thankfully, when they arrived at the pavilion, there was no one there, and they all crammed into the two elevators.

"I think everyone is inside already," Ella said. "Are you ready for your grand entry?"

"As ready as I'm ever going to be."

Giving her the thumbs up, Julian went ahead and opened the double doors to the banquet hall.

Two by two, her eight bridesmaids walked in, and then it was just her and Ella.

Threading her arm through Ella's, Vivian waited for the bridal march to start, signaling that it was time for them to enter. When it did, she took in a deep breath and started the measured walk they'd practiced.

The doors parted, held open for them by two Guardians who dipped their heads in respect. The rest of the force lined both sides of the broad aisle leading to the altar.

They were magnificent in their black tuxedos, two walls of powerful males and one female. Kri too was wearing a tux, and she was rocking the look.

Vivian couldn't help wondering how they'd managed to get so many tuxedos so quickly, but those random musings dissipated the moment she lifted her eyes to the altar.

None of the men looked as striking as her Magnus. Her heart swelling with love, she smiled at him and then at Parker who was standing next to him, looking very grown up in his own tux.

As she and Ella neared the steps, the goddess ascended the altar from the other side, and Vivian's step faltered.

Even though she'd been forewarned, and even though she'd seen Annani's portrait at Dalhu's exhibition, Vivian realized that no description and no painting could've done the goddess justice.

The unearthly beauty, and the immense power emanating in tangible waves from the small glowing figure could not be captured in a portrait.

Wow, Ella sent through their link.

Wow indeed.

As they climbed the three stairs to the top of the altar, the goddess smiled and spread her glowing arms.

"The Fates have blessed us with three wonderful new members, Vivian, Ella and Parker. Welcome to my clan."

An ear-splitting round of applause erupted, lasting until the goddess turned her palms out to signal for her people to hush down. "It is my greatest pleasure to preside over Vivian and Magnus's wedding, and hopefully, Ella and Julian's will follow soon." She glanced at Ella and winked. "It will give me an excuse to come visit again. So do not wait for too long."

Ella bowed her head. "Yes, Clan Mother." She moved to the side, joining the other bridesmaids.

Magnus stepped forward and took Vivian's hand. "You look stunning, my love. No bride could be more beautiful." He turned and motioned for Parker to come closer. "Come stand by my side, son. This is a family affair." He looked at Ella. "You too, daughter."

This hadn't been planned, but Vivian thought that it was perfect.

As Ella stood by her side, the goddess lifted her arms again. "I had a nice speech prepared, but I am very pleased to discard it and make a new one to bless this beautiful joining, of not just these true-love mates, but of a loving family. May the Fates smile brightly upon this joining and bathe your home with love and happiness." She looked down at the crowd and beckoned for someone Vivian couldn't see to come up. "Edna, please join us and bring the adoption papers with you."

Holding a thick stack of documents, the judge climbed up the dais and stood to one side, so her back wasn't turned to the goddess or to the family.

Julian produced a pen from his pocket and handed it to Magnus. "Good luck to you all."

Edna handed each one of them a packet. "To save time, let me summarize. Parker and Ella, by signing these papers, you accept Magnus as your father."

Parker took the pen from Magnus and scribbled his signature. "Here. It is done." He handed the papers back to Edna.

Ella was next.

Smiling at Magnus, she took the pen and signed on the dotted line. "I couldn't have wished for a better dad."

Edna took the forms from Ella and added them to Parker's. "Now it's Mom and Dad's turn. Vivian, by signing these papers, you give Magnus permission to adopt your children."

"As Ella said, I couldn't have asked for a better mate or father for my children."

A slight pang of guilt had accompanied her words. Josh had been a great dad, and he had loved his kids unconditionally, but he was gone, and Magnus loved her children too.

The Fates had been harsh on her and her family, putting them through one misfortune after another.

Magnus was their reward.

Taking the papers with her, Edna stepped down, and the goddess lifted her arms once again.

"By the power vested in me as this Clan's Mother, I pronounce Vivian, Magnus, Ella, and Parker as one happy family. You may kiss the bride, Magnus."

58

CAROL

*A*s soon as the ceremony was over, Carol pushed through the crowd to congratulate the happy family so she could slink out without feeling guilty about it.

The long hours without Lokan were starting to be intolerable, the invisible tether connecting them feeling more like a multi-tentacled appendage than a string. One tentacle was wrapped around her throat, constricting her air supply, another was squeezing her stomach, and a third one was tugging at her heart.

It was unbearable.

How did the other couples manage to function? Go to work? Leave on missions?

As much as she was giddy with happiness for having Lokan as her mate, Carol wasn't ready to be attached to him at the hip. Even if he weren't a prisoner and could join her in her activities, she'd been alone for far too long and doing her own thing to suddenly make a shift and do everything as a couple.

Maybe it was like that only in the beginning, and it got easier with time.

The worst part was that she didn't know how to interpret it.

It wasn't lust because Lokan had satisfied her and then some, sating her voracious appetite, and it wasn't love because they hadn't been together long enough for the seeds to sprout. Love, as opposed to lust, took time to grow.

Except, maybe she was wrong. After all, she hadn't been in love before, so perhaps that nearly painful need to be with Lokan was love?

Or was it part of the craziness of fated mates?

After taking off her bridesmaid's dress and the high-heeled shoes, she put on a loose blouse, a pair of leggings, and flip-flops. Too impatient to wash off the heavy makeup, she rushed out, hoping not to bump into anyone in the elevators leading down to the parking lot.

Thankfully, everyone was still partying, and she made it to her car without having to explain why she was leaving the wedding so early.

When she arrived at the keep, she texted Arwel to meet her in front of Lokan's cell.

"I didn't expect to see you back so early," he said as he punched the numbers on the keypad.

She waved a dismissive hand. "After the ceremony, there was really no point in me staying. I can do without the food and the booze."

Casting her a knowing glance, Arwel took a step back as the door started to open. "I told him that you were coming. He sounded just as anxious to see you as you are to see him. This matehood thing is too intense for my taste."

"You don't know the half of it. Wait until you find your one and only. This is impossible to explain until you experience it yourself."

"Oy vey. I'm not looking forward to it."

With a little wave of her hand, she headed inside. "I'm staying the night."

"I didn't expect anything else," he said to her back.

Leaning against the wall by the entry, Lokan pulled her into his arms as soon as she walked in. He didn't wait for the door to close behind her, crushing her against his chest. "This is terrible. I can't live without you." He sucked in a breath. "I felt like I didn't have enough air to breathe."

"Same here, but I still can't." She pushed on his chest.

"Sorry about that." He let her out of the embrace.

Taking her hand, he pulled her behind him to the bedroom. "I need to be skin to skin with you. Let's get out of these clothes."

He yanked his own T-shirt off.

Yum. Lokan's chest was a work of art, and his ferocity was a major turn on. Any other time, she would have been fully on board with jumping into bed right away and getting her hands on all those gorgeous muscles, but at the moment she was more curious than horny.

"Can you talk while I'm naked? Because I can't concentrate with you flexing your pecs at me, and I want to hear all about Annani's visit."

He looked conflicted. "Can't it wait for later?"

"No, because I'll be thinking about it and speculating, and it's going to take away from my enjoyment." She winked. "I'm not good at multitasking, and I don't want to think about anything else while we are making love."

"As you wish." Looking disappointed, Lokan pulled his shirt back on. "Let's go back to the living room. You will need a drink for this."

Her gut clenched. "Why? What happened?"

"It's nothing bad. Come on." He took her hand and led her to the couch. "Arwel is getting me a new supply of that fabulous beer. I should ask him to buy some good wine for you." He pulled out two beers from the fridge, popped the lids off, and handed her one. "Is there any specific brand you like?"

"I don't want to talk about wine. Tell me about the visit."

He sat next to her on the couch, took a long swig from his beer, and then cradled the bottle in his palms. "Annani thinks that my mother is her half-sister, Areana."

Carol had heard the story about Annani's sister who had taken her place as Mortdh's intended, traveling north with Wonder's little sister as her maid. Except, from what she had heard, the goddess didn't know whether Areana had even survived the nuclear catastrophe, and now she believed that her sister was Lokan's mother?

That was a strange leap of logic.

"Why? Do you look like Areana?"

"I don't. But I told your Clan Mother that as a young boy I had dreams of a blue-eyed, fair-skinned woman gazing at me lovingly. At that time, Navuh's camp was still in Mortdh's old stronghold, and everyone looked more or less like the local human population. Most of the immortal children born to the gods had olive-toned skin and dark hair. It wasn't until much later that other ethnicities were introduced into the gene pool."

"It's a huge leap of faith from dreams of blue eyes and fair skin to Areana being your mother. It sounds like a bit of wishful thinking on Annani's part."

"There is more." He took another long swig from his beer. "My father treated me differently, making sure that I spent most of my time studying instead of playing with the other boys. As far as I know, he didn't do it with his other sons. And then he moved my transition ceremony a year earlier."

"Maybe he just thought you were smarter and more mature than your other brothers."

"Or he was trying to hide the fact that I was born immortal and didn't need to transition."

"Because you are the son of a goddess."

"Right."

"Oh, wow. This is major."

"Annani asked the lie detector guy to bring in an artist who can draw Areana from my description, but I don't remember much besides those blue eyes."

"Eyes are the most important part. Maybe Annani can recognize her sister just from that."

"Even if she does, it's not going to be enough to convince Kian. Or me for that matter. I still can't wrap my head around this. If I'm the son of a goddess, shouldn't I be more powerful?"

"But you are."

"Not really. I have two special talents, one that works only on humans, and another that is useless for anything other than fooling around in dreamland."

A seed of an idea started forming in Carol's head. Perhaps sneaking a telepath into the harem was not the only way to transmit information out of there.

"Maybe it's not as useless as you think."

59

LOKAN

"I already explained why I can't dream-share with any other immortal but you. I would be signing my death warrant. Or semi-death in stasis." He glanced at the camera, remembering too late that their conversation wasn't private. "I'm such an idiot."

"No, that's okay." Carol patted his knee. "Don't worry about it. Once I present my idea to Kian, he is going to be very happy about your ability to dream-share with me."

"What idea?"

"If you can get me into the harem, I can tell you what's going on in there by dream-sharing with you. You and I can do exactly the same thing that Ella and Vivian would have done, but by using a different talent."

"That's the craziest idea I've ever heard. How am I going to get you in there?"

She shrugged. "The same way you planned on getting Vivian or Ella in."

"You are an immortal."

"So what? You said that only humans work in the harem. They wouldn't know the difference, and neither would the immortal females Navuh keeps in there. I don't trigger an alarm like the males do."

He shook his head. "Even if that was possible, which I'm not sure about at all, Kian would never let me take you to the island."

"What if he does? Annani is dying to find out if Navuh has her sister, and when Annani wants something, nothing stands in her way. Not even Kian. She can order him to let you go."

"I don't think she would. As much as she wants to find out if her sister is still alive, Annani is not going to risk the safety of her clan for that."

"She is not going to. The only one who will be taking a risk is me. You don't know where you are or where our base is. In fact, you don't know now any more than you did before."

"What if I betray you to my father? He can compel you to reveal that information."

"I trust you."

"I know, and I would never do that, but Kian and Annani are not going to trust me. Hell, if I were in their position, I would not trust me either."

She waved a dismissive hand. "I can persuade Kian. But to do so, I need to know how you planned on sneaking Ella and Vivian onto the island, and then getting one of them into the harem."

"That's the easy part. Since I am the one compelling the human pilots, I would have had no trouble getting someone on the transport plane. And since I'm my father's son, I don't go through the same checks as everyone else does upon entering the island."

"Okay. So, you can get me on the island. How are you going to get me into the harem?"

"I befriended the guy in charge of supplying the harem with new servants and made sure that he owes me some favors. I can ask him to help hide a girl I want to save from the brothel. He knows that I don't like what's going on in there."

Carol nodded. "That seems doable. The only problem I see is getting me out. When they attempt to thrall the memory of the harem away, they won't be able to enter my mind and will assume that I'm immune to thralling. They won't let me go, and you can't compel them to do so because this will be done by immortals."

Lokan rubbed a hand over the back of his head. It was time to fess up. "I didn't tell you the entire truth before. The only way to leave the harem is in a coffin. Once a human gets in, she or he never leaves."

"So how did you plan on getting Ella or Vivian out?"

"By faking her death. But I didn't figure out how to do that yet."

The truth was that it hadn't been an overriding factor. If he hadn't found a way to get the telepath out, he was going to leave her there. At that time, he had had no qualms about sacrificing one or both of them.

"Well, I can enter stasis somehow. I need to ask our doctor's advice on how that can be done. So, after they take me out of the harem in a casket, what happens next?"

"I sneak the casket on board a transport plane and whisk you away. That's also not difficult. As I said, I can compel the pilots to do anything I want."

"So, the only difficult part is going to be faking my death?"

"And getting you onto the island without anyone noticing that you are not like the other girls."

Carol waved a dismissive hand. "Not a problem. As long as I don't get horny, I'll be fine." She waggled her brows. "Which means that you'll have to make sure I'm well satisfied before we land on the island."

She made it sound so doable, but he knew better. It was

risky as hell and could get them both executed, or worse. His father might throw Carol into the brothel and sentence her to an eternity of suffering. He was willing to risk his own life, but not hers.

"It doesn't have to be you. I can do this with any immortal female because dream-sharing is not required. After she is revived from stasis, she can report what she's seen."

"Not really. There is no substitute for two-way communication. I can tell you in the dream what I see, and you can ask me questions or give me suggestions. What if Areana is indeed in the harem and we want to rescue her? If I am on the inside and communicating with you, we can organize it. Once I'm out of there, that door is closed."

"I don't want you to do it. It's too risky."

The hard look in Carol's eyes was chilling. It was the one that he'd seen only when she'd talked about the sadist, and it made it clear that his woman wasn't the soft angel she appeared to be. There was a core of steel inside her.

"It is not. If things go wrong, we won't be on our own. The clan will find a way to get us out. Don't you want to find out who your mother is? And whether she is Areana or not? Don't you want to get her out of there?"

Reaching for her hand, he cupped it between his own. "I do. More than you can imagine. But I'm not willing to sacrifice you to achieve that. There must be another way."

"There isn't."

"Kian will never agree. You won't be able to persuade him. Besides, pretty soon my father is going to realize that I'm missing and assume that I defected. I won't be able to go back to the island."

"How soon is soon?"

"I'm expected to report in person to him in twenty-five

days. If he or anyone else from the Brotherhood doesn't try to contact me before that, this is our window of opportunity."

She narrowed her eyes. "How likely is it for someone to try contacting you?"

"Not very likely."

"Then this is how long I have to convince Kian to let us go and to formulate a plan. That's plenty of time."

"Is there any way I can persuade you to abandon this crazy plan?"

She smiled sweetly. "Nope. You'd better focus that smart brain of yours on planning how to get us in, and then out, together with your mother."

His thoughts running a thousand miles per second, Lokan went over his options.

If Carol succeeded in persuading Kian to send them to the island, which he very much doubted, and they actually made it there, and Carol infiltrated the harem, and they somehow managed to get his mother out, what was he going to do next?

Come back to the clan and risk getting locked up again?

Would they do that after he helped Annani get her sister back?

Or would they welcome him with gratitude and open arms and give him a prominent leadership position?

Not likely.

If he was indeed Areana's son, Kian would feel threatened by him. After all, his cousin was the son of a human father, while Lokan was the son of the most powerful immortal in the world.

Blood-wise, Lokan outranked him.

In fact, Lokan outranked Navuh as well. His father was the son of a human female and a god.

Not that it mattered. Navuh was more powerful than him,

and it wasn't as if he could march into his father's reception hall and announce himself King.

Lokan chuckled. He would lose his head before he finished his proclamation.

"What's so funny?" Carol asked.

"This whole idea. Kian is never going to agree. But it was fun indulging in make-believe for a few moments."

Reaching for his hand, Carol looked into his eyes. "We can do this, Lokan. That's why the Fates have brought us together, so we can rescue your mother."

"We don't even know if Areana is indeed my mother. This entire thing is based on dreams and speculations as to Navuh's motives."

Carol's eyes sparkled with excitement. "If the portrait the forensic artist draws of your dream mom matches Areana, we will know for sure."

"What if it doesn't?"

"Then we will have to find another way to prove it or disprove it."

"How? There is no other way."

Carol shrugged. "I don't know, but I bet the Fates will come up with something."

To be continued...

COMING UP NEXT
The Children of the Gods Book 30
Dark Prince's Dilemma

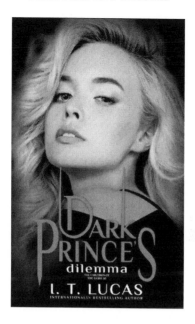

TO READ THE FIRST 3 CHAPTERS
JOIN THE VIP CLUB AT ITLUCAS.COM
AND GAIN ACCESS TO THE VIP PORTAL

(If you're already a subscriber and forgot the password to the VIP portal, you can find it at the bottom of each of my emails. Or click **HERE** to retrieve it. You can also email me at isabell@itlucas.com)

Dear reader,

Thank you for reading the ***Children of the Gods***.

As an independent author, I rely on your support to spread the word. So if you enjoyed the story, please share your experience with others, and if it isn't too much trouble, I would greatly appreciate a brief review on Amazon.

Kind words will get good Karma sent your way -:)

Click here to leave a review

Love & happy reading,
Isabell

RECOMMENDED READING BEFORE BOOK 2 & 3 IN
THE DARK PRINCE TRILOGY

1: ANNANI & KHIANN'S STORY
GODDESS'S CHOICE
2: AREANA & NAVUH'S STORY
GODDESS'S HOPE

DON'T MISS OUT ON
THE PERFECT MATCH SERIES
PERFECT MATCH 1: VAMPIRE'S CONSORT
PERFECT MATCH 2: KING'S CHOSEN
PERFECT MATCH 3: CAPTAIN'S CONQUEST
(READ THE ENCLOSED EXCERPT)

THE CHILDREN OF THE GODS ORIGINS

1: GODDESS'S CHOICE

When gods and immortals still ruled the ancient world, one young goddess risked everything for love.

2: GODDESS'S HOPE

Hungry for power and infatuated with the beautiful Areana, Navuh plots his father's demise. After all, by getting rid of the insane god he would be doing the world a favor. Except, when gods and immortals conspire against each other, humanity pays the price.

But things are not what they seem, and prophecies should not to be trusted...

THE CHILDREN OF THE GODS

1: DARK STRANGER THE DREAM

Syssi's paranormal foresight lands her a job at Dr. Amanda Dokani's neuroscience lab, but it fails to predict the thrilling yet terrifying turn her life will take. Syssi has no clue that her boss is an immortal who'll drag her into a secret, millennia-old battle over humanity's future. Nor does she realize that the professor's imposing brother is the mysterious stranger who's been starring in her dreams.

Since the dawn of human civilization, two warring factions of immortals—the descendants of the gods of old—have been secretly shaping its destiny. Leading the clandestine battle from his luxurious Los Angeles high-rise, Kian is surrounded by his clan, yet alone. Descending from a single goddess, clan members are forbidden to each other. And as the only other immortals are their hated enemies, Kian and his kin have been long resigned to a lonely existence of fleeting trysts with human partners. That is, until his sister makes a game-changing discovery—a mortal seeress who she believes is a dormant carrier of their genes. Ever the realist, Kian is skeptical and refuses Amanda's plea to attempt Syssi's activation. But when his enemies learn of the Dormant's existence, he's forced to rush her to the safety of his keep. Inexorably drawn to Syssi, Kian wrestles with his conscience as he is tempted to explore her budding interest in the darker shades of sensuality.

2: Dark Stranger Revealed

While sheltered in the clan's stronghold, Syssi is unaware that Kian and Amanda are not human, and neither are the supposedly religious fanatics that are after her. She feels a powerful connection to Kian, and as he introduces her to a world of pleasure she never dared imagine, his dominant sexuality is a revelation. Considering that she's completely out of her element, Syssi feels comfortable and safe letting go with him. That is, until she begins to suspect that all is not as it seems. Piecing the puzzle together, she draws a scary, yet wrong conclusion...

3: Dark Stranger Immortal

When Kian confesses his true nature, Syssi is not as much shocked by the revelation as she is wounded by what she perceives as his callous plans for her.

If she doesn't turn, he'll be forced to erase her memories and let her go. His family's safety demands secrecy – no one in the mortal world is allowed to know that immortals exist.

Resigned to the cruel reality that even if she stays on to never again leave the keep, she'll get old while Kian won't, Syssi is determined to enjoy what little time she has with him, one day at a time.

Can Kian let go of the mortal woman he loves? Will Syssi turn? And if she does, will she survive the dangerous transition?

4: Dark Enemy Taken

Dalhu can't believe his luck when he stumbles upon the beautiful immortal professor. Presented with a once in a lifetime opportunity to grab an immortal female for himself, he kidnaps her and runs. If he ever gets caught, either by her people or his, his life is forfeit. But for a chance of a loving mate and a family of his own, Dalhu is prepared to do everything in his power to win Amanda's heart, and that includes leaving the Doom brotherhood and his old life behind.

Amanda soon discovers that there is more to the handsome Doomer than his dark past and a hulking, sexy body. But succumbing to her enemy's seduction, or worse, developing feelings for a ruthless killer is out of the question. No man is worth life on the run, not even the one and only immortal male she could claim as her own…

Her clan and her research must come first…

5: Dark Enemy Captive

When the rescue team returns with Amanda and the chained Dalhu to the keep, Amanda is not as thrilled to be back as she thought she'd be. Between Kian's contempt for her and Dalhu's imprisonment, Amanda's budding relationship with Dalhu seems doomed. Things start to look up when Annani offers her help, and together with Syssi they resolve to find a way for Amanda to be with Dalhu. But will she still want him when she realizes that he is responsible for her nephew's murder? Could she? Will she take the easy way out and choose Andrew instead?

6: Dark Enemy Redeemed

Amanda suspects that something fishy is going on onboard the Anna. But when her investigation of the peculiar all-female Russian crew fails to uncover anything other than more speculation, she decides it's time to stop playing detective and face her real problem—a man she shouldn't want but can't live without.

6.5: My Dark Amazon

When Michael and Kri fight off a gang of humans, Michael gets stabbed. The injury to his immortal body recovers fast, but the one to his ego takes longer, putting a strain on his relationship with Kri.

7: Dark Warrior Mine

When Andrew is forced to retire from active duty, he believes that all he has to look forward to is a boring desk job. His glory days in special ops are over. But as it turns out, his thrill ride has just begun. Andrew discovers not only that immortals exist and have been manipulating global affairs since antiquity, but that he and his sister are rare possessors of the immortal genes.

Problem is, Andrew might be too old to attempt the activation process. His sister, who is fourteen years his junior, barely made it through the transition, so the odds of him coming out of it alive, let alone immortal, are slim.

But fate may force his hand.

Helping a friend find his long-lost daughter, Andrew finds a woman who's worth taking the risk for. Nathalie might be a Dormant, but the only way to find out for sure requires fangs and venom.

8: Dark Warrior's Promise

Andrew and Nathalie's love flourishes, but the secrets they keep from each other taint their relationship with doubts and suspicions. In the meantime, Sebastian and his men are getting bolder, and the storm that's brewing will shift the balance of power in the millennia-old conflict between Annani's clan and its enemies.

9: Dark Warrior's Destiny

The new ghost in Nathalie's head remembers who he was in life, providing Andrew and her with indisputable proof that he is real and not a figment of her imagination.

Convinced that she is a Dormant, Andrew decides to go forward with his transition immediately after the rescue mission at the Doomers' HQ.

Fearing for his life, Nathalie pleads with him to reconsider. She'd rather spend the rest of her mortal days with Andrew than risk what they have for the fickle promise of immortality.

While the clan gets ready for battle, Carol gets help from an unlikely ally. Sebastian's second-in-command can no longer ignore the torment she suffers at the hands of his commander and offers to help her, but only if she agrees to his terms.

10: Dark Warrior's Legacy

Andrew's acclimation to his post-transition body isn't easy. His senses are sharper, he's bigger, stronger, and hungrier. Nathalie fears that the changes in the man she loves are more than physical. Measuring up to this new version of him is going to be a challenge.

Carol and Robert are disillusioned with each other. They are not destined mates, and love is not on the horizon. When Robert's three months are up, he might be left with nothing to show for his sacrifice.

Lana contacts Anandur with disturbing news; the yacht and its human cargo are in Mexico. Kian must find a way to apprehend Alex and rescue the women on board without causing an international incident.

11: Dark Guardian Found

What would you do if you stopped aging?

Eva runs. The ex-DEA agent doesn't know what caused her strange mutation, only that if discovered, she'll be dissected like a lab rat. What Eva doesn't know, though, is that she's a descendant of the gods, and that she is not alone. The man who rocked her world in one life-changing encounter over thirty years ago is an immortal as well.

To keep his people's existence secret, Bhathian was forced to turn his back on the only woman who ever captured his heart, but he's never forgotten and never stopped looking for her.

12: Dark Guardian Craved

Cautious after a lifetime of disappointments, Eva is mistrustful of Bhathian's professed feelings of love. She accepts him as a lover and a confidant but not as a life partner.

Jackson suspects that Tessa is his true love mate, but unless she overcomes her fears, he might never find out.

Carol gets an offer she can't refuse—a chance to prove that there is more to her than meets the eye. Robert believes she's about to commit a deadly mistake, but when he tries to dissuade her, she tells him to leave.

13: Dark Guardian's Mate

Prepare for the heart-warming culmination of Eva and Bhathian's story!

14: Dark Angel's Obsession

The cold and stoic warrior is an enigma even to those closest to him. His secrets are about to unravel...

15: Dark Angel's Seduction

Brundar is fighting a losing battle. Calypso is slowly chipping away his icy armor from the outside, while his need for her is melting it from the inside.

He can't allow it to happen. Calypso is a human with none of the Dormant indicators. There is no way he can keep her for more than a few weeks.

16: Dark Angel's Surrender

Get ready for the heart pounding conclusion to Brundar and Calypso's story.

Callie still couldn't wrap her head around it, nor could she summon even a smidgen of sorrow or regret. After all, she had some memories with him that weren't horrible. She should've felt something. But there was nothing, not even shock. Not even horror at what had transpired over the last couple of hours.

Maybe it was a typical response for survivors--feeling euphoric for the simple reason that they were alive. Especially when that survival was nothing short of miraculous.

Brundar's cold hand closed around hers, reminding her that they weren't out of the woods yet. Her injuries were superficial, and the most she had to worry about was some scarring. But, despite his and Anandur's reassurances, Brundar might never walk again.

If he ended up crippled because of her, she would never forgive herself for getting him involved in her crap.

"Are you okay, sweetling? Are you in pain?" Brundar asked.

Her injuries were nothing compared to his, and yet he was concerned about her. God, she loved this man. The thing was, if she told him that, he would run off, or crawl away as was the case.

Hey, maybe this was the perfect opportunity to spring it on him.

17: Dark Operative: A Shadow of Death

As a brilliant strategist and the only human entrusted with the secret of immortals' existence, Turner is both an asset and a liability to the clan. His request to attempt transition into immortality as an alternative to cancer treatments cannot be denied without risking the clan's exposure. On the other hand, approving it means risking his premature death. In both scenarios, the clan will lose a valuable ally.

When the decision is left to the clan's physician, Turner makes plans to manipulate her by taking advantage of her interest in him.

Will Bridget fall for the cold, calculated operative? Or will Turner fall into his own trap?

18: Dark Operative: A Glimmer of Hope

As Turner and Bridget's relationship deepens, living together seems like the right move, but to make it work both need to make concessions.

Bridget is realistic and keeps her expectations low. Turner could never be the truelove mate she yearns for, but he is as good as she's going to get. Other than his emotional limitations, he's perfect in every way.

Turner's hard shell is starting to show cracks. He wants immortality, he wants to be part of the clan, and he wants Bridget, but he doesn't want to cause her pain.

His options are either abandon his quest for immortality and give Bridget his few remaining decades, or abandon Bridget by going for the transition and most likely dying. His rational mind dictates that he chooses the former, but his gut pulls him toward the latter. Which one is he going to trust?

19: Dark Operative: The Dawn of Love

Get ready for the exciting finale of Bridget and Turner's story!

20: Dark Survivor Awakened

This was a strange new world she had awakened to.

Her memory loss must have been catastrophic because almost nothing was familiar. The language was foreign to her, with only a few words bearing some similarity to the language she thought in. Still, a full moon cycle had passed since her awakening, and little by little she was gaining basic understanding of it--only a few words and phrases, but she was learning more each day.

A week or so ago, a little girl on the street had tugged on her mother's sleeve and pointed at her. "Look, Mama, Wonder Woman!"

The mother smiled apologetically, saying something in the language these people spoke, then scurried away with the child looking behind her shoulder and grinning.

When it happened again with another child on the same day, it was settled.

Wonder Woman must have been the name of someone important in this strange world she had awoken to, and since both times it had been said with a smile it must have been a good one.

Wonder had a nice ring to it.

She just wished she knew what it meant.

21: DARK SURVIVOR ECHOES OF LOVE

Wonder's journey continues in *Dark Survivor Echoes of Love*.

22: DARK SURVIVOR REUNITED

The exciting finale of Wonder and Anandur's story.

23: DARK WIDOW'S SECRET

Vivian and her daughter share a powerful telepathic connection, so when Ella can't be reached by conventional or psychic means, her mother fears the worst.

Help arrives from an unexpected source when Vivian gets a call from the young doctor she met at a psychic convention. Turns out Julian belongs to a private organization specializing in retrieving missing girls.

As Julian's clan mobilizes its considerable resources to rescue the daughter, Magnus is charged with keeping the gorgeous young mother safe.

Worry for Ella and the secrets Vivian and Magnus keep from each other should be enough to prevent the sparks of attraction from kindling a blaze of desire. Except, these pesky sparks have a mind of their own.

24: Dark Widow's Curse

A simple rescue operation turns into mission impossible when the Russian mafia gets involved. Bad things are supposed to come in threes, but in Vivian's case, it seems like there is no limit to bad luck. Her family and everyone who gets close to her is affected by her curse.

Will Magnus and his people prove her wrong?

25: Dark Widow's Blessing

The thrilling finale of the Dark Widow trilogy!

26: Dark Dream's Temptation

Julian has known Ella is the one for him from the moment he saw her picture, but when he finally frees her from captivity, she seems indifferent to him. Could he have been mistaken?

Ella's rescue should've ended that chapter in her life, but it seems like the road back to normalcy has just begun and it's full of obstacles. Between the pitying looks she gets and her mother's attempts to get her into therapy, Ella feels like she's typecast as a victim, when nothing could be further from the truth. She's a tough survivor, and she's going to prove it.

Strangely, the only one who seems to understand is Logan, who keeps popping up in her dreams. But then, he's a figment of her imagination —or is he?

27: Dark Dream's Unraveling

While trying to figure out a way around Logan's silencing compulsion, Ella concocts an ambitious plan. What if instead of trying to keep him out of her dreams, she could pretend to like him and lure him into a trap?

Catching Navuh's son would be a major boon for the clan, as well as for Ella. She will have her revenge, turning the tables on another scumbag out to get her.

28: Dark Dream's Trap

The trap is set, but who is the hunter and who is the prey? Find out in this heart-pounding conclusion to the *Dark Dream* trilogy.

29: Dark Prince's Enigma

As the son of the most dangerous male on the planet, Lokan lives by three rules:

Don't trust a soul.

Don't show emotions.

And don't get attached.

Will one extraordinary woman make him break all three?

30: Dark Prince's Dilemma

Will Kian decide that the benefits of trusting Lokan outweigh the risks?

Will Lokan betray his father and brothers for the greater good of his people?

Are Carol and Lokan true-love mates, or is one of them playing the other?

So many questions, the path ahead is anything but clear.

31: Dark Prince's Agenda

While Turner and Kian work out the details of Areana's rescue plan, Carol and Lokan's tumultuous relationship hits another snag. Is it a sign of things to come?

32 : Dark Queen's Quest

A former beauty queen, a retired undercover agent, and a successful model, Mey is not the typical damsel in distress. But when her sister drops off the radar and then someone starts following her around, she panics.

Following a vague clue that Kalugal might be in New York, Kian sends a team headed by Yamanu to search for him.

As Mey and Yamanu's paths cross, he offers her his help and protection, but will that be all?

33: Dark Queen's Knight

As the only member of his clan with a godlike power over human minds, Yamanu has been shielding his people for centuries, but that power comes at a steep price. When Mey enters his life, he's faced with the most difficult choice.

The safety of his clan or a future with his fated mate.

34: DARK QUEEN'S ARMY

As Mey anxiously waits for her transition to begin and for Yamanu to test whether his godlike powers are gone, the clan sets out to solve two mysteries:

Where is Jin, and is she there voluntarily?

Where is Kalugal, and what is he up to?

35: DARK SPY CONSCRIPTED

Jin possesses a unique paranormal ability. Just by touching someone, she can insert a mental hook into their psyche and tie a string of her consciousness to it, creating a tether. That doesn't make her a spy, though, not unless her talent is discovered by those seeking to exploit it.

36: DARK SPY'S MISSION

Jin's first spying mission is supposed to be easy. Walk into the club, touch Kalugal to tether her consciousness to him, and walk out.

Except, they should have known better.

37: DARK SPY'S RESOLUTION

The best-laid plans often go awry...

38: DARK OVERLORD NEW HORIZON

Jacki has two talents that set her apart from the rest of the human race.

She has unpredictable glimpses of other people's futures, and she is immune to mind manipulation.

Unfortunately, both talents are pretty useless for finding a job other than the one she had in the government's paranormal division.

It seemed like a sweet deal, until she found out that the director planned on producing super babies by compelling the recruits into pairing up. When an opportunity to escape the program presented itself, she took it, only to find out that humans are not at the top of the food chain.

Immortals are real, and at the very top of the hierarchy is Kalugal, the most powerful, arrogant, and sexiest male she has ever met.

With one look, he sets her blood on fire, but Jacki is not a fool. A man like him will never think of her as anything more than a tasty snack, while she will never settle for anything less than his heart.

39: Dark Overlord's Wife

Jacki is still clinging to her all-or-nothing policy, but Kalugal is chipping away at her resistance. Perhaps it's time to ease up on her convictions. A little less than all is still much better than nothing, and a couple of decades with a demigod is probably worth more than a lifetime with a mere mortal.

40: Dark Overlord's Clan

As Jacki and Kalugal prepare to celebrate their union, Kian takes every precaution to safeguard his people. Except, Kalugal and his men are not his only potential adversaries, and compulsion is not the only power he should fear.

41: Dark Choices The Quandary

When Rufsur and Edna meet, the attraction is as unexpected as it is undeniable. Except, she's the clan's judge and councilwoman, and he's Kalugal's second-in-command. Will loyalty and duty to their people keep them apart?

42: Dark Choices Paradigm Shift

Edna and Rufsur are miserable without each other, and their two-week separation seems like an eternity. Long-distance relationships are difficult, but for immortal couples they are impossible. Unless one of them is willing to leave everything behind for the other, things are just going to get worse. Except, the cost of compromise is far greater than giving up their comfortable lives and hard-earned positions. The future of their people is on the line.

43: Dark Choices The Accord

The winds of change blowing over the village demand hard choices. For better or worse, Kian's decisions will alter the trajectory of the clan's future, and he is not ready to take the plunge. But as Edna and Rufsur's plight gains widespread support, his resistance slowly begins to erode.

44: Dark Secrets Resurgence

On a sabbatical from his Stanford teaching position, Professor David Levinson finally has time to write the sci-fi novel he's been thinking about for years.

The phenomena of past life memories and near-death experiences are too controversial to include in his formal psychiatric research, while fiction is the perfect outlet for his esoteric ideas.

Hoping that a change of pace will provide the inspiration he needs, David accepts a friend's invitation to an old Scottish castle.

45: Dark Secrets Unveiled

When Professor David Levinson accepts a friend's invitation to an old Scottish castle, what he finds there is more fantastical than his most outlandish theories. The castle is home to a clan of immortals, their leader is a stunning demigoddess, and even more shockingly, it might be precisely where he belongs.

Except, the clan founder is hiding a secret that might cast a dark shadow on David's relationship with her daughter.

Nevertheless, when offered a chance at immortality, he agrees to undergo the dangerous induction process.

Will David survive his transition into immortality? And if he does, will his relationship with Sari survive the unveiling of her mother's secret?

46: Dark Secrets Absolved

Absolution.

David had given and received it.

The few short hours since he'd emerged from the coma had felt incredible. He'd finally been free of the guilt and pain, and for the first time since Jonah's death, he had felt truly happy and optimistic about the future.

He'd survived the transition into immortality, had been accepted into the clan, and was about to marry the best woman on the face of the planet, his true love mate, his salvation, his everything.

What could have possibly gone wrong?

Just about everything.

47: Dark haven Illusion

Welcome to Safe Haven, where not everything is what it seems.

On a quest to process personal pain, Anastasia joins the Safe Haven Spiritual Retreat.

Through meditation, self-reflection, and hard work, she hopes to make peace with the voices in her head.

This is where she belongs.

Except, membership comes with a hefty price, doubts are sacrilege, and leaving is not as easy as walking out the front gate.

Is living in utopia worth the sacrifice?

Anastasia believes so until the arrival of a new acolyte changes everything.

Apparently, the gods of old were not a myth, their immortal descendants share the planet with humans, and she might be a carrier of their genes.

48: Dark Haven Unmasked

As Anastasia leaves Safe Haven for a week-long romantic vacation with Leon, she hopes to explore her newly discovered passionate side, their budding relationship, and perhaps also solve the mystery of the voices in her head. What she discovers exceeds her wildest expectations.

In the meantime, Eleanor and Peter hope to solve another mystery. Who is Emmett Haderech, and what is he up to?

THE PERFECT MATCH SERIES

PERFECT MATCH 1: VAMPIRE'S CONSORT

When Gabriel's company is ready to start beta testing, he invites his old crush to inspect its medical safety protocol.

Curious about the revolutionary technology of the *Perfect Match Virtual Fantasy-Fulfillment studios*, Brenna agrees.

Neither expects to end up partnering for its first fully immersive test run.

PERFECT MATCH 2: KING'S CHOSEN

When Lisa's nutty friends get her a gift certificate to *Perfect Match Virtual Fantasy Studios*, she has no intentions of using it. But since the only way to get a refund is if no partner can be found for her, she makes sure to request a fantasy so girly and over the top that no sane guy will pick it up.

Except, someone does.

Warning: This fantasy contains a hot, domineering crown prince, sweet insta-love, steamy love scenes painted with light shades of gray, a wedding, and a HEA in both the virtual and real worlds.

Intended for mature audience.

PERFECT MATCH 3: CAPTAIN'S CONQUEST

Working as a Starbucks barista, Alicia fends off flirting all day long, but none of the guys are as charming and sexy as Gregg. His frequent visits are the highlight of her day, but since he's never asked her out, she assumes he's taken. Besides, between a day job and a budding music career, she has no time to start a new relationship.

That is until Gregg makes her an offer she can't refuse—a gift certificate to the virtual fantasy fulfillment service everyone is talking about. As a huge Star Trek fan, Alicia has a perfect match in mind—the captain of the Starship Enterprise.

"*T*he usual?" Gregg's favorite Starbuck barista smiled. "You know it. Any new sandwiches on the menu?"

He couldn't care less, but that would get her talking, and he loved the sound of her voice.

"Nothing new. But I recommend the cheese and basil."

"Then that's what I'll have."

"Toasted?"

"Naturally."

She took the sandwich out, put it in a paper bag, and wrote his name on it. "That would be ten fifty-two."

He gave her a twenty. "Keep the change."

Holding the bill, Alicia narrowed her eyes at him. "That's too much." She put it into the register and gave him back a five. "For your next coffee."

He knew better than to argue with her. "How about I buy you one?"

She laughed. "Coffee? I don't drink the stuff."

"You work here, and you don't drink coffee?"

"If I did, I couldn't sleep."

"How about decaf?"

She shook her head and then glanced at the next customer in line, letting Gregg know that his time was up.

"Oh well. Thanks for the sandwich suggestion."

"You're welcome. See you later, Gregg."

And that was it. He'd been coming there for months, sometimes twice a day, sometimes three, and the frequency had nothing to do with Starbucks's mediocre coffee and everything to do with Alicia.

Why hadn't he asked her out yet, then?

Because she wasn't his type.

Gregg didn't date tattooed and pierced rocker chicks. Hell, he didn't date at all if he could avoid it. His mother kept trying to set him up with the daughters of her country club friends, and sometimes he had to humor her and agree to a date.

But other than that he was perfectly satisfied with casual hookups.

He wasn't looking for a relationship, especially not with any of those spoiled rich girls who bore him to death. And if he brought home someone like Alicia, his mother would drop dead on the spot. He loved her too much to risk her fragile heart.

Besides, it wasn't as if he wanted a relationship with Alicia either.

She fascinated him, and he would have loved getting to know her intimately, but, unfortunately, she didn't seem interested.

"A double espresso and a toasted sandwich for Gregg!" the guy behind the counter called out.

Taking his order to a table with a good view of his girl, Gregg sat down and spent the next twenty minutes observing her from the corner of his eye while pretending to read on his phone.

He had to find a way to hook up with her so he could finally get her out of his system and stop wasting time at Starbucks. His partner was on his case about that, and although Gregg's money, or rather his parents' money, had been the seed investment that had funded their business, he still needed to put in the work.

Except, Alicia wasn't responding to the subtle hints he was throwing around. Today was as close as he'd ever gotten to asking her out, but her response or lack thereof had been pretty clear. She wasn't interested.

Would she change her mind if she found out how rich he was? Or if he lost the baggy shorts and flip-flops and wore something that made him look good?

Gregg didn't want to do either. She either liked him for who he was or not at all. The world was full of gold diggers and airheads who were impressed by fashionable clothing, and he wanted nothing to do with those types, not even for hookups. They tended to be as boring in bed as they were to talk to.

Was he jaded?

Kind of. Probably.

His mother was worried that he would never marry because he was too picky, and there was some truth in it. At thirty-two, he'd been with a lot of women, and none had captured his interest beyond a second date.

Which probably meant that the problem was his and not theirs.

Except, if wanting a woman that he could have an intelligent conversation with and could laugh with was being too picky, then so be it. He wasn't willing to compromise on that.

Besides, he was spoiled by the virtual world of the Perfect Match studios. He hadn't found his true love there like his partner had, but he'd enjoyed many satisfying virtual sex adventures, and he couldn't care less what the women behind the gorgeous avatars looked like in real life.

He enjoyed the fantasy. Hell, he was probably addicted to it.

"I knew I'd find you here." Sam clapped him on the back. "You have a serious coffee addiction, buddy." His partner pulled out a chair and sat across from him. "I just came back from a meeting with the Perfect Match board of directors. They are opening three more locations, and naturally they hired us to handle their cybersecurity."

"That's great. I'm glad Hunter and Gabriel are doing so well. A year ago they were still paying us with gift certificates."

Sam chuckled. "We can sell them. They are worth a lot of money today."

"I'm sure you are going to keep a few for you and Lisa."

Sam had met his wife through the service. But the funny thing was that he'd known Lisa for years because she worked in the same building their offices were in. Except, he hadn't ever spoken to her before meeting her in the virtual world of Perfect Match.

Uncomfortable, Sam straightened his tie. "We've only done it that one time. Real life is better than fantasy."

"I'm sure it is."

Well, maybe it was for Sam and Lisa, but not for Gregg. He would take fantasy over reality any day.

But as he glanced at Alicia, Gregg's conviction wavered. He could imagine having a virtual fantasy with someone like her. Perhaps he would design his next adventure with his tattooed barista in mind?

He could describe her in detail on his request form, and the program would create a lookalike avatar for him. He could then pretend he was playing with Alicia and not some random woman using that avatar.

Or he could do better than that.

What if he could find out what her fantasy was, give her a gift certificate, and then design his fantasy to match hers?

He knew how the algorithm worked more or less, and if he collected enough pointers from her wish list, he could fill in his questionnaire in a way that would ensure them getting matched.

That was the perfect solution.

Why hadn't he thought of that sooner?

He could have his cake and eat it too.

Was it a bit dishonest?

Probably. But Gregg could live with that.

Perfect Match 3: Captain's Conquest
JULY 13, 2019

Also by I. T. Lucas

THE CHILDREN OF THE GODS ORIGINS

THE CHILDREN OF THE GODS

DARK STRANGER

DARK ENEMY

KRI & MICHAEL'S STORY

DARK WARRIOR

DARK GUARDIAN

DARK ANGEL

DARK OPERATIVE

Books 35-37: Dark Spy Trilogy

Books 38-40: Dark Overlord Trilogy

Books 41-43: Dark Choices Trilogy

Books 44-46: Dark Secrets Trilogy

MEGA SETS

The Children of the Gods: Books 1-6—includes character lists

The Children of the Gods: Books 6.5-10—includes character lists

---

TRY THE CHILDREN OF THE GODS SERIES ON AUDIBLE

2 FREE audiobooks with your new Audible subscription!

FOR EXCLUSIVE PEEKS AT UPCOMING RELEASES & A FREE COMPANION BOOK

Join my *VIP Club* and gain access to the VIP portal at

ITLUCAS.COM

CLICK HERE TO JOIN

(OR GO TO: http://eepurl.com/blMTpD)

INCLUDED IN YOUR FREE MEMBERSHIP:

- FREE Children of the Gods companion book 1
- FREE narration of Goddess's Choice—Book 1 in The Children of the Gods Origins series.
- Preview chapters of upcoming releases.
- And other exclusive content offered only to my VIPs.